Praise for the Novels of Lydia Joyce

Voices of the Night

"Within the pages of *Voices of the Night*, you will find suspense, intrigue, love, and sensual scenes, but most of all, emotion." —Romance Readers at Heart

"Joyce's quietly chilling sense of suspense, expertly crafted Victorian London setting, and two beautifully nuanced, wonderfully complicated characters provide the key ingredients for a deliciously dark, superbly written tale of love, honor, and redemption." —*Booklist*

"A fascinating story . . . a wonderful storyteller." —Romance Reviews Today

Whispers of the Night

"Tantalizing, spellbinding, sizzling, and captivating, this novel lures readers into its depths, making them never want to leave. Joyce hones her skills as an erotic romance author of the finest caliber in a tale as dark and seductive as rich, decadent chocolate." —*Romantic Times*

"Ms. Joyce takes [a classic romance] theme and places it in exotic locales. . . . It makes for a fun and interesting change of pace. Readers who enjoy exotic locales will want to check out this dramatic story." —Romance Reviews Today

continued . . .

The Music of the Night

"Danger, deception, and desire all come together brilliantly in this sublimely sensual historical romance."
— *Booklist* (starred review)

"Complicated, challenging, sexy, and altogether adult."
— All About Romance

"Mesmerizing and fascinating. . . . Dark, intense, and with a surprise ending that will leave you breathless, her latest Gothic makes its mark on the genre."
— *Romantic Times* (top pick)

"Refreshingly different from the usual romance book offerings . . . intelligent writing . . . an excellent example of what a talented writer can accomplish if they choose not to follow the pack." — *The Romance Reader*

The Veil of Night

"Intelligent. Passionate. Filled with dark secrets and illuminating love. This is what romance is about!"
— Robin Schone, *USA Today* bestselling author of *The Lover*

Shadows of the Night

Lydia Joyce

A SIGNET ECLIPSE BOOK

SIGNET ECLIPSE
Published by New American Library, a division of
Penguin Group (USA) Inc., 375 Hudson Street,
New York, New York 10014, USA
Penguin Group (Canada), 90 Eglinton Avenue East, Suite 700, Toronto,
Ontario M4P 2Y3, Canada (a division of Pearson Penguin Canada Inc.)
Penguin Books Ltd., 80 Strand, London WC2R 0RL, England
Penguin Ireland, 25 St. Stephen's Green, Dublin 2,
Ireland (a division of Penguin Books Ltd.)
Penguin Group (Australia), 250 Camberwell Road, Camberwell, Victoria 3124,
Australia (a division of Pearson Australia Group Pty. Ltd.)
Penguin Books India Pvt. Ltd., 11 Community Centre, Panchsheel Park,
New Delhi - 110 017, India
Penguin Group (NZ), 67 Apollo Drive, Rosedale, North Shore 0632,
New Zealand (a division of Pearson New Zealand Ltd.)
Penguin Books (South Africa) (Pty.) Ltd., 24 Sturdee Avenue,
Rosebank, Johannesburg 2196, South Africa

Penguin Books Ltd., Registered Offices:
80 Strand, London WC2R 0RL, England

First published by Signet Eclipse, an imprint of New American Library,
a division of Penguin Group (USA) Inc.

First Printing, March 2008
10 9 8 7 6 5 4 3 2 1

*In memory of my Gran-Gran,
an original Southern lady*

Prologue

"Come back to bed." Emma's sleepy voice emerged from the pile of twisted blankets. "You have hours yet before the wedding."

Colin cast a glance over his shoulder as he gave his necktie a last quick tug into place. Morning light poured through the window, puddling across the bed to halo Emma's cherubic face amidst clouds of white linen. Her lower lip protruded slightly, an artificial expression that should have looked ludicrous on a woman of thirty-five, but Colin doubted that Emma had ever in her life looked anything but exactly as she intended. Flirting, dancing, cajoling, even during lovemaking she kept her face turned toward the most flattering angle, her expression intense but unmarred by any unaesthetic contortion.

Predictable, cultured, and undemanding, she was exactly what Colin had always wanted in a mistress. It was a pity their pleasant affair would be interrupted by his wedding so soon.

Colin shrugged at his reflection. "I have yet to dress and shave and be jocularly ridiculed by my brothers, and I am also expecting some important correspondence from my solicitor. I know how these events go; as dreary as they are, somehow there never is as much time as one needs to prepare."

"It would be so much simpler if marriage were settled without all this unseemly to-do, parading about as if the bride and groom had single-handedly invented the institution. A few documents passed between solicitors, the appropriate signature on the appropriate blank." Emma sighed.

Colin chuckled. "*Mon ange*, you were born a cynic." He squared his shoulders and straightened his gray morning coat before crossing the room to her bedside. Emma extended round white arms to pull him to meet her upturned face—not so carelessly that she mussed his suit—and kissed him with a faultless balance of passion and decorum.

"I suppose this is good-bye," she said when they separated. Her bottom lip, kiss-swollen and still jutting out slightly, began to tremble.

"For a few months, at least," Colin agreed easily.

The lip stopped trembling. "For at least half a year, I should hope. It isn't decent that a man should hurry too quickly from a wife's bed."

"Nor a woman from her husband's?" Colin returned coolly.

Emma delicately pulled a face. "I produced Algy's heir and a spare before I took my first lover. Now we live our lives, discreet and discrete"—her smile indicated the wordplay—"and well satisfied. I would wish you better, if I thought any better were possible upon this mortal coil."

Colin laughed again. "We shall see, I suppose." It wasn't as if he had any great aversion to marriage nor any great expectations going into it, really. He assumed that it would sort itself out, as his life always had. Eton, Oxford, the usual social clubs in London and hunt clubs in the country—his life had always fallen into place without a single conscious effort on his part. He had no reason to think that his marriage would be any different.

He had decided last year that it was an appropriate time for him to wed. As the heir to a viscountcy, he needed a son before he grew too old, and his cordial if distant relationship with his parents assured the stipend needed for an appropriate match. The debutantes that year were as callow and self-centered as they ever were, but this discovery scarcely put him off; after all, self-centeredness merely meant that a woman would spend more time thinking about herself than harrying him. All he desired was an accomplished hostess with a certain warmth and physical charm, traits that abounded among the daughters of his set. So when he found himself spending more and more time at Fern Ashcroft's side, as much by chance as by design, he rapidly made the socially required hints, and upon receiving the appropriate replies, he approached her father and requested her hand.

Colin had heard other young men of his set speaking in agonized voices of love and desire—the objects of which were, often enough, neither their wives in fact nor in potentia. But he did not seek such a match, either with Fern or any other woman. He had never experienced the heights or depths of a *grande passion*. He did not think it within his capacity to do so, nor even to miss such a disruptive and messy experience.

His only regret, and that a faint one, was that the engagement coincided with his discovery of the undemanding and ever-welcoming Emma Morel. But a mistress, however pleasant, was no reason to change the direction of his life, which had only one other shadow on the horizon—that of the matter of Wrexmere Manor, which his solicitor's letter should soon clear up.

Colin looked down at Emma and brushed a golden curl that had fallen across her forehead back to join the rest of the artfully tumbled mass. "Let's not put a time requirement to fidelity. It sounds so calculating, and you know I never calculate. Instead, I will merely say—good-bye, for now."

"I should cry, you know," Emma said, her cornflower blue eyes growing round and wet even as she spoke.

He raised one eyebrow. "Please don't. At least, not unless you intend upon pining after me until I return; if you do, I could hardly deny you the right to weep, however inconvenient. But you shall make me most abominably late if I must stay to comfort you."

Emma laughed, the dampness transforming into a merry glimmer. "Oh, you naughty thing! You know me too well. I've tried to pine before, but I simply haven't the constitution. Run along, then. I shall be here when you return, but whether or not there will still be a place for you, I can make no promises!" She paused, and for an instant, Colin saw a shadow of some real emotion in her eyes. Was it fear? "You're staying in Clifton Terrace, aren't you?" she asked.

"Yes," he replied cautiously.

She smiled brightly, and the shadow was gone. "Well, I shall hope to not see you back in my bedroom for a few years, at least!"

"Fair enough," Colin replied, and he turned away to face his wedding day and his bride.

Chapter One

The aisle stretched out interminably in front of Fern, lined with familiar faces and their smothering gazes. Distantly, she knew this should be the happiest day of her life, when her girlish dreams would finally be realized and she would emerge into womanhood on the arm of her new husband—the husband she had scarcely dared believe had chosen her. But she could muster no joy, and her smile felt more like a rictus. The heir of a viscount. It had seemed impossible that he had wanted her, impossible that she could refuse, and since Fern had never been one to attempt the impossible or even the indecorous, she had accepted. Now a stranger stood waiting for her at the end of the carpet, and the indifference of his gaze chilled her soul.

Fern's father stepped forward, and she found herself borne along in the wake of the bridesmaids and her flower-strewing nieces. The organ blast trembled in the vaulted ceiling, the vast space muddying the sound until it arrived as one great crash in her ears, and the scents of roses and toilet water crowded hot and cloying around her.

She wanted to press a hand to her roiling stomach. Instead, she tightened her grip on her bouquet and continued to smile for the staring faces, white as the orange blossoms that wilted in her grasp, and for the gray rapier figure that waited at the other end of the carpet.

Then she was there, beside him, standing unsupported, and the minister was speaking far too fast, the words tumbling together in her head until she could catch only fragments, like the falling shards of a stained-glass window: *Dearly beloved . . . a remedy against sin . . . wilt thou have this woman . . . this man . . . till death us do part . . .*

The man next to her was too cold, so gray and adamantine that she might break against him just as the pieces of the minister's words broke in her ears. Fern's stomach lurched again.

"Thereto I plight thee my troth." It was her own voice, and she felt it buzzing up her throat, but under what power, she could not say.

Then her bouquet was taken away and her hand enfolded in a broader one, cool and strong through kid gloves, a hand that seemed to fill her world . . . and upon her finger, it slid a ring.

Kneeling, standing, kneeling, standing. Fern wanted to shout, to clap her hands over her ears, to do something to stop the torrent of words that bore her helplessly along.

And then it was over.

The clash of the organ, the clang of bells, and they flew down the aisle toward the doors that spilled light like the gates of heaven into the hot cavern of the church.

The Honorable Mr. and Mrs. Colin Barton Jonathan Radcliffe.

Oh, God, what have I done?

And they lived happily ever after.

Was that not what was supposed to happen? Fern gazed out the carriage window—not the window of the flower-festooned landau that had borne the wedding party from St. George's to her parents' town house but Colin's discreet barouche, suitable for the quiet escape of the newlyweds. Around them, the city teemed under the thin drizzle that slid off the rooftops and dampened the streets, wheels rattling and hooves clattering as other vehicles pressed around them. But the interior of the carriage felt muffled, detached from the gray chaos beyond the door, and Fern had the fantastic sensation that the view beyond her window was nothing more than an illusion. The only things in the world that were real were the shadows in the carriage and the man across from her, whose figure was so trim in his perfectly tailored morning suit that he almost seemed edged, as if he could cut her.

Fern had been certain she had shamed herself during the ceremony by betraying something of the panic that she'd felt, but everyone had told her she was demure, beautiful, even radiant, and she wondered if terror gave her a special sheen. The day before, her elder sister Faith had cautioned her that eleventh-hour misgivings could be overwhelming, could even send her into a fit of hysteria or give her the vapors, but Fern had laughed away her warnings. After all, uncertainty was foreign to her nature. Why would her wedding be any different?

The more fool she, Fern thought. But it was over, the final, irrevocable step of matrimony had been taken, and now she could settle down . . . to being happy.

She tried to grasp the idea of happiness now that the terrible rush of the ceremony was over and she'd had the long line of congratulations and the even longer wedding breakfast to calm her nerves. Deliberately, she brought to mind how Colin, seated at the head table, had turned toward her for a moment to treat her to one of his calculatedly charming smiles. In that instant she felt the return of the small, awed thrill that had sometimes made her blush and drop her gaze during their brief courtship. Never mind that she had looked into his eyes and seen his smile reflecting nothing but emptiness. She had clung to that rosy glow with all her might, and even now, in the carriage, the sensation had not completely receded.

"Victoria Station." The words were Colin's, flat in a chilly statement of fact. Hating herself for it, Fern colored at his voice, her gaze still fixed unseeing out the window. She was a married woman, she told herself, and married women did not blush, but the knowledge that soon she'd be truly alone with him for the first time—would even sleep beside him that night—filled her with a combination of dread and a fluttery, discomfiting sensation that she neither understood nor could name.

Briefly, she wished she could be like her friends Mary and Elizabeth Hamilton, knowing and brash and beautiful. But that was not what she had been raised for. She had been raised to be an excellent hostess, a charming dancer, a capable household manager, a loving mother—in short, a good wife. And that was the way Colin wanted her, she reminded herself, or he would have chosen someone else.

The carriage pulled to a stop, and Colin waited impassively as the footman opened the door before descending to the pavement and turning to extend his arm to her. She grasped it, the soft gray cassimere wrinkling under her gloved fingers, and twitched her merino and velvet skirts into place.

Colin's arm was strong and steady under hers as he guided her into the station. Fern ventured a sidelong glance at him. His face was perfectly composed in the expression of impassivity she knew so well, wide mouth and powerful jaw relaxed, green eyes flitting about coldly, casually. No new awkwardness hung about him, no trepidation, just his usual indifferent self-assurance.

She envied him intensely for an instant but then told herself with a sigh that she could not blame him for her own frailty. A woman was not cast in the same mold as a man, as her mother had so often told her. A woman was made of finer stuff, both more delicate and more sublime, and so she should be like a climbing rose wrapping herself around a sturdy trellis, thereby embellishing it as it supported her.

A slight rebelliousness stirred at that simile, as it always did, but she suppressed it. She was no mythical Amazon to go charging about like a man, even if there was a small part of her—a very small part that seemed almost to belong to someone else—that whispered that it ought to be otherwise.

Her thoughts were terminated by their arrival on their platform, where the train to Brighton lay in an arabesque of iron and brass. Their footman gave their hand luggage to the porter, and Fern preceded Colin up the three steps into the train. They followed the blue uniform of the porter to their compartment.

"Tea, please," Colin ordered as the man lifted their handbags onto the rack above the seats.

"Straightaway, sir," the porter replied, and he departed, leaving Colin and Fern alone.

"Well," Fern said, feeling heat creep up her cheeks even as she tried to keep her voice light. "It should be a short trip to Brighton, at least."

"Are you weary, *mon ange*?"

The endearment—how easily said!—served only to make her blush more, despite the fact that there was no warmth in his voice when he spoke the words. "A little," she admitted. The heat of the compartment was stifling, and Fern loosened the ribbons that held her bonnet in place and unbuttoned her braided Zouave jacket as she settled across from him. Out the window, she caught one last glimpse of Colin's footman before he was swallowed by the crowd. It seemed to Fern that a piece of her life had been carried away with him, lost forever in the bustling confusion of the platform.

She looked back as Colin took the seat opposite her, setting his top hat beside him. His midnight hair was still perfectly arranged in a fashionable wave above his forehead, and in the close confines, she could smell the faint masculine perfume of his macassar oil. He suddenly seemed incredibly close to her, though they had been much closer every time she had waltzed across the ballroom floor in his cordial embrace. But always before there had been a restraint—the watchful eyes of a dozen society matrons, the proprieties that seemed to dictate their every move like steps in an intricate dance.

Surely the dance continued now; surely there were things she should say, ways she should behave, but she realized that she did not know what they were. She knew all the niceties of days at home and dinner parties, but what went on behind closed doors between a man and his wife—that, she could only guess. Her education, which had seemed so excruciatingly thorough only yesterday, now felt like a handful of gossamer threads suspending her over a chasm she had not even known was there.

"We shall arrive in time for a walk along the strand before supper," Colin said, as if the air did not stretch both heavy and thin between them.

"I should like that," Fern said. "A honeymoon in Brighton might not be as fashionable as a trip to the Continent, but though I have seen Paris, the Riviera, and all the great cities of Italy, I have never even been to Brighton." She was saying what he already knew, but such trivialities were familiar landmarks in a strange new land.

"It shan't be long now." Something stirred in the inscrutable depths of his eyes. Was that a spark of amusement? Or, dear Lord, was it contempt? Did he guess what uncertainties filled her mind? And yet he looked so unruffled. She tried to take courage from his sanguinity; as long as she could be certain of his lead, she had nothing to fear. This was how it was supposed to be, after all, the wife following the husband. It was not a fault of her education that she did not know what to do but rather a part of the plan. Like a climbing rose . . .

"Yes. It shall be nice to arrive," she said, stifling her

incipient surge of resentment. The words were meaningless—meaningless but safe.

Just then, there was a rap on the compartment door, and it slid open to reveal the porter carrying a tea tray laden with stark railway china. Skillfully, he set up the table between them and placed the tray on top of it just as the sound of the engine changed. Without even swaying at the jerk as the train chugged into motion, he asked if they needed anything else, and assured that they were comfortable for the moment, left again.

Fern hardly had room for another swallow of anything, but the tea was a welcome intervention, a reminder of things ordinary on what was certain to be the most extraordinary day of her life. Her hands shook slightly as she undertook the familiar ritual of serving, adding Colin's two lumps without asking, then her own single lump and cream.

Colin was no stranger, she told herself. Their families had known each other for generations. He couldn't be a stranger. Why was it, then, that she could not reconcile the image of the sober boy in knee breeches with the man who sat across from her now? Why was it that she could not shake the sensation that he was a mere simulacrum of a gentleman, that the real Colin, whoever he was, lurked somewhere deep behind those chilly eyes?

Colin raised the teacup to her in a mock salute, the irony of the motion not reaching his expression. "Thank you, Mrs. Radcliffe."

Fern made herself smile, deciding to take his words as a tender tease. "My pleasure, Mr. Radcliffe." But her gut tightened around the words.

He treated her with a thin smile in return, a twitch

of the lips that did not reach his dead eyes, and then he reached deftly into his coat and brought out a piece of paper, unfolding it and spreading it next to his teacup on the table between them. He bent his head over it, and Fern felt as if she'd vanished from his world—as if she'd been abruptly turned off. She stared at the top of his dark head, her mouth half opened to speak. But there was nothing to be said—nothing she could say—and so she took an unsteady gulp of her tea, her eyes watering as it scalded the back of her throat.

Colin looked up, his gaze distant, and for the first time, Fern read a true expression in his usually blank face: contempt. His hand, which had been resting lightly upon the leaf of paper, balled briefly into a fist, and her breath caught in automatic anticipation. But the hand loosened just as swiftly, and Fern read, involuntarily, the first few lines of the page beneath it: *June 8, Lincoln's Inn. Dear Mr. Radcliffe—*

Jerkily, Colin pulled the sheet off the table and folded it, sliding it back into his coat.

"What is it, dear?" she managed to ask in a slightly strangled voice, not so much because she wanted to know but because some part of her foolishly feared that she might disappear in truth if she did not reinsinuate herself into Colin's world somehow.

Colin's upper lip was still lifted in a sneer, and the gaze that he turned on her contained echoes of disdain. "It is business," he said distinctly. "It is no concern of yours. Do not ask me about such matters again."

Fern set down her cup too hard, the unglazed bottom scraping across the saucer. Colin did not wait for her response; he was already staring out the window, an uncharateristic frown creasing his brow. The letter had rattled him, and she had never seen Colin so much as surprised before.

Fern felt a chill slip up her spine. She had never been given to prescience, but she had the sudden feeling that the letter he had tucked away held a great and dire significance for their future.

Stones rattled beneath their feet as Colin escorted Fern along the beach. Colin kept an eye on his wife— his wife; what an odd thought, that, lying heavy and foreign in his mind—in case she took a misstep among the rounded pebbles in her smooth-soled, high-heeled boots.

Damn that letter, anyhow, he thought with bleak intensity. *Damn all the letters*, he amended. His solicitor was being singularly unhelpful in the investigation of the affairs at Wrexmere Manor, which, it seemed, had descended into an inextricable muddle. Now Mr. Barnes was attempting to convince Colin that perhaps an application to his father would be best. But Colin had been given direct management of his family's oldest estate upon his majority, and the solicitor had all the relevant records in his possession. There was no reason to disturb the viscount about it, even if, as Colin was beginning to suspect, embezzlement and mismanagement were involved. It looked increasingly as if the problem would require his own personal attention, however. He did not look forward to it. He had never been to Wrexmere, and from the distasteful manner with which his mother spoke of the place, he had no desire to go. But he knew his duty, and he would fulfill it, as he always did.

Beside him, there was a sudden clatter as Fern's

foot struck a stone and sent it skipping away, and Colin reached out reflexively to steady her elbow. But she shied away at his movement, and then, as if she had caught herself, she seemed to deliberately steel herself before moving slightly closer to him again.

Fern had been skittish throughout the train ride, and Colin had begun to wonder, with some displeasure, if he had misjudged the woman he had chosen to be his wife. She had seemed so placid and undemanding during their brief courtship, so pretty, plump, and conventional. He had imagined her not so often in his arms as at the head of his table and at the doorway to his ballroom, and the mental picture had satisfied him. But now . . . he was not certain what she was.

Nervous, he reassured himself. She was merely nervous.

At Fern's tentative request—and to his own thorough indifference—they had left the shrubbery-bordered promenade to walk closer to the edge of the water. The day had continued as it began: hot, nearly cloudless, with the pale June sun bleaching the grays, tans, and browns of the shingle until it stretched before them as a single motley band squeezed between the white seawall and the gray ocean. Around them strolled clutches of tourists, out for one last walk before supper, hands holding hats to heads and crinolines swaying like ringing bells in the breeze. It was too bright, too hot, and Colin could smell a warning in the wind.

"Look at the seagulls!" Fern said abruptly. Scores wheeled and shrieked in the air above their heads, while on the beach, dozens more stalked among the

feet and skirts of the passersby, their beaks darting out
to tear at an abandoned picnic lunch.

Colin gave them a distasteful look. "There are gulls
on the Thames," he reminded her.

"Yes, but they're such dirty birds, as sooty as any
pigeon. These are different. They're almost noble, if
such a word could be applied to a gull." Fern turned
her face toward his, and he saw the strain on it as she
delivered her little speech in a mimicry of light-
hearted chatter.

At least she was trying now. Relenting, Colin
looked up at the screaming, wheeling forms silhouet-
ted against the sun. "They are certainly less disrep-
utable." He did not add that he found them more
sinister than noble. Gulls, sinister? He immediately
chided himself for his foolishness at allowing his private preoccupations to color his view of the world.

He glanced back at Fern, and she flushed abruptly
and shifted her own gaze to the ground before her, the
side of her bonnet shutting out his view of her as effectively as a pair of blinders.

The blushing bride . . . Suddenly the cliché an-
noyed him, and he had to suppress the urge to scowl.
What was wrong with him? Why was it that he was
just as dissatisfied when she behaved exactly as he expected her to as he was when she surprised him? If he
could not even look at her without growing impa-
tient, this would be a very tedious marriage, indeed.

"When did you first notice me?"

The question pulled Colin abruptly from his
thoughts, and he refocused upon her. Fern was still
pink with lingering self-consciousness, but her gray
eyes were now steadily fixed upon his face. A single
light brown curl had slid from under her bonnet to ca-

ress her cheek in the sea breeze, and he reached out and brushed it aside experimentally, to see what she would do. Fern's color deepened at that gesture, but her gaze did not waver.

"I don't know," Colin answered, being honest without meaning to. *Why not her?* was a better question. Fern had always been in the background of his life, starting with house parties and country visits when they were children. But he could say the same of so many others, Fern's two sisters and the Hamilton twins among them. Why her, specifically, and when? There had been several young things that season who had seemed suitable to become his wife—and eventually his viscountess—but the choice of Fern had simply seemed the easiest.

"Oh, come now, you surely have a guess." A small smile flitted across her delicate rosebud lips. "You must tell me. After all, we're married, and husbands and wives keep no secrets from each other."

A pang of something—guilt? incredulity?—shot through him at that remark, but he answered lightly. "You are quite right. It must have been the day that you, Lady Mary, and Lady Elizabeth climbed an apple tree in the Rushworth orchard and you got stuck."

"Oh!" Fern exclaimed, her face thrown into lines of dismay. "I could have lived my life happily never having been reminded of that. I was trying so hard to be adventurous, like the twins. . . . "

"But you didn't have it in you. I know."

"And then two of your horrible brothers started throwing clods of dirt at me—"

"And I rescued you," Colin finished.

She shot him a disbelieving look, her first unchecked

natural reaction since their marriage. "You did no such thing!"

He was bemused by her uncharacteristic vehemence. "I called the gardener; isn't that close enough?" That small boy's feelings seemed so remote from what Colin was now, if his motivations could even be given the depth of emotion that such a word as *feelings* implied. He remembered his weary irritation at his brothers' undignified behavior and the indignant certainty that their malfeasance would reflect, inevitably, upon him as the oldest. As for Fern, he couldn't remember feeling anything about her at all except annoyance that she'd got herself into such a foolish predicament.

Fern giggled. "I suppose I can grant you that. My knight in shining armor, if a little tardy to save me from a torn dress and mud stains." She paused for a moment, her expression turning tentative again. "But still, I don't believe you took any special notice of me then."

He pressed his lips together. What answer would satisfy her? "Fern, I am afraid I cannot tell you what you want to know, for I do not know myself."

His chilly tone must have affected her, for Fern said, "Oh," and her face closed a little. "I apologize for my presumption. I should not have pressed you."

Abruptly, Colin was weary of walking upon the beach, weary of the conversation, and weary of her. He turned toward the promenade, catching her elbow before she could pull away as he flagged down a fly with his free hand. "I am hungry," he said, ignoring her slight stiffening at his touch. "Let us go in to supper."

Fern cast him a queer, unreadable look, and for an

instant, he almost thought she would demur. But her face cleared, and she nodded in agreement. "Yes. Let's."

The fly stopped in front of them, and Colin handed her up, steeling himself for the ride. As pretty as his wife was, he did not look forward to that evening.

Chapter Two

Colin had imbibed too much over supper, Fern thought miserably. He was not truly inebriated, not quite; no gentleman became drunk in the presence of a lady. But his voice was a shade too loud, his movements a fraction too expansive, and Fern had been enough in the company of men to know what that meant.

It was her fault. The awareness of her guilt settled heavily over her like a smothering drift of wool, making her movements dull and clumsy as she passed through the suite's drawing room into the bedchamber. She had ruined their walk on the beach, though she was not entirely sure how, and when they had stepped down out of the carriage in front of their rented Clifton Terrace row house, Fern had still felt stupid and awkward . . . and obscurely angry, which only made her more stupid and awkward. She had stumbled through the introduction to the housekeeper and the three maids who came with the house, and they had surveyed her with a kind of earnest pity and spoken very slowly, as if she were a half-wit. Supper had been delivered from the Grand Hotel and spread on the broad table in the dining room, and she had been left alone with Colin save for a single maid, which had made Fern even more tongue-tied than before.

Over the roast, she had even called him Mr. Radcliffe, not jokingly but as if they were once again in the first stages of courtship. After that, the evening had dissolved into long silences punctuated only by her inane observations about their accommodations, the weather, and the food, and his short replies. Fern had watched as Colin downed glass after glass of wine, conscious of his closeness, conscious of her failure. Colin was a viscount's heir; he needed a consummate hostess, a woman who could behave with grace and charm in any situation. Before that evening, Fern had thought she was that woman. Now, she no longer knew what she was.

The orange glow of the gaslights bathed the bedroom gently, making the green silk of the counterpane and the Oriental wallpaper shine like the inside of a Fabergé egg. Colin's valet, who had arrived ahead of them, and Fern's local maid were nowhere in sight. Automatically, she reached for the bellpull to summon them, but she started when a warm, large hand enclosed her wrist and arrested it midmotion.

"We have no need of attendants tonight." Colin's voice was laced with cool amusement that sent goose bumps across her flesh.

Fern turned to face him, her wrist still encircled by his broad fingers. She was too aware of his touch, of him standing there and looking at her with a distant, hooded expression. She could hardly guess at the meaning in his gaze, but it stirred up a heat in her midsection, part fearful queasiness and part something else entirely, prickly and disconcerting. The heat crept up her body, tightening her skin in its wake, and she knew with sudden mortification that her face was once again scarlet.

"I'm sorry; I didn't think to ask. . . ." She realized she was babbling and took a deep breath. "That is, you were quite right to stop me, Mr. Radcliffe—I mean, Colin." The familiarity of using his Christian name did not come as easily as it should to a wife. "I did not consult you before acting, and I apologize."

Colin's mouth twisted, his eyes narrow, and she caught a whiff of postsupper port on his breath, sweetly intoxicating. "Do you think that's what a good wife does? Consults her husband about every little thing?"

"Yes—I mean, no, of course not." Fern scowled at her stumbling tongue, but Colin's smile only broadened, taking on an edge that made her stomach flutter. He was diverted by his wife's foolishness, no doubt, she thought with a bitterness she hardly recognized as her own. Yet, like every expression she had seen on his face, his smile seemed more like an accessory than a reflection of genuine emotion. Every expression except for one—when he had read that letter in the train, then she had seen a trace of something that was incontrovertibly real. She suppressed a flash of apprehension and made herself explain. "But since you obviously cared about this, I thought I should have asked you in this instance—"

"*Mon ange*, my dove—it is our wedding night." His words were tinged with a faint amusement, whether sympathetic or mocking, she could not tell. He pulled her toward him, using his grip on her wrist to place her arm around his waist while cradling the back of her neck in his other hand. Her skin prickled at his touch; even though it was light, she felt that she would not be able to escape his grasp if he did not choose to let her go. "Don't you know what that means?"

Fern's instinct was to pull away and drop her gaze, but she forced herself to meet his eyes. His thumb brushed against the nape of her neck, and she shivered, that small movement reminding her how close they were as her wide skirts rustled against his legs.

"Yes." She was glad to find that her voice was steady, even if her nerves were anything but. "We will go to bed together." And more, she knew from the Hamilton twins' whispered stories and the vague hints her elder sister Faith had dropped. There would be kissing, too, and something else that Fern was too embarrassed to ask about, something that had made the imperturbable Faith blush and mumble and the twins burst into gales of laughter and exchange meaningful looks. *Trust your husband*, Faith had said finally, and that was what Fern must now do.

But he wasn't as easy to trust as Faith seemed to think he must be. In Colin's eyes was a light that made Fern wary, an interest that seemed to have cold intellect behind it rather than a warmer tenderness, and though the arms that held her were sure and strong, they felt like another kind of trap. As traitorous as it might be, Fern was not quite certain that she wanted to be defined by her husband's surety. He was, as always, every inch a gentleman, utterly self-composed and completely in command—of himself and, at that moment, of her, too.

The perfect husband. So why was she afraid of him?

His face filled her vision, and Fern realized abruptly that it was not some trick of her agitated mind: He was bending toward her. To kiss her.

Her breath quickened as heat flared anew deep within her center, shooting through her limbs and downward, deeper, with an intensity that made her jerk away without thinking.

But Colin's hand on her neck and the other that slid around her waist held her firmly, brought her up short, and in another breath his mouth caught her.

Astonishment froze her. It was like nothing she had experienced—nothing she had imagined. The restrained and formal kiss in her parents' parlor after she accepted his hand had left her pink and breathless for minutes after, little shivers of happiness dancing across her skin, but that—that was a spark to a bonfire.

Colin possessed her mouth, moving his lips against hers in an utterly thorough way that sent her senses whirling as tension curled tautly in her midsection. She had never thought that a man's mouth could be so *hot*. He pulled her tightly against him and kissed her again, harder. She could feel the contours of his chest against her hand, trapped between them—could feel the size and heat of his body that sucked her strength until her knees went weak and her mind plunged into confusion.

Her sudden twinge of fear was drowned in the roar of heat that followed, surging through every nerve and dimming her vision until nothing was left but the touch of him, the heat of him, the taste of him. His tongue was inside her mouth, and she sampled the

warm, rich aftertaste of port. She felt herself falling
into his arms, dissolving into him—

—and came to herself as abruptly as waking from a
dream. She jerked back so hard that she yanked herself
from his embrace, hardly feeling a twinge as half a
dozen strands of her hair, twisted around his fingers,
tore from her scalp.

Colin looked at her. His gaze made her heart race
even as she shuddered a little at how detached his expression was, as if nothing of what had torn through
her had even ruffled him.

"Is something amiss?" he asked, his tone as cool as
if he were asking for a dance at a ball.

"Yes. No. I don't know," she said as confusion and
embarrassment rose in a hot red haze around her. "It
just doesn't seem right. None of this seems right."

"Shhh." Colin placed one broad, rough finger
across her lips, and to her further mortification, even
that slight touch roused a tingling that spread across
her skin. "*Mon ange*, everything is exactly as it
should be. Do not be afraid. You have been doing
very well."

Rebellious rejection jolted through her at those airy
words, but Fern had no chance to incorporate it before
he stepped forward, catching her against the wall with
nowhere to go. Heat seemed to radiate from him, stirring her body into response, and she almost gasped
with the contact when he cupped the back of her head
in his palm. But he only lowered his forehead to rest
against hers. His gaze bore into hers, and she could tell
that he knew the shivering expectation that filled her
with that touch. His shadowed eyes, though, were as
still as a mirror, and as unreadable.

"You are doing just fine," he whispered, the breeze

of his breath making her own catch. "There is nothing, nothing at all wrong."

And then he kissed her again, and all thought fled. His mouth was on hers, his tongue against her teeth, his hands across her body, sliding to the row of pearl buttons along her spine.

He loosened the one under her satin belt where her bodice met her skirt, and she stiffened. Was he supposed to be doing that? It seemed too ridiculous to protest. If they were to share a bed, they could not spend the next forty years dancing around to avoid each other's naked bodies. Besides, Colin was a gentleman; he surely wasn't doing anything he wasn't supposed to. It felt so good, his mouth hot against her neck, his hands moving against her body. The efficiency of his motions frightened her a little for reasons she could not define. But he must be right, she told herself as a delicious heat shivered across her skin in the wake of his mouth. There could be nothing wrong at all. . . .

This was going to be a more pleasant duty than he had anticipated. Colin assessed the pliancy of the woman in his arms against his previous experience and arrived at a highly satisfying conclusion.

Why had he ever thought that passion didn't matter in a wife? After all, however many mistresses one kept on the side, it was always the wife one came home to, always the wife who was the closest source of relief. He kissed the crevice where Fern's generous breasts met, and she gasped. Smiling smugly against her soft skin, he congratulated himself on his choice, even though it was surely luck that had brought him this desire instead of stone. To think he'd been working himself up to this all night, as if it would be some sort of distasteful obligation! It was pleasant to know that his marriage bed would at least be a warm one.

The last button of Fern's bodice loosened under his fingers. The fine grenadine rustled, and the lace on the neck and sleeves bunched as he slid it down her arms, revealing her ruched and beribboned corset cover. It was wedding white, glaring in its purity, but it had no power to awe him, for its austerity served only to accentuate the thoroughly earthy pink-tinged flesh of the plump arms and lush bosom that escaped the confining whalebone. The golden haze of alcohol was scarcely necessary to appreciate such a sight.

He tossed the bodice aside, the sleeves fluttering as it fell, and looked up to meet Fern's gray eyes, wide with emotion. Surprise? Alarm? Desire? Maybe all three, wrapped into one.

He had the urge to rip off her corset and free those breasts, but her expression checked him. No need to scare her, he decided. He knew well enough how to seduce a woman into a satisfactory state of enthusiasm when it was best to do so, and he judged that now was one of those times. He unfastened her silk belt almost decorously, unhooking the waistband of her skirt beneath it. He fumbled a bit at the layers of petticoats—he seemed to have grown too many fingers—until he found the ties for her crinoline. Two tugs and it was loose, falling to the floor with a muffled clatter.

Fern giggled a bit breathlessly, and he lifted her free of it. She gave him a nervous, half-coy smile, more than a shade silly. *Well*, he thought, *if what she needs right now is a little silliness, I can give her that easily enough.* So he spun her around three times, her laughter filling the silken tent of the room, before he overbalanced and let her slide a little too abruptly to the floor.

"Oh, my," she said, grabbing his arm. She looked up at him through a fringe of brown eyelashes. He took her chin in one hand and tilted it up.

"You truly are a remarkable young woman," he said, looking into her eyes firmly, sincerely.

He felt her breath catch in perfect reaction, and her lips parted in anticipation and invitation. An invitation he had no intention of refusing.

He caught her mouth with his, his free hand moving down her waist to push her skirts over her round hips to slide to the floor in an unheeded froth of ruffles.

Fern made a little sound in her throat. His body tightened in reaction, and he held her harder against him as a jolt of lust buzzed up his spine, the stiff curves of her corset promising yielding flesh beneath.

She was willing now; he was certain of it—and he was more than ready. He lifted her into his arms and carried her over to the bed, ignoring the skirts as he trod on them. She gasped a little and giggled again as he set her down on the counterpane.

Her cheeks were pink, her lips still swollen and damp from his kisses, and her eyes were shadowed with innocent desire that made him feel decidedly lupine. Hurriedly, he stripped off his coat and necktie, his waistcoat, braces, shirt, and undershirt following. As he unfastened the first button on his fly, her gaze caught him again. He wanted nothing more than to have those eyes locked upon him as he shoved up her chemise and entered her right there as he stood between her legs beside the bed.

But trepidation was foremost in the welter of emotion he read on her face, and so he tamped down those urges and crossed to the doorway, where he turned the knob to shut off the gaslight. With only the glimmer of the lamps in the drawing room puddling in the doorway, he returned to the bedside.

"Are you sure this is right?" Fern whispered.

Colin couldn't hold back his laugh. "This is what married people do, *mon ange*." He stripped off his pants and drawers, pulling off his shoes and socks as he joined her on the bed. "You know that."

"Of course." Uncertainty still laced her tone, so Colin found her mouth to kiss it away. Beneath him, Fern tipped her head back, welcoming him. Her hands slid around him, her palms flat against his back. She held still for a moment, them skimmed them downward. He could feel her excitement at her own daring in the tension of her body, in the quickness of her breath and the slight quaking of the small hands splayed against his back. Her tremulous excitement was . . . heady. Dizzying. Wonderful, which was a sensation he scarcely recognized enough to name. It filled him with a sense of power, like a man about to gently pluck a precious flower, hesitating a moment with the petals against his palm, velvet, soft, and fragile.

Her hands reached his flanks and stopped.

"You *are* naked," Fern said, her tone split between awe and scandal.

"As you will be soon," he assured her. He reached underneath her and found the laces of her corset. He pulled the bow loose with a single tug, but with his hands sandwiched between her and the mattress, the lacing defeated him. "If you don't mind?"

"What?" Her voice was breathless in the darkness. "Oh."

She started to shift, the silk and linen of her drawers and stockings rasping against the embroidery of the counterpane, but there was a tug under his knee, and she stopped.

"Pardon me, Mrs. Radcliffe," he said in tones of exaggerated seriousness, knowing that it was the right thing to say, and she tittered predictably and pulled the lace edging of her chemise from under him as he shifted his weight away.

"No need, Mr. Radcliffe," she replied almost coquettishly. He could see only a vague outline of her body in the light from the parlor, but he could tell that she was smiling.

He sat back on his heels as she rose to sit, giving her room to twist around and turn her back toward him. His fingers found the naked skin of her back before encountering the corset, and he felt her delicate shiver against his hand. For a moment, he let it rest there, savoring the prickle as goose bumps sprang up on the smooth flesh. Desire shot through his body, making his erection ache with need.

Then he gave the laces a few expert tugs—well, semiexpert, at least, because there seemed to be a bit more clumsiness involved than he was used to—and reached around her to unhook the busk.

The corset came loose in his hands, and he eased it off her shoulders with a sense of deep satisfaction and almost ceremonious decorum. This would be the first time of many times, the first night of countless nights, and so some semblance of formality seemed only appropriate for the culmination of such a significant day.

The confection of lace came free of her arms, and Colin tossed it away—wincing when it clattered against something in the darkness beyond the bed—and pulled her back against him, her buttocks settling between his legs and his erection pressing against the small of her back as his arms settled around her small, soft waist.

She made a small startled sound and arched her back away from his groin, but he held her there, and with his mouth, he found the small indentation where her neck met the muscle of her shoulder, kissing it. Under the faintly acrid taste of her perfume, her flesh was warm and sweet, soft and smooth. After another moment of resistance, she sighed and settled back against him. But there was still a wary tightness in her body that warned him not to press too hard.

Go slowly, then, he told himself, though he wanted to do anything but. Still, he listened to his own advice and loosened his hold upon her, and she immediately pulled away.

He put his hands on her shoulders and urged her to face him. After a moment's hesitation, she did. He found an ankle by feel. Her foot was only stocking-clad; she must have slipped out of her shoes when he set her on the bed, proper lady that she was. He slid lower in the bed and found her garter ties just below her knee and tugged them loose. She stiffened, and he bent to kiss her plump calf.

"It is fine, Fern," he said against the silk.

"Of course it is," she agreed, but she didn't sound as certain as he'd like.

Slowly, he cautioned himself again.

He rolled down the stocking and pulled it off,

followed by the other, the fine hairs on her legs rising in the wake of his touch. Then, with great deliberation, he traced the outside of her drawers-clad leg up to her abdomen, then cupped a linen-covered breast in one hand and bridged the distance between them with his mouth.

Chapter Three

Fern gasped as Colin's hand closed around her breast, then again as his mouth—his mouth!—found her nipple through the thin chemise. Heat washed through her, humiliation warring with pleasure. Surely this wasn't how it was supposed to go. It must be a test of some sort. She should tell him to stop.

But she didn't want to, and when she opened her mouth the moan that emerged didn't sound anything like a protest. The wet linen scraped across her skin to the movements of his tongue. It should have been irritating, and it was in a way, but it was also . . . incredible.

She did protest automatically when he finally lifted his head, but he only released her long enough to find her other breast. He pulled her toward him, and she let herself come, awash in the pleasure that was half need, half emptiness where she was ashamed to admit to feeling anything at all.

He pulled her onto his lap, her legs on either side of his waist. Between them, even though she was not pressed against it, was that hot bar of flesh that somehow did not correspond to her memories of the statues she had seen in Italy. But there was no need to think of it now, not with his mouth on her body, his free hand sliding under the fabric of her chemise to press against the small of her back.

He released her breast for as long as it took to ease her chemise over her head. Fern thought she had been prepared by his caresses for the contact of his flesh against hers, but she was wrong. She shuddered at the shock of his rough palm against her skin, and her nerves hummed in expectation as she sensed him bend his head again. But he caught her mouth first, then worked his way down her neck. She leaned back against the hand at the back of her head and let him ease her onto the counterpane.

He tugged at her drawers, and she thought, *This is it*. But what exactly *it* was, she wasn't sure she knew. Still, a feeling of irrevocability accompanied the soft sound as her pantaloons dropped to the ground.

He kissed her forehead, her cheeks, her lips, murmuring incomprehensibly. He shifted between her thighs, and she felt the hot hardness against her belly and froze at its strangeness, at its weight that was somehow menacing. But Colin's murmurs continued uninterrupted, and she relaxed as he continued to coax her, to tease her with his mouth. His tongue traced a slow circle around her ear, his teeth catching at the hollow of her clavicle, then down, teasing circles around the sensitive skin of her breast before finally taking her nipple into his mouth. A shock ran through her body, setting her nerve endings to tingling as heat swirled dizzyingly in her head.

He lifted his head, and she was still panting and dizzy when she felt a hard, round prodding at the intersection of her legs.

No, she thought, *that can't be right*. She started to object, but then he pushed, and she felt herself opening to the invasion. That rod of flesh was too hot, too large, stretching her, hurting her. She floundered, unable to spin her unraveling wits into a thought, to wrap it around what was happening to her and her denial of it. The ache became a pain that lanced through her, and her protest was lost in a hiss. Then he pulled back, and she managed to get control of her voice again.

"W-wait." But it was hardly a whisper, swallowed in the horror and lingering pain.

Colin paused, and she thought for an instant that he had heard her, but then he thrust into her again, deeper.

This time, there was only a slight burn of discomfort and then something new and strange, a kind of pleasure that came unexpectedly, so much like the pain that it was hard for a moment to tell them apart. The aching hollowness within her was filled, satisfying a different kind of ache, but how it was filled! Something in her rebelled—rebelled against the pain and pleasure that Colin stole from her, spiraling her own body out of her control, but most of all, against the invasion of that shaft of flesh and its possession of her body.

I am mine, mine, mine. But Colin's body pinned her against the bed, his thrusts summoning from her sensations that she had no power to control or even understand. Part of her body crowed with a ravenous delight, welcoming the mastery and the pleasure both, lifting her legs to encircle his waist and tightening her hands around his biceps. But the deepest part of her ran away, curled up and hid from that pillaging of her body.

With that retreat, the traitorous welcoming built with every thrust into a sizzling heat that threatened to overwhelm her, pushing her higher as his rhythm increased. But it wasn't without a price. She felt it taking—felt *him* taking—and she closed her eyes against it as she tried to shut her mind to his insidious invasion.

He was heavy against her, demanding, asking for a part of her that she did not want to give, and suddenly that anger within her, the part so distant she hardly felt it to be a part of her, boiled to the top. Her hands, which had been lying limp against the counterpane, lifted to the chest that was hanging over her and pushed.

Colin's breathing changed abruptly, but he didn't so much as shift. He thrust into her again and again and again, and then he gave a low moan and a shudder that shook his whole body; and then he lay still.

Stunned, she let her hands drop. A moment later, with a chilly kiss on her cheek, Colin pushed away, leaving Fern with a dampness between her legs and the feeling that she had been used. She lay there limply, staring at the ceiling, while beside her, her husband's breath returned to its normal pace. A minute passed, then two. Colin rolled out of bed. She watched his naked silhouette as he stepped into the light of the suite's parlor, and then she heard the noise of a door open and shut.

The water closet, she realized numbly. He was going to the water closet. For some reason, the mundanity of that action seemed absurd, even insulting. After what had happened between them, that unspeakable, wonderful, horrible thing that he had done to her, he went to relieve himself?

It came to her as she lay there, motionless, that this was what Faith and the twins had meant by their titters and innuendos. Fern knew now the reason for their blushes . . . but their smiles? That she could not fathom. How could a woman give in to the pleasure with the violation that accompanied it? The brutal, unsubtle assertion of power and ownership? She grabbed a corner of the rumpled counterpane and scrubbed it between her legs as if she could wipe away the memory, too. Maybe there was something wrong with her. Maybe it was that part of her that never could be still when she was lectured on the duties of a wife, too strong and too stubborn to fall into easy subservience. It couldn't be right. Not in a virtuous, upstanding woman.

But Fern was not so sure anymore exactly how virtuous she wanted to be.

Faith would probably just shake her head if she knew what Fern was feeling, and the twins . . . Who ever knew what the twins were thinking? Perhaps they were so used to sharing with each other that they didn't imagine such an encounter an invasion. Fern knew what the rector at Dunville would have advised: that she pray for a softer heart so that she would welcome the mastery of her husband.

But she didn't want a softer heart. She wanted to be whole again, to be herself again, with Colin safely on the other side of her skin.

She heard the parlor door open, and the light in the parlor dimmed. Quickly, she wriggled under the covers, pulling them up to her chin, counterpane and all, despite the muggy night. Staring at the vague folds of the window curtains with her back to the doorway, she heard Colin stumble in through the darkness.

He hesitated for a moment, and she could feel his gaze sweeping across the room, trying to make out the shapes of the furniture in the darkness. Footsteps again. They reached the opposite side of the bed, but instead of stopping, they followed the bed's perimeter around. Fern could feel his hand dragging against the counterpane through the mattress as he used it to guide him.

She closed her eyes as he rounded the corner at the foot of the bed, half fearing and half hoping that he would come up to her and . . . what?

But whatever incipient expectations she harbored were disappointed, for he came no closer. He took two steps away from the bed, and then the curtains swished back and the sash grated up, first on one window, then on the other. A damp, salt-laden breeze, marginally cooler than the close air of the room, drifted through to touch Fern's cheek.

The footsteps retreated as Colin circled back around the bed. For an instant, there was nothing, then a weight settled on the mattress, enough greater than hers that Fern's body began to tilt toward him before she realized what was happening and shifted to settle more firmly in her crease in the bed.

She felt a brush on the back of her neck, Colin's fingers catching slightly in the disarray of her coiffure. But she did not move, and the hand retreated. Soon his breathing eased into the slow rhythm of sleep, occasionally punctuated by slightly drunken snores.

But it was a very long time before Fern found any rest.

Fern woke to a yellow dawn and the shrill cry of a gull. She lay still for a moment, looking through the twin rectangles of the windows at the slate-tiled roofs across the street, the long blue sky stretching above them. The emptiness of it echoed something new within her, something so raw and wide that she could not encompass it.

Already, the day was warm, and sweat dampened her body beneath the sheets. The blankets and counterpane were bunched at the foot of the bed; she must have pushed them off in her sleep.

She slipped out of bed, careful not to disturb her husband, who lay sprawled on top of the sheets in warm, buttery light like some slumbering, capricious Greek god. His perfectly molded muscles were softened in unconsciousness, his lean flanks bare, his side-turned face hidden in the crook of his elbow. She regarded him for a moment with a mixture of feelings that she could put no simple name to. Fear was part of it, and uncertainty, and some instinctive thrill that she alone could see the embodiment of masculine power lying unaware . . . and almost defenseless. And, to her shame, desire was part of it, too.

Fern turned away from him to look down upon the street, the slight, salt-tainted breeze cooling her skin. A few stray pedestrians passed in the thin light below, servants and laborers already at work even at this early hour. She ought to draw the curtains: If one of them looked up, there was a chance he might see her through the open window.

But she began to understand, now, that emptiness that she felt upon awakening; whatever part of her had held the modesty of innocence was no longer there. That piece of her had been hers alone, but now it was gone, stolen past all recovery, so what did it matter who saw what remained? She wanted, in some bizarre way, for the world to know what had happened to her. She wanted to shout it aloud, and whether the impulse was anger, betrayal, or something both more obscure and more wild within her, she did not know.

But she was used to ignoring that unconventional corner of her mind. So instead, she crossed the room softly, the jointure of her legs aching slightly with every step. The pain was like a brand left in her flesh, a tangible echo of what Colin had taken: *It is mine. I have claimed you.*

No, I am mine, she thought, with fierceness and hopelessness. Why had no one told her this was what marriage was? There was, of course, a great deal of talk about two people becoming one flesh, but no one had ever explained what that meant. No one had ever told her that the flesh they would become was the husband's, the wife's annihilated in the heat of that thrusting ego.

Fern stopped in front of the dresser and lifted the transferware water pitcher that waited beside a small stack of crisp white cloths. The blue and white Chinese ladies in the basin seemed to look at her reproachfully as the water swirled up to drown them. Fern leaned over the basin and splashed her face, fragmenting their images in a cascade of drops and ripples. She tasted salt as the water flowed across her lips, and she felt lightened when it had gone. When she washed between her legs, the linen came away spotted with the rusty brown of dried blood.

There was a stirring from the bed, and Fern raised her eyes to meet Colin's gaze in the mirror. He was on his back, his head propped up on the pillows and his long, lean body stretched out across the bed. His private parts lay exposed, and Fern could not help but look, remembering the night before. His member was nothing like the huge, hard, heavy thing she had felt then, but it still bore little resemblance to the paintings in the British Museum or the statues in the less bowdlerized Italian villas. It was darker than the skin around it, almost purple, and it lay, bloated and strangely limp, pillowed on a nest of hair and lying slightly over his thigh.

A sense of shame at their nakedness stole over her, but there was something hot and proud and brittle in the feeling, too, like a beggared queen brought before her conqueror. The look he gave her was thorough, possessive, and abruptly, she wanted no part of it. She wadded up the damp linen cloth so the stain was hidden and dropped it on the dresser.

Her untouched dressing gown had been laid out on the bench at the foot of the bed, and now she picked it up and slid her arms into its ruffled sleeves, a shield of lace and linen.

Colin lifted an eyebrow. "The view was pleasant."

"If you wish me to remove my clothing, you need only order me to do so. I did promise to obey." Those words came unbidden, and Fern was almost startled to hear herself say them.

Colin's eyes narrowed, and her breath caught a little at the coldness in them. No man should be so formidable with sleep-ruffled hair. "I would hope that I needn't ever order you to do anything."

Fern regretted her words instantly. "Of course not. I was only teasing."

But she felt the empty space curl up into a hot, hard kernel in a distant corner of her mind, and her fingers seemed to act of their own accord, for they finished buttoning up her dressing gown before she turned away again to see to her toilette.

Colin grimaced as Fern turned her back to him. He had lain awake for some time, staying in bed in the vain hope that his nausea and headache would disappear before his new wife woke. Despite the too-bright light that streamed in through the windows and made his eyeballs ache, Fern's soft face was a pleasing enough vision, if only her brow didn't knit in such an unbecoming way when she looked at him. He would have liked it even better were the room decently dim.

He swung his legs out of bed and stood up—and immediately regretted it. Rubbing his aching forehead, he circled around the bed and shut the windows with two quick swishes of the velvet curtains.

Much better.

It had probably been a bad idea to get drunk on his wedding night, he admitted to himself. But he hadn't been so drunk that the memory of it had been obscured, and from everything that he recalled, it had still been a satisfying encounter. His lust had been sated, and Fern had been willing and enjoyable enough. Perhaps she hadn't indulged in the acrobatics that some women of his acquaintance prided themselves in, but that was no flaw; he was glad enough to have an innocent as a wife, and he'd always found such elaborations unnecessary and undesirable in his quest for a satisfying release.

He turned too quickly, sending another bolt of pain through his head. "You look lovely, *mon ange*, but you are the only lovely thing about this blasted morning," he said, hiding his wince.

She laughed, her face relaxing, and he realized that it had been tense.

Yet more honeymoon jitters, he thought with a very private mental snort. Must he spend the next month coaxing her out of herself every night? He couldn't see what she could possibly still be nervous about. With everything taken into account, their wedding night had gone well enough. Almost perfectly satisfactorily, if she hadn't gone so rigid there toward the end. He turned away from her and shrugged on his dressing gown.

"I had planned for us to see the Pavilion today." He tied the sash of the dressing gown around his waist in two efficient movements. "Somehow, though, I am less enthusiastic than I was." He glanced at the window, where sunlight painfully gilded the edges of the curtains where they did not meet properly.

She smiled again, and this time, he could see the strain in it. "Visiting the Pavilion sounds delightful."

A properly agreeable response. Why, then, did it rankle him? "As soon as we finish breakfast," he promised. Her glazed expression did not alter. He crossed to the bedside again and tugged the bellpull.

"I will meet you downstairs in half an hour," he said, opening the wardrobe to pull out a morning suit and searching in the drawers until he had socks, underclothing, and a starched white shirt to match. He shoved his feet into his shoes without bending down. "Williams will attend me in the parlor so that you may dress in privacy with that maid, whatever her name is."

"Lucy." Her expression changed, but the shift was inscrutable, so he could not fathom what it meant. Then she thanked him with enough sincerity that he dismissed his lingering doubts as he left the room.

"You're quite welcome, *mon ange*," he replied

automatically, but he shut the door behind him with a feeling of uncertainty. He wasn't sure anymore what this marriage was going to be, and it was the first time in his memory that he had been uncertain about anything that mattered.

He decided that he disliked the feeling, and he only hoped that he would not dislike his wife, too.

Chapter Four

Fern stared blankly at the door that Colin had just closed, feeling as if the world were falling away under her feet.

To him nothing had changed. He had no idea what he had done to her, what she had felt. He had done it to her and she didn't even *know*.

The door opened again, and Fern stiffened. But it was her temporary lady's maid who entered.

"Morning, m'm," she said, bobbing and giving Fern a boldly curious glance through her lashes despite her down-tilted head.

"Good morning," Fern said with as much dignity as she could muster. She turned away and jerked open the window curtains, letting the light and the sea breeze back into the suddenly stifling room. She turned back to meet the maid's scandalized expression.

"But, m'm, someone might see in!"

"Then I will stand away from the windows," Fern said firmly.

The woman opened her mouth as if she wanted to argue, then shut it again. "Yes, m'm."

Fern unbuttoned her dressing gown and stood like a mannequin while the maid dressed her, pretending she did not see the knowing glances the girl cast at the scattered clothing from the night before and the disarray of the bed.

More knowing than I, she thought with abrupt resentment. But she said nothing, did nothing, just allowed herself to be clothed in her blue taffeta walking dress and then sat obediently at the vanity to permit the maid to repair the ravages of her hair.

As the girl worked, Fern looked at her reflection for the first time in a very long while. She had sat like this for a lady's maid a thousand times since she had come out, and at least half a dozen times a day, she stopped at a mirror to straighten her hat or smooth her hair. But that wasn't the same as truly looking, as she did now.

Through fresh eyes she saw a young woman, plumply pretty, with a soft face, soft, wisping hair, and gentle gray eyes. She looked conventional. Predictable. Safe. Looking into those eyes, Fern would never have guessed the thoughts she knew lurked beneath.

But that didn't make them any less legitimate. Nor, she felt with a growing conviction that filled her with a trepid kind of euphoria, could they be dismissed for long.

"How far is it to the Pavilion?" she asked Lucy.

"Couldn't say, m'm. Not too far," the woman answered promptly.

"I think I shall ask to walk," she decided. She had a morbid aversion to being trapped in a carriage with Colin, though she was aware of the vast difference between asking for a thing and getting it and had no reason to believe that he would accomodate her. In fact, she was more than half certain that he would refuse, and she took a perverse kind of satisfaction in forcing Colin to actively deny her in his neat ordering of her life, to make him oppose her rather than to simply acquiesce quietly to his every whim. At some level, such an action only emphasized her powerlessness, but it also required that he take the role of a managing bully instead of a magnanimous benefactor, and that differentiation was obscurely critical to her now. She could only hope that it would make some difference.

The maid finished and left, and as Fern was about to follow her out the door, she saw Colin's waistcoat from the afternoon before, now draped over a chair. She remembered the letter that he had read on the train, and she hesitated. She had no right to look at it—in fact, Colin had specifically instructed her to stay away from all business matters. But that hurt, angry corner of her mind stirred, and she set her chin and stepped toward the waistcoat, her heart beating hard in her ears. With jerky movements, she rifled through the outer pocket—and came up with two letters, not one.

Ignoring the stab of guilt, she pulled them out and opened the top one. Familiar writing greeted her.

June 8
Lincoln's Inn

Dear Mr. Radcliffe—
 I have continued to make with the utmost diligence the inquiries that you requested in respect to Wrexmere & c. However, my ability to discover anything is still hampered by the unfortunate circumstances of the ledger-books, and the difficulty of

achieving any sort of meaningful communication from Joseph Reston.

   At this point, I would strongly recommend an application to your father, in order to better assess the circumstances of his history with the place before taking any direct action of your own.
I remain,
Yr. obt. serv't.,
        James Barnes

The next letter was no more enlightening, but it was far stranger. It began:

Dear sir,
   Youve' ben asking after us again, but there's no need for it. Becaus we do what we're ment. We do what we promise evry bit. We hav evry Thing still and we have ben keeping our part of the agree-ment. Dont' be harrying after my man hes' a fair man. He wonnt' ever go to the Queen with less he be pushd.
Yr srvt,
        Dorcas Reston

With a little surge of guilt and more than a little foreboding, Fern quickly returned the letters to Colin's waistcoat. She'd had no right to read them; now that she had, she was more troubled—at herself and their import, both—than self-satisfied. She left the room, and it felt like an escape.

Colin granted that if Fern's request was out of spite, perhaps it was deserved, since he *had* possessed the tastelessness to get rather pissed on his wedding night. He'd had his reasons, of course—he'd never get smashed without good reason—but all things considered, perhaps Fern had some cause to resent it. But he felt rather pleased with himself at how easily he forgave her and how generously he took the blame.

Taking the blame, however, did not mean that he was willing to walk. And so he swiftly denied her petition even as he made airy allusions to a vague sense of regret, ordering a coach to come as he had already planned.

As they descended the stoop into the pitilessly brilliant morning light, Colin offered his arm to his wife, and she hesitated for a moment, looking at him under the shade of her beribboned hat with an inscrutable expression in her pretty eyes. Then she stiffly placed a small gloved hand in the crook of his elbow and stepped out silently beside him. The driver swung the carriage door open, and Colin handed her up automatically before mounting the steps himself.

It had to be more than just his being drunk that had her on such edge, since that had seemed to bother her so little the night before. He must have insulted her in some way, he decided as he leaned back in the seat across from her. But he could think of nothing that he might have said or done to create this brittleness in her.

No matter; she would forget whatever trifling concern she had as soon as she saw the Pavilion.

They approached the palace from the rear, but as soon as the first onion dome appeared over the top of the Unitarian church, Fern's eyes lit up predictably, and she craned to see better.

"Why, it must be just like India," she said with a touch of awe in her voice.

Colin chuckled, lingering uncertainties swallowed

in a wash of self-assurance. "Perhaps." He patted her hand tolerantly.

At that touch, though, she stiffened against him, her eyes darting penetratingly across his face before returning to the street in front of them.

What? Colin thought, his irritation coming back as quickly as it had disappeared. But he kept silent. He hated arguing, and already the beginnings of a foul mood and his lingering headache promised the start of a very bad day. The knowledge that Fern could sway his natural detachment in a darker direction served only to feed his irritation more.

They reached the arched and domed gate of the Pavilion's grounds, and Colin handed Fern down out of the carriage. She made a sound like a delighted child, too bright to be real, slipping free of his elbow to dart through the entrance.

"We must see it from the front," she declared.

Colin lengthened his strides to catch up with her, but she skipped merrily past the other clumps of visitors on the walk and headed across the wide expanse of lawn toward a small oval pond. She reached it and turned around, her pale blue skirt swinging out over the water as wisps of hair, already pulled free by the stiff sea breeze, blew across her face. She looked like an emminently fashionable china doll, and just as fragile.

"How extraordinary!" she said as he reached her side, her eyes wide with exaggerated enthusiasm. "I could hardly think of a construction that could be more out of place."

"Indeed," he said, rather more to be agreeable than because he had any particular opinion. Her display of girlish delight was clearly manufactured, but why she would create such an air of near hilarity was beyond him. He decided to ignore it in hopes that it would simply go away. Most things that irritated him did, if he ignored them long enough.

She looked at the long building consideringly, the latticed porticoes under delicately fluted columns supporting an absurd fantasy of a roof, all domes and ribbed minarets. "It should be painted fantastic colors. That would fit the architecture better. Or even white. But there is something about that staid, restrained buff that makes it all the more incongruous."

To Colin, nothing could improve the appearance of the strange thing sprawled in the middle of a perfectly respectable English town. It wasn't that he disliked it, exactly. It certainly had a kind of whimsy about it that was attractive in a queer way. But to change its appearance to make it other than what it was seemed like an exercise in pointlessness.

He just nodded politely. "Ready to enter, *mon ange*?"

She shot a smile at him, bright and glassy. "Rather," she said, and she began to cross the well-groomed lawn, little tendrils of hair flying loose in the wind in defiance of her smart coiffure.

The Pavilion's lavish interior was a cacophony of color, red and yellow warring with green and blue. Ladies and gentlemen—and those who were neither—trailed along the gallery between the banqueting room and the music room. He and Fern joined them, Fern finally coming to light on his proffered arm, tense and flighty. She appeared to be riveted by their surroundings, but he knew he was the source of her unease, however ludicrous it was. Her gaze lingered on the fantastic chandeliers.

"They look like they must be gas. Are they original?"

she asked, as if they were the most fascinating things in the world.

He raised an eyebrow. "The prince had gas laid on by the twenties. The pattern is of lotus blossoms in the Egyptian style."

"How appropriate," Fern murmured.

He cast her a sideways glance. The lotus was the flower that the ancients claimed would bring forgetfulness when eaten. That it was built into the very lamps that had shone upon the frivolous, excessive entertainments of the then–Prince of Wales was indeed appropriate, a coy reference, however unintentional, to the oblivion of decadence. Could Fern have meant that?

He stopped just inside the doorway of the music room and cast a look at his wife. Her wide, soft face was open, her lips sweetly good-natured, her eyes clear and bright . . . but surely not clever. Surely.

Suddenly she laughed and slipped her arm away, crossing to stand in front of one of the scarlet panels that encircled the room. "It is like the china at the house we're letting," she said, nodding at the drooping Oriental trees painted in gold. "And our suite, too, with all that green and gold and red. I do believe that our landlord is an admirer of the last King George!"

Colin chose to reply in the same inconsequential vein. "At least he did not prefer the chrome yellow," he said with a nod at the garish medallion that hung over their heads.

Fern glanced up. "More likely he could not find it."

She did not return to his arm but led the way through the rest of the chambers—the bedrooms, the red drawing room, the tearooms, even the great kitchen.

He followed her because he had no particular desire not to, but he could not stifle a sense of disconsolation. It wasn't that he minded drifting along a course set by someone else. He'd found that was the easiest way to live, for all anyone would demand of him was that he go through the motions expected of a viscount's heir, while he watched the world from behind his eyes as his mouth spoke the words it should and his body took the actions that were expected of it. He had no desire for more.

But following his wife was not the course laid out for him. His wife was meant to fall in behind him, to conform to his life, making the moves he made and smiling at the people he smiled at. She wasn't meant to go flitting about with her eyes too bright and her laughter too shrill.

Despite her forced gaiety, she seemed more vibrant and alive, to his jaded eyes, than he thought he'd ever felt. She took the exploration of the Pavilion as a kind of mission, regardless of how trivial the task and how many people had gone before, as if she could find deep meaning even in the palm-leaf pillars of the great kitchen. Colin had never seen her like this before; in all their conversations during tea or waltzes, she had never seemed to have a mission to become possessed of.

When there was nothing left to explore, she seemed to deflate slightly, the high color leaving her face, the purpose falling out of her step, leaving the curling bits of flyaway hair around her face as the only lingering hint of the energy that had so recently possessed her. She looked at him, a brittle glitter in her eyes.

"What precisely were you looking for?" Colin asked, driven by an uncharacteristic curiosity.

Fern blushed and gave her head a shake that would have set her curls atremble in the maidenly coiffure she had worn up until that day. "I don't know. Anything there was to find, I suppose. I forget that none of this is new to you. I hope that you haven't found it too terribly tedious."

"I've been everywhere in Brighton," Colin said, his indifference returning. "You should think of the entire trip as a wedding present and enjoy it as such."

"Thank you, Colin." Her words were delivered simply, but there was something in her sideways glance that disturbed him. Not hostility, exactly, but maybe just a hint of resentment.

"What is it, *mon ange*?" he asked automatically, knowing from experience that it was more pleasant to swiftly allay a woman's feelings of dissatisfaction than to allow them to fester. He offered his arm and she took it, but her expression was abstracted as she allowed herself to be led back through the curious crowds toward the entrance.

"Nothing," she said, her tone utterly unconvincing. He cast her a skeptical look, and she ducked his gaze, turning her attention to the golden designs in the carpet in front of them. "I just wondered if everything that I ever spend a farthing on from today forward should be considered a gift from you."

There was an edge in her voice he did not understand. He curved his lips in a display of indulgent reassurance. "I do hope your expenditures won't be too extravagant, but I suppose you could consider everything to be my gift, if you'd like."

The small frown bowing her plump lips deepened; that was clearly not what she wanted to hear. Colin sighed mentally. He had never enjoyed the games that the more temperamental of her sex seemed to thrive on, and he hoped this was not evidence of a side of her he had not yet seen.

He tried another tack. "Your parents did settle a certain sum on you when you married. Apart from your dowry."

Her expression cleared a little. "Yes. Three hundred per annum should be more than enough to keep me in gloves and lace."

Colin nodded, pleased that she had been so neatly mollified. "I should hope so."

They stepped into glaring daylight and crossed the lawn toward the gate. There, Colin paused and pulled out his pocket watch. Still two hours before noon. What did one do with a wife all day long? He was already weary of this honeymoon, ready to return to his usual routine, in which their spheres would decidedly separate, to intersect only in the evenings. Somehow, he had a feeling that matters would not resolve so easily. First Wrexmere and now Fern. It seemed like his life, which had been so pleasantly predictable before, was taking a decidedly nastier turn.

"Let us walk over to the Old Steine," he said, nodding to the broad triangle of grass bisected by a walk. "It may not be as fashionable as it once was, but it has historical appeal."

"That sounds lovely," Fern said, but he could tell that her gaze, no longer caught by the strange delights of the Pavilion, was being dragged out to sea.

Yet she voiced no protest as she followed him to the fountain that dominated the Old Steine. Jets of water leapt out of the basin as it tossed a sparkling spray into the air. The wind caught the shining droplets and blew them across her walking dress.

"It shall be ruined!" Fern said, but she moved out of the way leisurely, belying her declaration of concern.

While Fern pulled off her glove and held her hand out toward the spray, Colin surveyed the tourists that stood in clumps along the walks crisscrossing the triangle of grass. Most were strangers, wearing awkward suits and cheap dresses—the rail had made Brighton almost startlingly democratic, and despite the conveniences of the train, Colin missed the refinement of the company that had been the rule in his childhood.

Colin did recognize a few of the people, but he made no attempt to hail them. While he was by no means averse to society, he felt that as newlyweds, they should conduct themselves with tasteful retirement. Which was why he had chosen Clifton Terrace for their temporary domicile, even though there were far more houses to let along the fashionable Adelaide Circle of Kemp Town. While being eminently respectable, Clifton Terrace was slightly removed from the whirl of entertainments, and with their having taken a house there, society would expect little entertaining of them.

"Let's go down to the water," he said to Fern, extending his arm. "Soon there will be an unbearable crush."

"I would like that," said Fern, putting on her glove once more.

As they descended the road leading down along the tall seawall, the beach itself came into view, and Fern made a small sound of surprise. "There are so many people!"

Colin looked across the expanse between the wall and the water. Yesterday, it had stretched out like a pebbled highway, spotted with groups of early evening walkers. Today, however, only patches of gray were visible among the teeming crowd below. A thousand children dodged among pedestrians at the edge of the waves, ignoring the cries of their mothers and nurses. Two thousand belled skirts swayed in the breeze beside their gentlemen escorts, upright and unruffled by the wind. A hundred boats for hire rocked on the waves, the occasional higher billow causing the passengers to shriek with glee or terror as their rower expertly and stoically guided them through.

"I thought . . ." Fern began, and then she shook her head and smiled. "Never mind. It was silly of me."

"You thought that yesterday evening was typical?" Colin furnished.

She opened her mouth to say something, but just then, a familiar voice rang out.

"Why, I do say! It's Radcliffe!"

Colin turned around to meet the slightly reddened face of Algernon Morel, with Jack Wakefield, Lord Gifford, looming over his shoulder.

"Gifford, Algy," he said slightly stiffly. He didn't dislike either man, and Gifford in particular was welcome in all levels of society because of his smooth manners and his impeccable pedigree. But together, they could be up to no good, for Gifford's morals were notably malleable, and Algy's reputation eclipsed any activities that his wife might even dream of. Colin thought, distantly, that he should perhaps be disconcerted at meeting his mistress's husband, especially so soon after leaving her bed for his new wife's, but he could not work up enough feeling to care much about it one way or the other.

"Ah, so this would be your little woman," Algy observed, as oblivious to hints as always. He waggled a bushy blond brow. "And how are you taking to married life, *madame*?"

Colin winced at Fern's sharp intake of breath and looked over, expecting to see shock written across her face. To his amazement, though, she was trying not to laugh. She extended her free hand to Algy, and he pressed it eagerly.

"One day of marriage is hardly enough to tell," she said, her voice bland.

Algy let out a guffaw, and if he had been close enough, Colin knew the man would have tried to nudge him in the ribs. Delicacy and propriety were utterly unknown to Algy. Whether he knew about Emma's liaisons, Colin had no idea, and Colin was even less sure about whether the man would care.

"Quite a charmer you have there, Radcliffe!" Algy chortled. "She'll make an impression in this afternoon's parade."

"Parade?" Fern turned large eyes on Colin.

"Every afternoon, Brighton society—and those who wish they were—gather at the north end of town and ride their carriages to the south end," Colin supplied.

"Why?"

"Why do people promenade in Hyde Park? Because it's done. I was going to wait a day or two before going out into society, but"—he gave a small bow to Gifford and Algy— "it seems that society has found us."

"It sounds interesting," Fern said, but her expression lacked enthusiasm.

"Not half as interesting as the dance that I am hosting tonight, if you consent to come, Mrs. Radcliffe." Gifford's dark, rich voice came out unexpectedly, and to Colin's irritation, Fern pinkened.

"I don't think that we shall be able to make it," Colin answered before she could speak.

"Ha!" Algy exclaimed. "Look at him, Gifford; he's gone prudish on us. Not to worry, old chap; it's no bachelor affair. Gifford's mama has come to commiserate with him on his most recent expulsion from the family bosom. Jolly straight, and all that rot."

That was marginally better, but even so, Colin disliked the hungry gaze Gifford gave Fern and the motives that it hinted. Friend or no, the earl's heir was notorious for his interest in any woman who was claimed by another man. An innocent new wife would be his ideal prey, and Fern . . . she could be trusted as much as any woman, he supposed, but women were notoriously weak-minded about flattery.

"I'm sure I would love to see Lady Rushworth again," Fern said before he could react. "It's such a shame she's been staying away from London for her health, for we all missed her at the wedding."

For a moment, Colin was so taken aback by her rebelliousness that he could not speak. His world was truly going mad. Giving her a narrow look, he pulled her more firmly against his side. "I'm sure that Lady Rushworth would not expect you to go out in society so soon. We can call on her tomorrow when she is at home."

"Oh, rubbish," Fern said, with a good deal more spirit than he had ever seen from her. "Tomorrow, she will be swarmed with all the guests from tonight's ball. And I would like to dance. It's been ever so long."

It's been one week, thought Colin, but he did not say it aloud in front of Algy and Gifford, who were watching their exchange with a little too much interest. And far too much amusement.

He swallowed his irritation and decided to play the line of the indulgent husband—for now. There was no need for them to know how intolerable he found the situation. "Well, my dear, if you are so eager, we'll see." He smiled benignly at all three. "Now, if you will excuse us, gentlemen, we will continue our stroll." He turned his back to the men, pulling Fern with him, and walked away before the two could offer to join them.

Fern felt giddy as she walked along on Colin's arm. She had defied that stamp she felt embedded in her flesh, Colin's mark of ownership over her, and the sky had not come crashing down. *I am my own person*, she thought. *Discrete, whole within myself.* She kept her silence for fear that she would begin laughing even as she felt Colin lowering like a storm cloud beside her. She would pay for her actions, but at that moment, the fierce, dissatisfied corner of her mind was uppermost, and she could not care.

They reached the promenade, but Colin did not guide them onto the beach. Instead, he raised his free hand to hail a carriage—not a little open fly but one of the black closed carriages that invalids rode in—keeping her pinned mercilessly against him. The coach stopped, and Colin opened the door, guiding her inside with a hard grip on her arm that chilled her bones, smothering her sense of victory with a wave of dread.

She knew then that the payment for her rebellion would be far more than she had bargained for.

Chapter Five

The air in the closed black carriage was dank and stifling. Fern's clothes chafed at her sweat-damp skin as soon as she stepped inside. Still gripping her arm, Colin spoke a word to the driver before stepping in behind her. He brought a breath of cooler air with him, but he shut the door with a snap before most of the heat could escape. Sweat sprang up on her forehead and upper lip as she blinked to adjust her eyes to the oppressive darkness that was relieved only by a sliver of light that slid between the velvet curtains.

Colin's face, impassive at the best of times, was unreadable in the dimness. His eyes were black holes surrounded by a rim of pale green, the void behind them pitiless and disdainful. Fern's stomach clenched, her blood pounding in her ears as fear and defiance warred within her.

"Where are we going?" Fern asked. She meant to make it a demand, but her voice trembled slightly, and she flushed at that self-betrayal.

Colin did not answer, only tightening his grip on her arm until it hurt. Fern pressed her lips together, determined not to say anything. He pushed her onto the bench and sat beside her. The carriage lurched into motion.

"You are not to contradict me," Colin said finally, each word sharp-edged, precise. His face was a blank. "You are not to make decisions that will affect both of us. And you are never to voice a definite opinion on any subject of importance that may differ from my own."

"Never?" She blurted the question, the heat in her cheeks flaring hotter.

"Not ever," he agreed flatly. He tightened his grip on her arm, and she winced. "Not in private, and certainly never in public. I chose you to be my wife because you seemed modest and reserved, able to add to my comfort by creating a pleasant, harmonious household as you fulfill your duties as hostess and mother. You did not behave in a manner in keeping with those expectations a moment ago, and I do not expect a repetition of such an event."

All the anger and shame and disappointment of the past two days came rolling over her. *He is going to destroy me*, she thought, panic rising in her throat. *He is going to shut me away in a little box until all the air is gone.*

Her entire being revolted from the idea—revolted from him and his power over her. Her blood swirling, Fern opened her mouth, but nothing came out except a ragged sound that might have been a moan or a cry of rejection. She clamped her jaw shut, her heart beating wildly. His hand on her arm was like a vise.

Trapped, trapped forever . . . She had to get away *now*. Without thinking, she threw her body weight away from him, but his grip was too tight. She couldn't escape. Fighting down a sob of hysteria, she lashed out blindly, her free hand striking his face with a ringing slap.

Colin felt the pain, sudden and sharp, cutting through layers in his brain that he hadn't known were there. Layers wrapped *around* his brain . . . It was like a jolt of light to eyes that had always been in darkness, burning into his mind and flooding it with color that he could never have imagined.

Colin released Fern with a shove that knocked her hard against the side of the coach. In the sudden silence, they sat frozen, staring at each other. Fern was incapable of speech, shocked at what she had just done but unable to apologize as fury and rebellion still roiled, choking, inside her. Colin's expression was frozen, the livid lines that her fingers had left already outlined in red. But under the dark slashes of his brows, his eyes flared, and for the first time, Fern felt the presence of a person at the bottom of their dark depths, looking back at her.

Her breath caught. *This is not the man I married*, her brain wailed in warning. But she had not married a man at all—she had married a title in the form of a man, with nothing inside. Now there was something there, and she couldn't recognize it.

"Who are you?" she whispered into those eyes, the eyes of a stranger.

His gaze only burned into hers with more intensity, and he extended his hand. Fern pressed back harder into the corner away from him, but he merely held it there, the white kidskin palm glowing in the dimness. Seconds ticked by. What could the man want? More to the point, what could he want that he couldn't take?

Tentatively, Fern placed her hand on top of his.

He closed his hand suddenly and pulled her hard

against him, his mouth coming down to meet hers so abruptly that her lips were bruised against her teeth. He took her mouth instantly, wholly. There was no finesse in this kiss, no refinement. He crushed her against him as his mouth moved hard against hers. Fern fought a wave of panic even as her center tightened in reaction and her heart beat a confusing tattoo of fear and desire.

No—this is not what I meant when I took his hand, she thought wildly. She tried to jerk free, but he held her too tightly against him. She pushed against his shoulders, and when that did not work, she took his lower lip between her teeth and bit down hard. The coppery taste of blood hit her tongue as he shuddered and cursed against her mouth, but instead of releasing her, he pinned her back into the corner of the carriage with his weight as he jerked at her bonnet strings. The hat came free, and he yanked it off.

"What are you doing?" She gasped, her heart thrumming with the rush of their encounter as her stomach made little shivering flips. She licked the taste of his blood from her lips, and, swearing again, Colin closed his eyes for an instant before fixing her with a piercing gaze. Fern wedged herself farther into the corner. She had become so accustomed to the blankness behind his green eyes that this attention was unsettling.

"I am kissing you." The words were spoken with such tenseness that they scarcely sounded like his. Fern opened her mouth to rebut his announcement, but he put actions to words, catching her mouth, his hands tangling in her hair.

The taste of his blood sent a disturbing shock through her, half horror and half titillation. Was he punishing her? She couldn't breathe! She pushed at him, bracing against the corner of the carriage and shoving with all her strength. He broke away, rocking back.

"Do you want me to hurt you again?" she said, between a snap and a plea.

Colin simply looked at her, his eyes burning in the dimness. "I cannot," he said distinctly, "remain in Brighton with you."

Fern swallowed hard, fighting against the sensation that she was falling. "You are going to leave me?"

His lips curled up strangely. "No. We will both leave. Wrexmere is at my disposal, and I have business that needs to be attended to there, anyhow. We will travel by post." He gave her a searching look. "Tonight."

As he said the word, the carriage came to a shuddering halt. Without waiting for a reply, Colin jerked the door handle down and pushed out. Fern was still immobile in shock at his announcement. She blinked in the dazzling wash of light that flooded through the carriage door. They were in Clifton Terrace. Colin did not pause to help her down but tossed a coin to the driver as he strode swiftly up the stoop and disappeared into the house, leaving Fern to push unsteadily to her feet, collect her hat, and follow.

Wrexmere. The name shot through Fern. She stumbled up the stoop. Suddenly, that was the last place in the world that she wanted to go.

Inside, the house was already in an uproar. The housekeeper was running about, and Fern could hear hurried footsteps on the first floor above her head. She climbed the stairs slowly.

Fern stepped through their bedroom door. Colin

stood against the wall, his arms folded over his chest as her maid and his valet dashed back and forth from the wardrobe to the open trunks in the middle of the floor. He was a stranger, so dark and glowering, a shadow that lorded over the servants who scurried to do his bidding. He glanced at her, and his eyes were dead again.

A thousand questions burned in her mind, but she could not speak, dared not speak, for the brief flame of her rebellion had been lost in confusion, and all that was left was her fear.

Who was this man whom she had married? Was he the creature she had seen so briefly, lurking within the emptiness? She did not know, and suddenly, she was afraid to find out, longing for the blank smiles and hollow words that had so disturbed her only a day before even as a part of her wanted almost as badly to make him kiss her like that again. Instead, she simply stood mutely in the doorway, fraying the ribbon of her new bonnet in her hands.

In minutes, their trunks were packed and carried down to a waiting post chaise. Colin's commanding glance sent Fern down after them. The valet and the driver heaved their luggage onto the roof of the coach and bound it in place.

Fern could do nothing but watch. She wanted to ask about their destination, for she had no idea where this Wrexmere was. She wanted to demand that she have a chance to write to her mother and sisters, or at least to change into a traveling dress. But she was frozen into silent acquiescence by the sheer towering authority of the man who stood behind her. A good girl—that was what she was. A good girl who would become a good wife, a good hostess, and a good mother. She had no place in this burst of strange activity, no background that could give her hope of controlling any of it.

The valet opened the door to the coach and stood aside. Colin touched Fern for the first time since he had left the carriage, taking her arm in his, the strength and heat of his grasp sending a small shock down into her center and up through her brain. She hated herself for it—not for the sensation itself but for the multitude of indecisions and uncertainties that came with it. If she wanted his touch, why did it make her mouth go dry with fear? And if she was afraid, then why did a dark, secret part of her mind keep replaying that last, brutal, blood-tinged kiss with a shivering relish?

She was not a good girl. She was not a good anything. Helplessly, she let Colin lead her forward, into the dark mouth of the coach. He released her as she sat and stepped in behind, shutting them in the hot darkness with a click of the door.

Fern could not bear to look at him. She did not know whether she wanted to beg for forgiveness or deride him, whether she wanted him to kiss her hard and wildly or whether she wanted to slap him again. So she took the coward's way out. She shut her eyes, leaning her head against the back of the squabs, and tried to make her mind as blank as her vision as the coach rocked into motion.

And she tried not to think of what Colin would do about it.

Chapter Six

It was hot. Intolerably hot. Fern struggled to hold still, to keep up the pretense that she was resting or even asleep. But a trickle of itchy sweat had rolled down between her breasts, and another was making its way down her spine even as her eyes stung from salt that had worked its way under her closed eyelids. She could feel the heat of her face, radiating into the still air around her. She would have to move to wipe away the sweat and retrieve her fan from the chatelaine at her waist, or she truly would swoon in a moment.

When she could bear it no longer, a whisper of air brushed across her skin. Had Colin opened the window? The noise of the wheels on the road, which had changed from the sharp rattle of cobblestones to the more muffled rumble of dirt and gravel, had grown no louder. There—there it was again, a faint, soft gust against her neck. But it wasn't cool. In fact, if anything, it was damper and hotter than the air within the coach.

Fern's brain made the connection just as Colin spoke, his words low and compelling, each one accompanied by the soft wind of his breath against her skin.

"I know you are not sleeping."

What was he doing? Kneeling? He was not a man to kneel. She hadn't felt his weight settle next to her, had not felt his body press against her skirts. Fern kept her eyes tightly shut, but she could not control the quickening of her heartbeat.

"I don't know why the hell I'm here," Colin continued, rough and quiet. "I don't know what it is that you did to me. But I do know that I will not allow such a—an *irritation* to be unilateral."

Fern gave a sharp intake of breath as Colin's mouth came in contact with her skin. She kept her eyes shut hard—out of stubbornness now, and a fearful curiosity that would not be denied. His lips moved across her skin with the studied seduction of the night before, but there was a new urgency under it that made her blood rush to her head as her skin burned with every movement of his mouth against it. He moved lower, to the hollow of her collarbone that was barely exposed by the high neckline of her dress, and the air in the coach seemed to thicken in her lungs. With a groan, she opened her eyes and pushed herself away from him even as she ached for more. He stood in the center of the carriage, balancing on the balls of his feet and stooped over her.

"Why are you doing this?" she asked. "You shouldn't kiss me like that—not here. What do you want of me?"

Colin stooped lower, looming over her. Fern pressed into the corner formed by the seat back and the carriage side so hard that the back of her head ached, but there was nowhere for her to go. His face came closer and closer to her own until she found herself staring at his strong throat as his lips brushed her forehead. "I would think that the answer to both questions would be obvious."

"Well, it isn't to me," she burst out, her confusion, frustration, and desire overwhelming her usual rectitude. "I don't understand any of this. Last night, in the bedroom, you kissed me and told me that I was pretty, but then you did that . . . *that* to me. Then today, when you yelled at me until I hit you, instead of yelling more or beating me, you kissed me again, and that time it was like you meant it differently. . . ." She trailed off helplessly.

Colin shifted so that his dark eyes were staring directly into hers from only a few inches away. Fern fought against the dizzying fear that she could be sucked into those depths and lost forever.

"Are you saying that you do not know what happened last night?" he asked. His voice was quiet, holding neither incredulity nor scorn.

"I know what happened," Fern countered, feeling stupid and hating it. "I was there."

"Did you not know what it was? What it meant?"

Fern stared at him, trying to discern the meaning of his words, but she might as well have been looking at a painting of a man, for all the reaction that he betrayed. "It was terrible," she whispered. Those words loosened her tongue, and she found herself saying far more than she had meant to. "It was most terrible of all because it was not as terrible as it should have been. You hurt me. You took . . . some part of me, and I will never get that back. But a part of me wanted it. Reveled in it. I knew you were stealing from me, but I couldn't refuse until it was too late, and even then . . . a part of me didn't want to."

There was a long pause as Colin's face remained as

still as a mask, and then he gave a low chuckle that raised the hairs on the back of her neck. "Oh, Fern, you have so much to learn. A day ago, I would have been peeved at such a misapprehension, but now, I find that I am relishing the opportunity to be your instructor. Perhaps I was a bit ham-fisted last night. If so, I can promise that tonight will not be the same." He paused. "No, I don't think it will be the same at all."

"What are you talking about?" Fern asked, the words half a question and half a demand.

"What we did last night, Fern, is what a man and his wife are meant to do."

Fern shook her head spasmodically. "I can't believe it. Women could not live with that."

He straightened slightly, still looming over her with his head and shoulders brushing the roof of the coach. "It is not a terrible thing, Fern. You were understandably surprised and confused, but I don't believe that even you truly think that it is terrible."

"I couldn't stop you," she said, avoiding the implicit question.

"Did you want to?" he retorted.

"I don't know." The answer slipped out before Fern could stop it, and she bit her lip.

"Did you not enjoy it?" Colin pressed. "Just a little?"

She dropped her eyes, unable to lie. "Yes. Yes, I did."

"Then what was wrong?" he pursued.

"I couldn't stop you," she repeated helplessly. "I couldn't do anything. I was powerless. I couldn't stop anything."

His face took on a curious expression, clouded and inward-turning. "You were not powerless earlier today when you bit my lip."

Fern flushed and looked at the lip in question, which bore a faint purple bruise. She reached out tentatively, touching it. "Does it hurt?" she asked.

"Why? Do you want it to?" His mouth brushed her hand as he spoke.

Fern froze, startled at the question. "I don't think so," she said. She dropped her hand.

"If I kissed you like that again, would you do it again?" His eyes were strangely bright.

"Yes," she said with a surge of resentment. "Of course I would."

"Of course you would," Colin murmured. "I will keep that in mind."

"Why did you have us leave Brighton?" Fern asked suddenly, eager to change the subject.

Colin's expression shuttered, growing cold. "I could not stay any longer. That is all you need to know." He bent over her again and kissed her, softly, on the lips.

"I don't understand," Fern whispered against his mouth in the moment before he pulled back.

"Don't worry. I promise that you shall." Then he kissed her hard, pushing her bruised lips against her teeth, pressing her back into the corner of the carriage.

Fern battled confusion and her body's mindless reaction to his mouth against hers, moving roughly and desperately. What was he doing? Why? His hands were pulling at the row of tortoiseshell buttons down the front of her dress, his tongue pushing insistently at her teeth. *If I kissed you like that again, would you do it again?* The words echoed in her head.

Do you want it to? He had asked her that question, but she could have just as easily posed it to him. Why was he playing these games?

Whatever the reason, she would win, she thought

with sudden ire. Her hand around the back of his neck turned into a claw, her nails sinking into his skin. Ruthlessly, she raked her fingernails across the nape of his neck, and his frame shook, the frenzy of his kiss turning to a more methodical insistency, his hands slowing in the unbuttoning of her dress.

"I won't do this," Fern said, finding her voice as he broke away. "And I certainly won't do it here."

"Don't tell me that a part of you doesn't want it," Colin returned, tugging her bodice down over her shoulders.

She made fists with her hands so that the sleeves could not be pulled over them. "I don't want to hurt you. But I won't let you steal from me again."

He leaned close, so that his chest was pressed up against her breasts as he whispered into her ear, "It is a gift, not a theft. You end with more, and I with less."

Shocked as she grasped his meaning, Fern jerked back, rapping her head against the wooden wall of the coach. "Sir!"

"How do you think babies come into this world?" Colin asked, tugging at the last buttons of her dress.

"I am quite sure that I don't know," Fern said crisply. She pushed his hands away.

"A babe looks like both its parents because it is begun with a piece of the man entering the woman," he said, his voice tinged with a mocking kind of amusement. "It is true. You steal from me, not I from you."

"I don't care about physiology," she insisted, even though she knew he was telling the truth. "I know what happened."

"You were surprised."

"I was sane," she returned.

"You were confused."

"I knew what was happening to me. I didn't like it. I don't like it now." *Oh, God, if only that were true . . .*

"Why not?"

"I don't like being powerless . . . helpless . . . " She made a frustrated noise, capturing his hands between hers. "Female, you will say."

"As I have already said, you were not powerless in the carriage earlier today."

"I don't know what you want from me!" The exclamation came from the pit of Fern's frustration, blasting past all her contrary impulses and desires.

"Neither do I," he murmured, "but I am sure that we can find out together." He freed his hands and reached for her bodice again. Fern braced to fight him, but this time he began buttoning it up. "What I want would be close to impossible in a crinoline in a coach," he said simply. "We will stop for the night soon enough, and you and I will have ample privacy and space." His gaze flicked up coldly to meet hers. "And believe me, this time, you shall want anything that we do at least as much as I."

Fern could think of nothing to say that would not end in a round of fruitless argument, so she sat mutely as he finished with her last button and sat back against the cushions—next to her this time, instead of across from her. He flicked aside the curtain and stared mutely at the passing countryside. After watching him for several minutes, Fern did likewise.

Chapter Seven

Fern opened her eyes, realizing as she did so that she had fallen, however improbably, asleep. The coach had stopped moving. She blinked at Colin, but he was already reaching for the door. He swung it open, and Fern saw that dusk had arrived.

She followed him unsteadily down the iron steps. "Where are we?" she asked. They stood in the courtyard of a livery stable and a public house, which were also the only buildings visible along the rough track. The buildings were solid and stark in the fading light.

"Rotherham," he said. "If we were continuing on, this would be our fourth change of horses."

"But we are not?"

"I have decided to stop here for the night," he said. "We will not be able to change horses so often after this point, so our rate will slow somewhat. There is no need to press on through the night."

"It sounds like we are going to a very remote place," Fern said, her stomach fluttering with apprehension.

"I wouldn't know," Colin said, sounding bored. "I

have never been there. But I suppose it is remote enough."

He began to walk as Fern digested that declaration. The publican met them at the door, and Colin made arrangements for taking two of the four bedchambers above the public room for them, the valet, and their driver. Then he handed two sealed letters over to the publican. At Fern's inquiring glance, he gave her a dry smile. "It is not good for an heir to a viscountcy to disappear. My brothers might get the idea that one of them shall be the next viscount."

"Oh," said Fern, uncertain as to how much he was joking and even less certain as to the appropriate reply.

Colin gave the publican a final order to have supper brought up and guided Fern to the stairs with a firm hand on her back, mounting them behind her with the key securely in his palm.

He unlocked their room and Fern entered, followed by the valet and driver bearing their trunks. The servants stacked their baggage in the corner, Colin's on top of Fern's, where they took up nearly half the open floor space.

As the servants left for the final time, Fern looked around the little room. There was no fireplace—there was no room for a fireplace—but even though the suffocating heat had lessened, it was still too warm for her to feel its lack. A bed and a chair comprised the total furnishings, and Fern examined the threadbare counterpane with a muted sense of trepidation. Colin pushed past her, setting her skirts to swaying, and jerked down the blankets. His body blocked her view of the bed, but she saw him nod in satisfaction.

"Clean," he said briefly.

Fern eyed the bed distrustfully—her concern about

vermin had been only distantly secondary to her fear of her husband and what they might do there that night. "You seem experienced in such determinations."

The corner of Colin's mouth quirked up, but his gaze stayed flat. "Indeed," he said without elaborating.

Fern looked at the trunks, piled one atop the other in the space opposite the chair. Hers was on the bottom, and there was no place for them to be set next to each other for her to reach her clothing. Only her hand luggage, with the supplies for her personal toilette, was free. Colin followed her gaze.

"I will have Davies move the trunks tomorrow so that you may dress," he said. "You can do without for the night."

"I don't care to do without," Fern found herself saying. She blushed, but she was too tired, cross, and irritated to apologize for her words. "I haven't changed or refreshed myself since this morning."

"The second can be taken care of easily enough," Colin said, ignoring her protest and her tone. "The publican will bring up wash water with dinner."

"Where shall we eat?" Fern asked helplessly. There was scarcely enough space for them both to stand in the tiny room.

"Remove your crinoline," Colin said without inflection.

"What?" Fern bit the inside of her cheek when the word came out shrill.

"Remove your crinoline." Still not a trace of emotion flickered across his face.

"I should dress for dinner, not undress," Fern said, grasping at a normality that seemed to be swiftly fleeing. "It is a nasty, vulgar thing to not wear a crinoline to dinner." That was a narrow-minded, almost child-ish assertion, but uncertainty made her cling to the familiar. She might not know why she was here, or where she was going, or even who her husband was, but she was certain of proper dinner attire, and a walking dress without her hoops was certainly not it.

"Remove it, or I will remove it for you," Colin replied evenly, as if she had not spoken.

"You wouldn't!" Fern said, though she was nowhere near as sure as her words.

Colin's eyes narrowed, not the squint of anger that other men might have given a defiant wife but a half-lidded expression of ennui. He reached out, and Fern jerked away, but she had nowhere to go, for the door was a mere step behind her. Colin caught her bruised arm, and she winced, but he spun her away from him without reacting. He let go of her, and she stood stiffly as he unhooked her wide velvet belt and tossed it on top of the trunks, seething inside but not daring to voice a further protest as her traitorous body reacted to the nearness of his hands. He loosened her waistband and unceremoniously pulled her bodice from it to expose the tapes of her petticoats. Methodically, he untied them until he reached her crinoline, which he freed and pulled from her hips with a jerk as her entire being reverberated in reaction to his touch. The contraption clattered to the floor.

"There," he said. "Sit now. There is plenty of room."

Stiffly, Fern edged past him to take the single chair, stepping over her deflated hoops. Colin kicked them under the bed just as there was a knock upon the door. Fern froze in the act of refastening her disarrayed skirts, quickly moving her hands to her lap. Colin gave her an expression that was almost a smirk and opened the door.

"Wash water and dinner, sir," said the slatternly maid who stood in the narrow hall, thrusting a tray toward Colin. He took it and set it on the trunks, crushing Fern's belt. He started to close the door, and then he paused.

"What's your name?" he asked.

"Pegoty, sir," the girl muttered.

"Pegoty," he repeated. "This is my wife, Mrs. Radcliffe."

Fern just stared at him, baffled as to why he would make the pretense of introducing a village servant girl into her acquaintance.

"She is quite a proper lady," he continued, "and she is deeply offended that your establishment affords her no opportunity to dress for dinner. But she is not nearly offended by that as she will soon be by this." And with that, Colin bent down over Fern, pressing her back into the chair, and forcibly tilting her head up with both hands, he kissed her fully upon the mouth.

For an instant, Fern was frozen with shock. Then she hit him, hard, with her clenched fists against his chest, tried to kick his shins and bite his mouth. But she could not move him, and so she did the last thing she could think of, grabbing a handful of his hair and yanking with all her might.

Only then did Colin pull away, and he was smiling ferally, his green eyes flaring dark under his black brows. He looked up at the gaping maid. "Thank you, Pegoty," he said, and with one hand, he swung the door closed in her face.

"Are you intent upon humiliating me?" Fern burst out.

"Let that be a warning to you: Whenever you embarrass me in public, I will serve you the same," Colin said evenly. "And believe me, as a woman, you will always suffer more."

Fern just shook her head. She could have sworn that her behavior, exceptionable or otherwise, had no part in that display. Colin took a plate from the tray, placed the silverware upon it, and thrust it at her. It was cold tongue. Fern hated cold tongue, but the strain of the day had made her ravenous, so she cut into it anyway, trying not to taste the rubbery flesh as she chewed and swallowed.

Colin watched his wife as she ate, the strange tumult within him still seething just below his skin. The instant that Fern had struck him in that closed carriage, something in him had come alive. No one in his memory had ever struck him before. Not a lover, not his brothers, not his nurse or teachers, certainly not his father—not even his fellow students at Eton.

Colin had found that sudden shock of pain . . . stimulating. Not in some simply crass and carnal reaction, though carnality certainly had something to do with it, but in a more fundamental way, as if his nerves were waking up for the first time. He had felt like a blind man who had suddenly woken up one day to clear sight and a glorious sunrise. And so he had seized upon that sensation hungrily, provoking Fern irrationally into hurting him again, and each time it was like a sizzling brand shooting across the darkness of his soul. . . .

It was wrong, terribly wrong of him, he knew, but whether the wrongness was in the sizzle or the darkness, he could not say. He wanted to feel it again, but he could not ask her to hurt him. He was incapable of it.

Wrexmere. The idea of the place hung like a memory of a dream in his mind. There were other small estates he might have visited, hunting lodges unused this season and obscure cottages that had wandered into the family's property but had never been properly used. But instead he had blurted out his intention to go to the one place that was plaguing him, that would not fit into his neat life any better than his wife and what was now between them did. Did he have a desire to redouble his doubts and tortures? Or was it an instinctual equivalence, pairing his marriage with the mysteries and difficulties of his family's most ancient estate?

He did not know. So he cut the cold tongue and ate it slowly, washing it and the potatoes down with the dark bitter ale and saying nothing as his mind turned the matter over and over.

The clatter of flatware on crockery made Colin turn to his wife. She had finished her meal, and now she sat looking at him with a feverish light of realization in her eyes and the plate perched across her knees.

"You like it when hurt I you." The words had the cutting precision of a razor. "You *enjoy* it."

Colin started to reject her bald statement, but a quirk of Fern's head cut him off.

"Be careful of how you reply," she said with a steadiness that he had never seen from her. "If you tell me that I am deluded, I will be very, very careful to never hurt you again."

Colin narrowed his eyes, nonplussed by this strange self-composure from his usually flustered bride. Where had she found her backbone—and why must she find it now, of all times? He folded his arms across his chest, glaring at her, and he was pleased to note that she blanched slightly. "Never?" he demanded, testing her.

"Not ever," she said, her voice quavering slightly. She cleared her throat quickly to cover her weakness, but her eyes dropped.

"No matter what I do to you?" he pressed, driving home the advantage.

"No matter," she whispered.

Despite her patent fear, Colin did not doubt that she meant what she said, as far as she was capable of upholding it. He waited a moment longer while she studied the empty plate in her lap before finally deigning to give a reply. "I do not enjoy it."

She looked up quickly, disbelief in her eyes.

"I do not enjoy it," he repeated with emphasis. "Not exactly. But I do want it. I almost feel like I need it," he added, half to himself.

"But why?" Fern asked helplessly.

Colin chuckled without humor. "It changes me somehow." For some reason, he felt compelled to share a piece of what he had been turning over in his mind. "I could not stay in Brighton anymore, among society, knowing that might change, that other people might see . . ."

"See what?" Her expression was baffled.

"That they might see me," Colin finished nonsensically. "I want you to hurt me. Which is why I asked: Do you want to?"

Fern's eyes tightened, growing intense. "It makes me feel like I'm buzzing inside, like one of those traveling lectures on electricity."

"Then you will do it again," Colin said with satisfaction.

"I shouldn't," Fern said. "And I don't want to do . . . that thing again. Between us."

"I believe what you mean is called *making love* among polite circles."

"I do not care what it is called," she insisted. "There is nothing lovely about it."

"You do not mean that."

"Of course I do." Her retort was swift—too swift.

Colin stepped closer to her, and Fern leaned back, her eyes widening and her lips parting slightly. He plucked the empty plate from her lap and set it on his trunk's flat lid. "You want it again. Your body tells me so. Even when I kissed you in front of the maid, your body told me that you wanted it."

"That is not true." Her words were breathless.

"Then we will try again, and you can try to make me stop." He leaned over her. "Bite me. Scratch me."

"I don't want to do this." She clutched the chair rigidly and licked her lips.

Colin pulled her up with one hand, pushing the chair away from her with the other. She was stiff in his arms. He pushed her down onto the bed, making no pretext at being gentle.

"No!" she said, the word coming out a yelp. But her hands gripped his arms rather than pushing him away, moving up to cling to his neck as her thighs gripped his hips.

"If I believed you meant that, I would stop," Colin said. "It only hurts the first time."

"I don't care about the pain," she said, the words coming out in a rush. "I might even want it, just a little, so that I could have the . . . the rest. I just don't want to be stolen from!"

"Then take back from me," he growled. "Take more than I do. You know how to do it. It makes you sizzle. I can feel it. I'd wager that it makes you sizzle all the way down here." He followed the line of her outer thigh up under her petticoats and down to the slit of her pantaloons, pushing the fabric aside until he met the smoothness of her thigh and the hot, damp opening at the jointure of her legs. Fern was panting, her body rigid and her eyes wide.

"Stop me," he ordered.

Her face contorting, Fern shook her head. "I can't," she said, the words scarcely audible.

He pushed two fingers into her roughly, and her body shuddered even as she opened to welcome him. "Stop me," he repeated.

Gasping, she shook her head again, and he began to move the fingers inside her. Her face twisted, her hands curling until her fingernails dug sharply into the back of his neck.

Colin stilled as his body's response shot through him, the information his senses were sending him suddenly immediate, insistent, the world opening up within him like a flower. The subtle gradations of pink and white of Fern's skin seemed suddenly to glow with an intensity that was almost painful in its astonishing complexity, the fine tracery of lines in the creases of her brow as intricate and beautiful as the chase work on an Oriental bowl. He could smell the faint mustiness of the bedclothes under the sharp, insistent scent of Fern's femininity and desire, each scent vibrating with a vigor he could hardly understand. And he could feel so much more, too—the stitches of the sheets under his palms; Fern's body, hot and hungry, through their clothes; the sweet slickness of her secret places against his fingers; and most of all, himself. Every nerve in his body sang with life. What it sang was a need for her—not a general, vague urge for release but an immediate, pounding drive to consume the source of this new experience.

Fern's gray eyes were narrowed, catlike almonds. Her lips drew back slightly from her teeth, and she dragged her nails across the back of his neck. Colin could feel the scores that she was making in his skin, a latticework of fire that seemed to writhe deliciously over his body. Traceries of life.

"You like that," he told Fern hoarsely.

"You like it more." Her rasping whisper seemed to go through him.

"You are not so powerless now," he noted.

She looked almost surprised, and she smiled slowly. "I suppose not." She moved her hand almost tentatively to his earlobe. She squeezed it between her nails, experimenting. A new, fine jolt of heat went through him, and he kissed her impulsively.

For the first time, she seemed to expect it and to know instantly what to do, without a lapse between thought and instinct. Her mouth was small and slick under his, her rosebud lips indecorously demanding. He drank her kiss even as she took back. He unbuckled his belt with a hand still slick from her, unbuttoning his fly and freeing his erection. She tangled her fingers in his hair.

"I do want this now. But go slowly," she said, half an order and half a plea. "More slowly than last time."

He said nothing, but instead of throwing up her skirts as he wanted to, he pushed them up gently until they mounded on her belly between them. He ran a hand softly up the outside of her thigh, and she made a small mewling sound as he circled to the softer bare inner flesh. He guided himself into her, savoring the tightness of her body as it clasped him and the pang as she tightened her grip in his hair. He buried himself inside her, and she shuddered, whimpering slightly against him as her hands tightened into fists in his hair, pulling taut against his scalp. He moved within her, the pain wakening his deadened nerves to pleasure, going faster and faster—

"*Slow down.*" Fern's jerk upon his hair almost made him lose control right then. But he obeyed, hardly recognizing the words coming from his mousy little wife. Her eyes were shut tightly, her face a mask of absolute concentration, as if she were trying to remember something or find something. Her breath grew more and more ragged, and then her lips drew back as she arched against him.

"There!" she cried, and then she jerked his head down to meet hers, crushing his bruised lip against her own, and Colin let himself drop to the white-hot release, spending himself in her as his veins burned and his head pounded with blood and desire.

The sensation was fleeting, as it always was, and yet it had been more than he knew what to do with, and it left him feeling changed. He rolled to the side as a wave of irresistible lassitude overtook him, only the ingrained politeness of many previous encounters keeping him from slumping bonelessly on top of her.

This must be what it is supposed to feel like, he thought, his heart still racing. Was it like this for everyone? No wonder so many young bucks could think of nothing else. Before, lying with a woman had been like scratching an itch, pleasant largely because of the relief it gave. He had thought of intercourse as a kind of draining off of excess pressure. But this . . . this was beyond his experience. It made him unsure of himself, unsure of everything.

Which was why he had to get to Wrexmere as soon as possible. He would deal with the fiscal irregularities there and expunge any lingering ghosts of the past, and with any luck, he would be able to deal with these strange feelings in an equally straightforward manner. The sooner he got everything sorted out and neatly put away in its place, the sooner he could go back to his regular, compartmentalized life, with no one the wiser that it had been shaken so badly.

But as he lay there, panting and fog-brained, he wasn't sure that was what he wanted anymore.

Chapter Eight

"That did not feel so much like a theft." Fern's voice was a hoarse whisper full of wonder.

"I assume you enjoyed yourself." Those words came from some automatic part of Colin's brain that seemed to tick along regardless of everything that was happening to him.

"Yes," Fern said, sounding rather perplexed. "Yes, I did." She took his hand, which had been draped across her waist, and turned it palm up. Colin felt the heat of her breath against it. "Tell me more about where we are going, or I won't bite you." Her voice shook a little—probably at her own daring.

Colin pulled his hand back and rolled away. He pushed into a sitting position and looked at her, sprawled crosswise on the bed. "Wrexmere was in the family four generations before the death of a distant relative brought its master to an unexpected barony."

"Why are we going there now?" She frowned at him, and he had the strange urge to smooth the delicate lines in her forehead that this caused.

"Because it is the most remote place that I have at my disposal," Colin said, a half-truth. "I have never been there myself, but my father gave its use over to me at my eighteenth birthday. No one should be there except the steward and his wife, though there is a little village some distance away."

"That is the only reason?" she asked guardedly.

"It is reason enough."

"Is there really no one there?" Fern straightened up. "Not even a maid?"

"Of course not," Colin said. "Why would there be a maid when none of my family have lived there for generations?"

Fern shook her head. "But what am I to do? Mother found a regular lady's maid for me and has already sent her to your town house so that she would be waiting when we returned—but now I'll have no one."

"I apologize if it inconveniences you," Colin said stiffly.

Her brow creased. "Who shall fasten my clothes? Who shall dress my hair?"

"I will fasten your clothes if you need assistance, and as for your hair, surely it won't hurt you to wear it in a slightly simpler style for a short while," Colin said, growing tired of her shallow preoccupation.

"Simpler!" She shook her head. "I haven't any idea of how to dress it at all. I've never done so much as brush it on my own. I have been taught how to arrange a dinner party for sixty guests, and I can make a lace cap and booties for a new baby and create a pillow with thirty-two types of embroidery stitches, but I haven't the slightest idea about what to do with my hair."

"You'll learn. Just as you learn anything," Colin said brusquely, ignoring the strange and unfamiliar pang of guilt that he felt. Her life was so small, so very narrow in its scope and significance . . . and he had been glad of it. It was what he had wanted, but now everything had changed; they'd both been jerked from the paths that had been intended for them, and Colin knew that, fundamentally, it was his fault.

Fern blew out a huff of air, pressing her lips tightly together as if she'd explode with a retort if she did not.

"What is the matter?" Colin said—tried not to demand, for it was not fair to take out his frustration with himself upon her.

"That's easy for you to say, because you still have your valet to shave you and polish your boots," she said, something in her tone betraying that she knew how much like a sulky child such a statement made her sound.

"Do you want me to send him away?" he asked evenly.

"Yes, I do. It might be silly, and it might be petty, but yes, I want you to send him away. You've robbed me of a maid to haul me halfway across England to a place I have never heard of, so why should you keep your valet?" Her gray eyes flashed defensively.

Colin looked at her coldly. "I will send him back tomorrow, then."

"Good," she replied shortly.

Why are we really squabbling? Colin wondered. It wasn't that their argument had any content, to speak of. Fern pushed a strand of hair back from her face and shifted restlessly. When they came together, everything had seemed right, somehow, but now, Colin did not know what to do with the young woman who sat next to him. He didn't really know her at all—he'd had no intentions of ever getting to know her except in the most superficial way, in discussions about social banalities and empty domestic arrangements during their dinners.

And now he was shut in with her in a room so small that they could barely move, there to remain until morning. The minutes seemed to heap around him like smothering drifts of snow. What was to be done with all of them? How were the two of them to spend them together, with no other diversion than their own company?

They could try to spend as many as possible in the one activity certain to require no extraneous meaning. Despite the violence of his last climax, his body was already beginning to stir again. Yet he should be able to talk to his wife. It was wrong that there was an intractable barrier, for he did not even know enough about her to ask her a more significant question than how her sisters and parents were doing. She fidgeted next to him, staring at her hands, avoiding his eyes.

Finally he said, "You look uncomfortable. Let me help you undress for the night."

"I have no nightdress to wear." Her tone carried traces of resentment. "It is in my trunk."

"I know," he said. "Stand up."

Slowly, she obeyed.

"Come here."

She stepped forward, and he stopped her with a hand splayed against her waist. He stood and began unfastening her bodice one button at a time. He could see the flutter of her pulse in her throat, could see the tightening of her jaw. Colin's movements became provocative without his making a conscious decision to do so. It was easier this way, when their bodies could talk and nothing else mattered, even if he knew it would not be enough. . . .

He freed the last button and traced a line from the shadow of her throat downward, between her breasts and along the stiff steel busk of her corset. Fern gripped his elbows as if to steady herself.

"I think I am better than any maid," he said softly.

"It depends upon one's objectives," Fern said, but her trembling voice belied the tartness of her words.

"What are yours, then?" he asked, suddenly serious. "What do you want out of all of this?" His nod encompassed everything that was between them.

Her eyes were bright and round. "Happiness."

"Happiness." He blew out a rush of air. "The ruby of a maharaja I might be able to procure for you, but happiness . . . I feel inadequate to such a demand. What is happiness? Who can say?"

"You can't?" She looked curiously at him. "Why, happiness . . . just is."

"Do you make it?" he demanded.

She shook her head. "Make it? Of course not."

"Then why did you look to me to provide it for you?"

Fern stared at him silently for a moment. Then she burst out, "Oh, you think I am a dolt!"

"No," Colin disagreed quietly. "I think I don't know what you want or why."

She made a frustrated noise. "I have this picture in my head of how my life is supposed to be—me a contented wife with a pleased husband and a well-mannered brood of children, cheerful servants, and friends from good society. And it's all rosy and lovely . . . except I am afraid the woman in the picture isn't really me. She looks like me and she smiles like me, but inside, she doesn't feel the things I feel, doesn't have the thoughts that I have or the anger or the fear. She's perfect. The perfect wife, and she has the perfect husband." She stopped. "That's what I thought you were. You seemed like the picture I had in my head. And if you were enough like the picture, then maybe I would be like it, too."

A man in a picture. The flat appearance of social perfection. She was right about him, precisely correct—that was what Colin had made himself to be. But what was behind the stiffly painted physiognomy? It would not have occurred to him that there might be something else until that day, but now he had the sudden fear that he would find himself incomplete.

"I wish we were at Wrexmere," he said abruptly. He pushed her bodice from her shoulders. Her hands lowered with deliberation to her sides, and the garment slid off, revealing the smooth curves of her shoulders.

"I still don't understand," Fern pressed. "What is at Wrexmere?"

"Nothing is there except an estate that needs attention. It's what isn't there."

Fern stared at him blankly, and Colin spun her away from him and unbuttoned her skirt so that he could get to the ties of the petticoats beneath. He forced himself to focus upon the fabric under his hands, ignoring the soft flesh that was a mere corset's thickness from his fingers. He could still smell her on him, like a drug. He clenched his jaw. "There isn't anyone there. No one I know. No one who knows me. Not of consequence, anyhow." The strange steward, with his cryptic letters, hardly counted.

"Why don't you want to be among people?" There was a strained note in her voice, one that he instinctively knew had nothing to do with their conversation and everything to do with the fact that he was undressing her and their mutual awareness of that fact.

"People!" He snorted. "People don't bother me. Society bothers me." He tugged the skirts downward, trying to ignore the tantalizing path they took from her neat waist over the curve of her hips. He was silent for a long moment, savoring her body so close to his. She was going to ask him more if he did not provide a better answer; for all the tentativeness of many of her questions, she had a remarkable persistence. Finally, he spoke the words aloud. "I am not myself right now. Or, more properly, I have just realized that I don't know who I am. I would prefer to have no one scrutinizing my actions until after I figure that out."

"Until you can fashion a new facade, you mean." The response was quiet.

Colin stared at the back of her chemise, which was slightly creased with sweat from being pressed against her body in the heat. He grasped her waist in both his hands and pulled her back against him. She fit so well there, the top of her head resting on his throat just below his chin. She trembled slightly—she was still afraid of him, or herself; he wasn't sure which. She, who had shaken his world, was afraid of him because he was larger, stronger. A part of him was very glad, for it seemed to be the only advantage he had over this small coddled woman.

"A facade," he repeated, amusement making him honest. "No, I have no facade. If I had a facade, I would not have needed to leave Brighton."

"But you are so empty," Fern whispered. She grew stiffer against him, inclining away without actually moving.

"It is no facade," Colin repeated.

She made a ragged sound and pulled away, turning to face him. "I can't believe that. You are merely distant. Hard to know. Shy, maybe. My sister Flora is shy, and many people think she's aloof."

"Fern, I am not lying," he said wearily. "What you saw was what I was."

"But I look at you now, and I see . . . you," she whispered. "You are there, looking back at me."

Colin closed his eyes, and the words came almost unbidden. "I feel different. I feel alive. I don't think I knew what that meant. But I also feel dissatisfied."

Fern's face shuttered. "With me?"

"With everything." He chuckled quietly. "Except . . . not with what you do to me."

Fern nodded slowly, her soft face shadowed. "I do not think that I dislike it quite so much anymore. I'm scared it may be wrong of me, but it feels good now. Extremely good, most of the time. Sometimes it felt bad, but that was good, too." She lifted a hand to his neck and caressed it softly. The salt on her skin burned a little in the raw scratches. "I liked that," she whispered. "I needed it, just as you said you did."

"Yes," Colin said. She placed her hand flat against his throat as he spoke, her eyes going half-lidded at the vibrations against her palm.

"I could squeeze," she breathed.

His heart quickened. "You could," he agreed.

Her eyes got wider. "I can feel that." She smiled. "I can feel what I do to you."

"I can feel what I do to you, too. I can feel your heat from here," he said. "I can smell your desire."

Her brow creased. "This is all we have, isn't it?"

"But we do have this," Colin insisted. "This is important."

"This is a start," Fern said, as if only half convinced of her own words.

"We will have more." It was a promise. "We might not have it now, but we will."

"Oh, I do hope so, Colin," she said earnestly.

He quirked a corner of his mouth. "For now, let us at least enjoy what we have."

"I couldn't refuse you. Not last time, and not again." Another shiver went through her, and this time, it held more desire than fear. "I want it too much."

"Good," said Colin.

She sat on the bed, drawing him with her, and it was a long time before either of them spoke again.

Chapter Nine

"There it is."

The words jerked Fern awake. She blinked woozily out the coach window and saw . . . nothing. Fog eddied low across the road, gathering in the hollows and tangling the occasional twisted shrub that rose on the higher hillocks of moorland intertwined with the bog.

Bog land. Fern's father had once mentioned the numerous schemes to exploit the peat or fill in the low places that various entrepreneurs had undertaken in order to try to wrest a fortune from the poor land. But the bog had defeated them all. As they had traveled on from the inn where they had spent the night, the countryside had grown more and more damp and desolate, and it seemed as if they were traveling farther back in time the deeper they went. The last livery stable had been many miles ago, and the old man who ran it seemed suspicious to see a stranger there. The cold chicken lunch that Colin had bought had at least been hearty, if unflavorful, the remains of it in the hamper that lay on the floor between them.

"I don't see anything," Fern said. She looked at

Colin. As the land grew more bleak, he had seemed to become more forbidding. He sat across from her in pristine and chilly elegance, his green eyes dark and inscrutable, and she could not truly believe that he had been the man with whom she had shared such a confusing, tumultuous night. But she knew that under that crisp gray superfine and white linen were her marks—the marks of her nails and her teeth, the proof that she was not without power over herself and over him. She still ached from their encounters the night before. It was easier to do . . . that . . . than to talk, and even easier to try not to think—about anything. Thinking was dangerous.

They could not lie easily next to each other, and when they spoke, they got tangled in each other's words and hopes and mangled dreams, and so they had consumed the night with action in which no words were needed. Their bodies had spoken, but what had it all meant? The next morning, Colin's valet had attended upon him one last time before being sent away, and Colin had helped Fern to put back on a fresh traveling dress, as he had promised. Her efforts to dress her own hair had resulted in less success, though, and already the unkempt bun at the nape of her neck was beginning to slide.

"I saw a sign," Colin said. "Wrexmere. There is supposed to be a village—"

Even as he spoke, the coach lurched, turning off the main road onto a rutted lane. Fern grasped the balance strap to keep from being pitched into the far wall.

She peered anxiously out the window. "I don't see anything but more moor and bog."

"It should be here," Colin repeated, in the tone of voice of a person for whom *should* always became *is*.

They rounded a corner. Fern would have sworn that the landscape was too flat to hide anything, but the fog must have distorted her perceptions, for there, on a slight rise, was a cluster of cottages around the cold gray block of a stark country church.

Fern watched it fixedly, glad to have the excuse to look at something other than her husband. They were already quite near, and as they drew even closer, she could see the ruined outlines of the foundations of other houses that had once stood among the survivors.

"What happened here?" she asked.

"Enclosure, most likely, probably before the property came into my family." Colin's tone was indifferent. "On land like this, it was better for the lord to have half a dozen shepherds than one hundred farmers. We should have been ruined in a few more generations if we hadn't come into Radcliffe proper, for all that it was only a barony when the title came to our line."

"Oh," Fern said. She and her sisters often stayed at their uncle's estate, and though her father had acquired enough wealth through his investments to make him a rich man despite his status as a second son, Fern was deeply aware that one generation was enough to separate her from the history that the land gave the true nobility. The skeletons of the houses were forlorn, Colin's dry facts an insult to their desolation.

In the village, nothing moved, and Fern wondered how many of the houses that remained were occupied. As they passed by the moss-rimed church, the bell rang slowly twice, the tolls shuddering the still air and making the silence afterward even more profound. The coach rattled, the horses' harnesses jingled, but beyond their little globe of life and heat, the world seemed dead.

"There could not be more than a dozen habitable houses there," Fern said.

"I don't know," Colin replied. "The tenant's cottages are in New Wrexmere, about half a mile distant, and they should be in much better repair. No Radcliffe property would be allowed to fall into such a state."

Fern continued to stare until the village passed out of sight. No one responded to the church bell. No one came out to look at the coach. The village maintained a breathless stillness.

The driver tapped on the sliding conversation door, and Colin reached behind his head to slide it open.

"There it is, sir," the driver's voice came. "Wrexmere Manor. I promised to get you there before nightfall, sir."

Colin nodded out the opposite window, and Fern followed his gaze. Ahead and in the distance, a sudden granite tor pushed out of the boggy land to form a dome that seemed to bear down upon the surrounding countryside. At the top, an ancient, crumbling keep speared bluntly into the sky.

"That?" Fern said.

Colin slid the door closed. His expression was remote. "It could be."

"We can't stay there!" she protested.

"The caretakers will be there," Colin reminded her.

"We can't stay," she repeated.

"I can't go!" Colin shot back, displaying the first trace of emotion that she had seen from him since they had left the inn. "I need to come here."

"There must be a hotel—"

"No," he said firmly. "No hotel. We are going there." He pointed to the bleak gray structure.

Fern sat back against the squabs, her trepidation mounting. "I have a bad feeling about this."

As they mounted the hill, Fern felt a wash of relief as she realized that there was more to the manor house than the old gray keep. A half-timbered hall butted up against it, its many-paned windows flat and dark. Even its somber bulk, with its skeletal timbers and damp, pallid walls, seemed more welcoming than the mass of rock beside it. In its shadow was a smaller structure, an old plaster and limestone cottage. No smoke rose from the chimney, and its small windows were tightly shuttered.

"Does the caretaker live there?" Fern asked, pointing to the cottage.

"I haven't the slightest idea," Colin said. "We will see when we arrive."

Just as he spoke, the muffled sound of the wheels on the too-soft dirt track changed to the sharp clatter of stone, and the coach jolted and rocked from side to side. Fern looked at the ground outside the window—between the weeds, she could make out the faint, irregular shapes of an old cobblestone drive that had sunk into the damp earth unevenly, throwing the cobbles up in strange angles.

The coach stopped, and for a moment, Fern just sat white-knuckled in the silence, looking at her expressionless husband. The coach swayed as the driver swung down, and after a pause, the door was opened.

Colin stepped down and offered his arm to Fern. She recoiled before she could stop herself. Compared to these bleak surroundings, the familiarity of the coach seemed like a refuge. Suddenly, passionately, what she wanted more than anything else was to travel straight to her parents' town house and pretend that none of this had ever happened, that she was still the blithe girl she had been only a few days before.

But she could not do that. There was no going back. As Colin held his hand out to her silently, patiently, part of her stirred and yearned to join him, no matter how foolish the endeavor. No matter what secrets he was keeping about this place.

Fern took his hand and stepped down.

She had hesitated long enough that the driver had already had time to lower the first trunk to the ground. Colin paid the man and then strode purposefully up to the cottage door. He rapped upon it, the sharp sound cracking in the silence. Fern approached and hovered, not knowing what else to do, a few feet behind him. The house was in worse condition than it had looked from a distance. The plaster was coming away from the wall in chunks, and slimy green algae had advanced several feet up the facade. If the residents of this hovel were maintaining the rest of the property, it did not bode well for the conditions inside the manor house itself.

There was no response. Colin waited for half a minute, and then he knocked again, louder this time. Fern suppressed the urge to say that she supposed that no one was home; the comment was one of the inane noises she always felt the need to make when she was nervous. Instead, she bit her lip to keep her silence, wrapping her hands hard around her middle.

Colin rattled the lock, and his glove came away

covered with rust. "No one has lived here for some time," he said. Fern could hear the frown in his voice. After examining his hand for a moment, he snorted and turned on his heel, avoiding colliding into Fern only because she dodged to the side. He strode across the short, weedy turf to the broad door of the Tudor wing of the manor house. He rapped again, harder.

The sound reverberated within, and then . . . nothing.

Colin rattled this lock, and this time the door came open. "Perhaps they can't hear me," he said, but his tone contained a cold note that sent a chill through Fern. He stepped inside.

Casting a wistful look at the carriage, Fern followed and plunged into stifling darkness. In the dim light from the doorway, she peered at the walls. Thick curtains muffled the windows and strangled the light. Stumbling in the blackness, she went to the nearest one, groping under the heavy velvet for the drapery pull. She found it, and a shower of dust flew from the curtains as she opened them, gilding the pale, foggy light with silver motes.

Fern began to cough, and Colin turned around.

"It doesn't seem that the caretakers have done much caretaking," he said, his expression stony.

Fern wiped her streaming eyes and looked around the cavernous Tudor hall. The oak wainscot had darkened to black, and the white plaster above was grimed to gray. Under the oppressive coffered ceiling huddled a vast jumble of furniture, thick with dust and festooned with silken sheets of cobwebs. Colin frowned at a grotesquely ornate Louis XIV settee.

"I think I recognize this from Norwood," he said.

"My grandmother set up house there after my grandfather passed away. I suppose the old furniture was sent here." He swept the room with a glance. "Not only from there, I would say."

"Where do you suppose the steward is?" Fern asked tentatively, though any hope of his existence had been dashed at the sight of the room.

"I don't know," Colin said shortly. His jaw tightened, and Fern had to consciously force herself not to quail before his reaction. *I have power, too*, she reminded herself.

"I am going to look around." Colin put action to words and disappeared through the single interior doorway.

Fern cast one last look at the coach. The driver was lowering Colin's trunk to the frost-heaved cobbles. She tore her gaze away and hurried after Colin, into the interior of the house.

There was not much more of the ground floor to see. A short hallway led past the stairs to the dining room, equally dingy, crowded, and forlorn. There was a door at either end of that room, one to a small square room that Colin curtly identified as a cabinet, and the other to the kitchens, which occupied the ground floor of the old keep. Fern could not shake the sense that she was being watched—a nonsensical sensation, to be sure, since she would have sworn that no one had disturbed the dust there for years.

In grim silence, Colin led the way upstairs. Fern followed, his behavior frightening her less than the house did. The four bedrooms on the first floor were filthy, crowded, and pervaded with a dank, unused smell that seemed to creep under her skin and make her bones itch. Above, the servants' rooms under the eaves were entirely bare, and large chunks of plaster lay on the floors, loosened from the ceiling by leaks in the roof.

"I don't think there is a steward anymore," Fern said softly.

Colin stood at the highest point of the last attic room, half stooping under the slope of the roof. His face was set in an expression of deep incredulity and disapproval, as if such a disappointment were foreign to his experience and intolerable. "I believe you are right, but it would be of deep interest to me to meet the man whom I have been paying two hundred pounds a year for the maintenance of this property." Though the words were mild, she could hear the steel beneath.

"Embezzlement," Fern breathed.

"Outright theft," Colin retorted, his face dark.

"We can't stay here," Fern said, voicing what she had been thinking since she stepped into the hall. "It's filthy, and the servants are gone."

Colin gave a short laugh. "We don't have much of a choice for tonight, at least." He nodded to the narrow window, set into a dormer in the roof.

Fern's stomach sank as she peered through the grimy glass to see the coach already rattling down the long drive, away from the house. "You couldn't catch it?" The question was almost a plea.

Colin's eyes narrowed. "No. I am afraid, my dear wife, that we are stuck here for the moment. And, since I sent my valet away at your request, without a single servant."

Panic welled up in Fern's throat. They had no candles, no servants, no clean place to sleep, no transportation, and no food. "Whatever shall we do?"

Colin's smile was chilly. "Make do, my dear; make do."

Colin went downstairs to fetch their luggage. He brought in the wicker hamper that contained the remains of their lunch first. There was enough left to make a light dinner, but if they wanted breakfast, he would have to go down to the village the next morning to find it.

With luck—and for the first time in his life, that phrase carried some doubt—he'd be able to get more than food: He and Fern both needed servants, and he needed a damned good explanation not only for those ridiculous letters but also for what had been done with the money that was meant to maintain the property.

He returned to the first floor and found Fern moving between the four bedrooms with a preoccupied expression. He left her to whatever she was doing until he had brought all their luggage in, stacking it in the corridor. The first two bedrooms he looked into contained pulled-back bedclothes but no Fern. He found her in the third, scowling down at the bed. She looked rumpled, tired, and dissatisfied, and Colin couldn't stifle another pang of guilt. Fern wasn't a woman raised for adversity. She was made for an orderly, predictable life. And yet everything between them had been anything but predictable, and she was rising to the challenge despite every aspect of her upbringing being calculated to make her helpless.

"This is the only bed we can sleep in. The rest have gone moldy," she said.

"Aren't you supposed to sun them or beat them . . .

or something?" Colin said, a vague recollection of the activities of maids rising in his mind.

"Sun them for damp, beat them for dust," Fern agreed. "But it would take more than that to get these beds really clean, and there isn't any sun today, anyhow." She pulled off the sheets and blankets with a single jerk, then looked at him. Something glinted deep in her gray eyes, a sudden intense flash of emotion that he had seen several times before it was just as quickly smothered.

But this time, it didn't instantly disappear. "If you want to *make do*, then don't just stand there—help me with the doing," she said.

The unexpected asperity of her demand surprised a chuckle out of him, and he stepped forward to help.

"The ground is wet, too. We can go into another bedroom and try to beat the dust out of it in there," she said.

"How is that done exactly?" he asked.

"With a beater." She paused. "Or, if we can't find that, a broom. If you will take this into another bedroom, I'll look for a broom. . . ." Her voice trailed off, her certainty sliding.

Abruptly, he pitied her. She had not asked for this, and she was bearing up remarkably well, considering. She hadn't yet blamed him for making a decision that was looking increasingly disastrous, and since Colin himself wasn't sure why he had become so fixated upon staying at Wrexmere, he took her lack of accusations with an unfamiliar sense of gratefulness. He could hardly blame her for not wanting to search through the darkening rooms of the manor alone—

there was something about the house that lifted the hairs on the back of his neck, too.

"Fern," Colin said.

She looked up, and he noticed a smudge of dirt on her nose that was, quite incongruously, incredibly alluring. He wanted to pull her into his arms, to kiss her into forgetting her fears, and then into forgetting everything else. But he knew that would not help anything, however attractive that solution was.

"Devil take it," he muttered. "It would help me."

"What?" Fern asked. Colin circled the chaise that separated them and grasped her shoulders. She looked up at him, and for once, he knew that he was not the cause of the fear in her eyes.

How had he ever thought this woman conventional? Her soft face, yes, that might fool a man by its prettiness, but those eyes, which shone with a hundred depths and gradations of feeling, were nothing short of extraordinary.

He bent his head slowly toward hers, watching her expression change to expectation, feeling her breath hitch through his hands. Their lips met, scarcely brushing, and she trembled. Anticipation lanced into his groin, and he let his mouth take hers, covering it, her uncertainty and need tangling in the desperation in her lips, her teeth, her tongue. Her mouth was hot with her fears and her desire, the slickness of it begging him for more, the hard nip of her teeth demanding it.

Finally, he pulled away, and she leaned against his body, panting slightly as her eyes glittered darkly.

"You can do it," he said softly. "We can do it."

She let her forehead rest against his chest, as if she were drawing certainty from him. Certainty!

There was nothing that he possessed less of. He didn't know what was going on in this strange, neglected place, didn't know what was going on between him and his wife. But he did know, with a swiftness that dizzied him, that some things were worth fighting for.

He spoke reluctantly. "Come help me here, and then we will find a beater together."

She pushed off him. "Of course," she said with palpable relief.

Together, they wrestled the mattress into an adjoining bedroom. Fern pushed the casement open, then retreated hurriedly. "It's beginning to drizzle," she said in a tone of dismay. She rubbed her arms briskly. "It's so clammy."

"Indeed." It was still warm enough that the dampness was stifling rather than chilly; Fern's reaction was one of pure unease. "We should find that beater now, and perhaps some candles or oil for the lamps."

"In the kitchens, I suppose," Fern said, her voice laced with doubt.

"Let's go, then," Colin said, before her unease could overtake her common sense. He headed toward the stairs, Fern following so close behind that the edge of her skirts sometimes brushed the back of his legs.

They went through the dining room and toward the kitchens, passing through the entryway to the ground floor of the keep.

"I don't like this place," Fern said. Colin offered his arm, and she clung to it as they advanced.

Colin couldn't help but agree. Light filtered in from arrow slits high around the perimeter of the room, and a draft fluttered the cobwebs in the great groin vaults that supported the floor above, the thick supporting pillars obscuring their view more than half a dozen paces in any direction. As they penetrated more deeply into the room, Colin caught glimpses of two enormous stone fireplaces that dominated one wall, with pots and utensils hung from dozens of hooks between, a sight that seemed as forlorn as it was encouraging to their quest for a beater or broom. Trestles, thick with dust and bleached and scarred with centuries of scouring, lurked between the pillars.

"The floor plan must never have been changed since the keep was built," Colin said as they crossed the room, looking for anything that might promise a beater.

"What do you mean?"

Colin didn't know whether Fern was truly curious or simply filling up the silence. He answered anyway. "In the Dark Ages, the kitchen and storage rooms were on the ground floor of a keep, with the great hall above. There weren't any doors to the kitchen from the outside—you had to climb up an exterior wooden staircase to the first floor to get in. When the keep was attacked, the stairs were burned."

"Oh," Fern said. "Was this ever attacked?"

"In the days of Margaret of France, and now and then during the Wars of the Roses."

She looked around the room, and her haunted expression told him that she was imagining the air shaken by the clash of arms and the cry of men. Now the empty room reverberated with nothing more than their footsteps, caught in the high vaults above.

They reached the far wall of the kitchen, where four doors lined up beside a staircase that led to the upper reaches of the keep.

"A pantry?" Fern asked.

"I don't know," Colin said.

The first door opened onto a narrow flight of stone stairs that led downward into darkness. A breath of cool, dank air slivered up the steps to caress his face.

"The cellars," Fern said. "Let's not go there."

Colin simply grunted, frowning, and opened the second door. The light from the high windows around the kitchen penetrated the gloom. It was a tiny, cell-like chamber, just large enough to contain an ancient bed box that was still filled with moldering straw.

"Third time's a charm?" Colin suggested. He opened the next door, and Fern screamed.

Chapter Ten

The chamber was like the room they had just seen, only a version reflected through a horrible, twisted mirror. Spidery writing scrawled from the walls and ceiling down onto the bed box and across the floor, covering everything in tangled layers of words, the dark crimson of old blood twining with black and angry orange. Some words were written out in huge brushstrokes two feet high; others were written so small that the letters blurred into incomprehensibility. The one thing that united them all was their hate.

. . . they shall be brot to accompt' . . . and the WRATH of the Lord . . . mine anger as the seas . . . day of judgement . . . evildoers . . . evildoers . . . EVILDOERS

Colin shut the door so hard that the air shook in the vaults. Fern clung to him, making strangled, half-sobbing sounds.

"What was that?" she said, the words almost a plea.

"It was nothing to be frightened of." His heart was beating hard and fast against his chest in defiance of his own assurances. "It was old—very old. No one has written like that in two centuries."

"It was horrible," she said. "I don't care how old it

is—I could feel the hatred. This whole place is infected with it." The last was said in a wild rush, and Colin drew Fern closer to him, hoping that she would sense a steadiness that he did not have.

"We won't go in that room again," Colin promised, as much to himself as to her. He began to move toward the fourth and final door, and Fern stumbled along beside him. When he reached for the handle, though, she cried out.

"Surely you don't mean to open another door!"

"It was only words," Colin said. "They can't hurt us." Still, he braced himself as he swung open the door.

He was confronted with a pantry. An ordinary pantry, filled with mundane pantry things, thick with dust and corroded by age, but completely and thoroughly unexceptional.

Beside him, Fern gave a short laugh that had a hysterical edge. He reached onto one of the shelves and took out a jar of lamp oil.

"I am ashamed to say that I do not even know what a beater looks like," he said in the most normal tone he could manufacture.

Fern took a shuddering breath and loosened her grip enough to reach past him with her free hand and grasp a long-handled tool with a curled wire head on one end. "This is it."

"Good," Colin said. "Let us go." The words carried more force than he'd intended, and Fern nodded fervently beside him, gripping the beater like a weapon. It should have been funny, but Colin found himself incapable of amusement. All he wanted was to set this manor to rights and to leave it behind him forever. He had never been given to superstitions or irrational fears, but he wanted as little to do with this place as possible.

He guided Fern back into the Tudor wing, and when she had to release his arm in order to precede him up the stairs, she did so with a reluctance that he could feel. When they reached the first-floor bedrooms, her shoulders seemed to unwind a little.

"Half an hour ago, I would not have believed you if you'd told me I would be grateful to see these rooms again." She squinted up at the ceiling, where water infiltration had made wide stains in the plaster. She went to the bedroom where they had laid the mattress out onto the floor. Outside, the rain had increased from a drizzle to a steady wash that whispered against the half-timbered walls. "Who do you think wrote all that?" she asked abruptly.

Colin didn't have to ask what she meant. "I don't know. A crazed person, no doubt, but I assume you already came to that conclusion yourself."

Fern shuddered. "Could it have been a prisoner?"

"A prisoner?" Colin frowned. "Not here. That was a servant's room, though why anyone would keep a mad servant on . . ." He shook his head. "It is also likely one of the only bedrooms without a window, so if one of the family members became ill . . ." He trailed off. "But there are no family stories of mad relatives— not that I know of, anyhow."

Fern was silent for a long moment, her expression hooded. Finally, she spoke with an air of decision. "I don't want to think about that anymore. Let's get this mattress clean." She hefted the beater, then paused. "Did you realize that these last two days are the only times since we have known each other that you have actually spoken with me?"

Colin raised a skeptical brow, allowing the change of subject. "I can't imagine how I managed to gain your consent to wed me if I had never spoken to you."

She shook her head earnestly. "That is not what I meant. I meant spoken *with* me, truly talked about something together. We have had dozens of meaningless exchanges of pleasantries, but it doesn't count when the topic is idle speculation about what dress your sister-in-law will wear to the soirée or when the swallows will come back this year. Those aren't real conversations. They're a charade—noises that people make to hide the fact that they are not talking to one another."

"And what would the purpose of such a charade be?"

"For me, its purpose was to hide how much you frightened me and to conceal the fact that I had no idea of what to say to you," Fern answered, her gaze dropping despite the evenness of her voice. "What its purpose was for you, I cannot say."

Colin took her shoulders, forcing her to look at him so that he could read the truth in her eyes. "I scared you—really scared you—that much?" He was not sure whether the idea appalled or intrigued him.

She closed her eyes, swaying slightly in his grasp. He could feel the trembling attraction in her body, and it roused a response in his own. "You still scare me. But now I am just as scared of myself, so it seems pointless to hide from you when I cannot hide from me." She opened her eyes and smiled thinly. "And I am even more scared of this place. I think."

The allusion to what they shared sent a twist of desire lancing from his groin outward. He pulled her against him, sliding his arm about her waist so she could not back away. "We have only just begun, *mon ange*," he whispered into her hair. "If we are such frightening creatures now, imagine what we will become in the fullness of time."

Fern shivered, leaning into him as the beater slid from her fingers. "Terrifying," she whispered back. She lifted her hands to the back of his neck, digging her fingernails into the base of his skull as she pulled his head down to meet her upturned lips. He took the offering as greedily as he reveled in the fire across his neck, crushing her skirts against him. When he pulled away again, she smiled at him—breathlessly, tremulously, but a genuine smile of happiness, the first he'd seen from her since their marriage.

He did not know what else his future held in store for them, but that they would have something worth keeping, he was certain, and was glad of it. Gladness. The emotion fizzed like champagne in his brain, strange but welcome.

Time would tell, people said, and it certainly would. But for the first time since that ringing slap had woken him from his dream of a life, he considered that the result might just be better than what he had begun with.

Fern watched Colin flail at the featherbed through the inch-wide door opening, holding her handkerchief tightly over her mouth. She had made her best effort at beating the mattress as she had remembered seeing the maids do, but it made her eyes and nose stream, and her hands quickly grew raw even through her gloves. She hadn't dared complain—she did not want Colin to think her as soft and useless as she was half-afraid that she was—but she had been more than happy to give the task over to him when he offered.

She watched the fabric of his coat move across his broad back with every swing of the beater as he balanced on his wide-set legs. He should be made ridiculous, reduced by doing such a menial and feminine task, and yet to see his hard body in motion was an experience to savor. A new, fat puff of dust rose up at each stroke, hazing the air and drifting with sullen reluctance out of the open window and into the steady rain. Finally, the mattress had been hit to the point where it was impossible to tell whether there was more dust entering the air or if the new swirls of dust were just eddies in the clouds that already filled the room.

Colin paused and wiped his coat sleeve across his forehead. Then he grasped two corners of the mattress and pulled, sliding it toward the doorway.

Fern quickly opened the door, and together, they wrestled it through the doorway. She shut the door again, closing the dust inside, and looked up at Colin. He was frosted with dust, from the his grayed hair to his dulled shoes.

"You look as if you were carved of marble," Fern said. "All except your eyelashes. No artist has ever been able to work stone so finely."

"I do not know whether the correct response would be to thank you for the compliment or apologize for the insult of appearing before a lady in such a state," Colin said.

"You cleaned the mattress for us both, so there is no reason to apologize," Fern said. "Besides, I doubt that I am better."

Colin heaved, sliding the mattress to the door of the

bedroom that Fern had chosen for them. She got caught up in the doorway, battling her crinoline as she tried to fold the mattress so it could fit through. Suddenly, her skirts and feet were tangled, and with a yelp, she toppled onto the mattress, her hoops flying up and sending a cloud of dust into the air that made her sneeze.

Colin blinked at her for a moment, then gave a short bark of laughter. The sound thrilled up Fern's spine even as she wiped her streaming eyes.

"I suppose I don't make such a good chambermaid," he said.

Fern tried to get up, got twisted in her skirts, and fell over again. This time, though, she was close enough to grab hold of Colin—which she did, and, possessed by a sudden impishness, pulled as she toppled backward.

Taken by surprise, Colin overbalanced and sprawled atop her, sending her hoops into new chaos. Fern looked into his astonished face and began to laugh herself, the sheer release of it feeling so good that she gave herself up to it, peal after peal ringing from her until she slumped, breathless, pinned beneath Colin's weight.

"You think that is funny, do you?" Colin asked, a note of challenge in his voice.

"At this point, I am desperate to find anything funny," Fern retorted. "Besides, you were the one who began laughing first."

"Ah, but now you have made yourself helpless." His eyes glittered in a way that made her pulse speed up.

"I am never helpless," Fern shot back, and to her amazement, there was some grain of truth under the bravura. She was not just a passive receptacle, and though her ignorance—unsuspected only days ago—was still a source of constant frustration and limitation, she had found the ability within herself to act, even with regards to the astonishing and frightening being that was her husband.

He kissed her then, and it was a long time before they resumed the process of getting the mattress back onto the bed. Once it was in place, Fern picked up the linens she had found in the press at the bed's foot and frowned.

"I've never made a bed before," she confessed.

Colin raised an eyebrow. "Give the sheets to me."

Fern blinked at him, and he took them from her unresisting arms. "How . . . ?"

"Eton, *mon ange*," he said, setting the stack aside as he unfolded the topmost sheet with a snap. "Come. Take this side, and I will show you how."

Fern took direction with bemusement, and when they finished, Colin sprawled upon the bed, loose-limbed in repose as he stared at the dust-grayed hangings above his head. Fern took up some rags that she had found and, with the windows open to the increasingly heavy rain, pushed around the dust that coated the jumbled furniture within reach. Soon the air was full of motes, the rag leaving shiny tracks on the wood that dulled as the dust settled immediately upon it again. She sneezed.

"Put it away, Fern," Colin said, his gaze still upon the hangings. "You aren't doing any good."

Trying to sniff in a ladylike way as she wiped her streaming eyes, Fern could do nothing but nod.

"It's getting dark," he added.

"I'm getting hungry," Fern admitted.

Colin took out his pocket watch. "No wonder. The hamper's in the corridor. If you fill the lamps, I'll get it, as well as wood, water, and a kettle to wash with. It shall be a light dinner, but it must hold us until I go to the village in the morning."

Fern nodded again. Colin pushed upright in an easy motion and tossed a packet of matches on the bed as he strode through the doorway.

As soon as the door closed, she regretted agreeing to letting him leave her, even if following had meant a return to the kitchen. She shifted, trying to shake the feeling of foreboding that overtook her. From the window, the rocky tor sloped down to the village, moor and bog interwoven into a treacherous tapestry of heather, sedge, and mosses. The wash of rain was constant, not the ominous roll and crack of a storm but a steady, drowning, suffocating shower that oppressed everything under it, leaching the color from the world and draining it down into the deep peat.

She dusted and filled one of the lamps, waiting for the ancient wick to darken with the new oil before carefully striking a match and setting the leaping orange flame to the end of it. The wick caught, and though it gave off the low glow of sperm oil rather than the strong white paraffin light, she was grateful for the cheerful ruddiness of it, driving out the gray of dust and rain. But the rosy globe of light attenuated swiftly, leaving the crowded corners of the room in gloom and making the hulking furnishings strange in the flickering shadows. Not threatening, exactly; it was more lonely than anything. That thought was so ludicrous that Fern made herself laugh aloud in a stiff "Ha ha!" But it didn't feel funny. It was a sense that wore on her nerves, dissipating when logic was brought to bear upon it but coalescing again in the corners of her mind whenever she thought of anything else.

Fern determinedly sought to occupy herself. She found towels in the linen press, clean though musty, and laid out their nightclothes. Going through Colin's trunk felt wrong: The scent of his clothes was now familiar to her, a combination of laundry soap, sandalwood, and cedar, but she still felt like an invader for pawing through something so fundamentally private as his unworn clothing.

With no productive tasks left, she occupied herself shoving around more dust with the rag, trying to keep her hands busy and mind away from the dark, silent kitchen cell and the words written there. . . .

The noise of the door opening again made Fern jump and spin around, her crinoline swaying against her legs.

"Startled you, did I?" said Colin mildly. There was a spark of humor in his eyes that made Fern's heart beat fast. It was so real, so alive—it was part of the new Colin that stirred and frightened her and made her want to seize on to him and never let go.

He carried a bucket, a kettle, and a hamper over one arm and a big block of peat under the other. He set down everything but the hamper on the hearth, carrying it to the bed to unpack the leftovers from their lunch.

"I found a door in back of the kitchens that led to a well yard," he said. "There was an internal cistern, but it was dry."

"In all this rain?" Fern asked, watching him bring out the remains of the roast chicken and potatoes.

"Broken, I suppose." He paused, surveying the food. "There isn't much left over, I fear."

"It shall have to do. Now I am glad we didn't stop for luncheon," Fern said. When they had been on the road, she had resented Colin's hurry.

Colin split the food evenly onto the two plain, heavy earthenware dishes that were still marked with the remains of their luncheon. Fern's stomach growled in a very unladylike way, and Colin gave her an amused glance that made her belly do a flip-flop for a very different reason.

She took her plate hurriedly and began to gnaw on a wing. Her sister Faith would have said that since he was a man, he should have the lion's share of the food, and it would only be ladylike to pretend to be full after a few bites and offer him the rest. But Fern wasn't Faith, and she was also ravenous.

She ate as neatly as she could in such rough conditions. Colin consumed his share more slowly, as if to make the food seem to stretch further. He watched her with half-lidded eyes, and she kept her own gaze fixed to her plate as much as she could. She still wasn't comfortable with him, not the new Colin and not the old, either, despite the moments when she forgot her awkwardness and simply felt like herself with him.

He sighed when he finished the last bite. "I wish we had twice as much," he said.

"I saw a sack of flour in the pantry, but I dare not speculate upon its age," Fern said.

The edge of his mouth quirked. "What would you do with a sack of flour?"

"Find someone to cook something with it," she retorted.

"That's my Fern," he said, the jocular words tempered by an ironic twist of his lips. She must have betrayed some reaction in her face, for he added, "What is it?"

"You said my name again. You have said it several times today, but almost never before. You always just said *mon ange*."

The handsome lines of his face drew into a faintly puzzled expression. "I suppose you are right. I had never thought of that."

Fern shrugged, feeling embarrassed. "It is nothing."

His look was keen. "Apparently not to you."

She shrugged again and looked away. When he said *mon ange*, she felt like blushing, but when he called her by her name—well, that woke a very different part of her, one that was more fundamental to herself. But she could not explain to Colin what she meant.

"I would like to wash and change clothes," she said, to switch subjects. "I am covered with dust, though not so thoroughly as you."

"Fair enough," Colin said. He rose and began to arrange the peat on the grate as Fern packed the scanty remains of their dinner back into the hamper.

"I hope we don't start a chimney fire," Fern said nervously.

"Only one way to find out." Colin took the jar of lamp oil. Fern backed away, getting the wide circumference of her hoops well clear of any splashes. He quirked an eyebrow at her caution and poured a good measure onto the peat. Taking the matches from Fern, he struck one and flicked it into the fireplace with the same motion. Fern yelped and recoiled.

The flames did not roar up as Fern had feared but swiftly formed a hot, straight column of flame. Colin stood beside the hearth, holding the bucket at the ready with an expression of complete self-possession. Fern watched him—watched his penetrating attention, the way his jaw worked slightly as he anticipated the worst—and a hand rose automatically to the quiver in her stomach.

After a moment, Fern cleared her throat. "We haven't begun to smoke ourselves out yet."

"The draw seems good," Colin agreed, setting the bucket down and swinging a hook over the fire to hang the kettle on.

Fern watched the flames a moment more. Their cool, capricious yellow tongues danced across the peat, eating into it slowly—too slowly. She sighed.

"What is it?" Colin asked.

She smiled ruefully. "It will be fifteen minutes or more before the water is ready."

His eyes narrowed. "They needn't be wasted."

Fern's heart stuttered at the note in his voice. "I don't know . . . " she said. *I don't know if I should want this. I don't know what it means between us, and I am afraid to find out.* But she did not say those words aloud. When she did not have to think—or could not think— she could give herself up to her . . . her *other* side. She was thinking now, though, and not simply reacting, and she found that she could not make herself consciously choose.

"Come here, Fern." Colin's eyes were as green and fathomless as the sea.

Fern stepped forward, one hesitating step at a time.

"I have been your maid since last night. Now it is your turn to be my valet."

Fern's mouth went dry as she realized what he meant. She looked at him for a long moment, but he simply stood there, as if he could wait forever. Slowly, she raised her hands to the top of the fastened buttons of his coat. The first one resisted for a moment, then released at a slightly stronger tug. The second soon followed. She slid her hands underneath its fabric, up to his shoulders. She could feel the contours of his muscles under his waistcoat. She raised her eyes to meet his. His face was set, as impassive as always, but his gaze burned her. Breath quickening, she pushed the coat off his shoulders and down, so that it slid off his wrists. She caught it before it hit the ground and draped it on the nearest chair. Still trapped by his gaze, she loosened the buttons of his waistcoat mechanically. When she put her hands against his shirt to push it off, the heat of his skin startled her, and she jerked away as much at her body's own swift reaction as at the initial surprise.

"Do it," Colin whispered hoarsely.

She nodded, swallowing, and obeyed. The shirt followed. She stood, staring at the shape of his chest beneath his fitted undershirt. A sparse V of curly black hair disappeared beneath it, almost familiar now yet still fundamentally alien. And arousing, for it stirred a flutter of awareness deep in her center, the instinctual recognition of his consummate maleness.

"You must take it off," she said, her voice raspy and shaky in her own ears. "I cannot reach over your head."

Colin raised an eyebrow slowly, and even more slowly, he pulled his shirt over his head. Fern closed her eyes for a moment, swaying. She could feel the heat from his skin, and it made her body ache and itch. He was looking down at her when she opened them again, standing half-naked with a brazenness that couldn't be right. He was not kissing her or caressing her or pulling at her clothes. So why, then, did she feel so suffused?

His chest was covered with a fine tracery of red scratches—her work from the night before. They scared her and fascinated her at once. She extended a hand, placing her palm over one of the marks across his chest. She could feel his heart beating against her hand.

"Do they hurt?" she asked.

"No more or less than I want them to."

Colin's even reply sent a shiver across her. "I should not want to really harm you."

"And I should not want to be harmed." He paused. "I have heard of a place in London where some go to be beaten and whipped for their pleasure."

Fern pulled back. "Do you want that?"

He shook his head. "No. Only this much. Enough to remind me that I am alive."

"I don't understand," Fern said. "I don't understand any of this at all."

"You have never been the heir to a viscountcy," Colin replied. He captured her hand and placed it over his heart again. "A peer is a thing, not a person, and I learned to be the perfect future peer."

Fern just shook her head again. Colin slid her hand across his lightly haired chest and belly to the denser curls above his belt line.

"Finish it," he said.

Fern hesitated for a moment and then ducked her head over his belt, unfastening it even as she could not help but notice the distinct bulge just below her hand. She pulled the end of the belt loose.

"The trousers," Colin said.

With mounting trepidation and burning cheeks,

Fern unbuttoned the top of his fly. She reached out to unfasten the second one, but she yanked her hand back after brushing against that hard bulge.

"I can't," she said, unable to express the combination of humiliation, fascination, and arousal that battered her.

"You shall," he countered. "It is nothing to be afraid of, Fern." He captured her hand again, and though she tried to pull away, he placed her hand flat against the hard ridge of flesh.

"It's so hot," Fern blurted. She bit her lip. "What . . . is it called? Your private part?"

Colin chuckled, a sound so strange coming from him that Fern jumped slightly. "The medical term would be *penis*. Most men use more vulgar terms."

"Oh," Fern said. "You do not want to tell me what they are?"

"No, I don't think so," Colin said flatly.

Fern stared at her hand where it touched him. "Does it hurt when it gets so . . . swollen?"

"Do you hurt when you are swollen with wanting me?" At Fern's automatic exclamation, Colin quirked the corner of his lips. "I am in a position of some knowledge of your reactions, just as you are in a position of knowledge about mine."

"I think I understand what you are saying," Fern said, blushing furiously.

"You did not answer my question."

Now he was baiting her; she was sure of it. "If it shall make you stop talking, I will do what you want!" She unbuttoned his fly the rest of the way as quickly as she could. "There. Now, I am quite sure your valet doesn't do *that* for you."

Colin did not reply, instead taking a step away from

her and bending over to pull off his shoes and socks. He straightened, and knowing what was coming next, Fern averted her eyes, licking her lips nervously.

"Fern."

She turned back around to see him standing naked before her, his . . . his penis jutting from between his legs in a way that should have been ridiculous. Yet somehow, it was anything but. A little frightening, yes. A little threatening, even. And certainly titillating in a way that made no sense to her, for it was not a beautiful part of his body, as his back and shoulders and thighs were. Fern wrapped her arms around herself as her skin prickled with awareness.

"Now it is your turn," Colin said.

Fern did not move, and after a moment, Colin closed the distance between them. Fern found herself staring at the shadow in the base of his strong throat as he deliberately loosened the row of buttons extending from her neck to her belt. The cool air slid through the lengthening gap in her bodice, insinuating itself between the folds of the fabric to brush the skin of her arms. He unfastened her belt with a quick twist, and it slid across her belling skirts to the floor.

He stepped back. "Now you must undress for me."

Chapter Eleven

"What?" Fern stared at him.

"Undress," he repeated. "For me."

Awkwardly, Fern raised her hands to the open throat of her bodice and pulled it down across her shoulders. She grasped one cuff with the opposite hand and slid it over her arm, then pushed the other off. She dropped the garment on top of his pile of clothes and then looked at him in mute question.

His eyes seemed to burn in the darkness, devouring her, and a spiral of heat twisted out of her center and down her limbs, making her skin tingle and her muscles ache in its wake.

"No more," she whispered. "Please, Colin."

"Your skirts, now," he said.

She hesitated, then reached behind herself for the hooks that held her skirt on. It took her a moment to unfasten them—she was not used to undressing herself—but she managed to free them one at a time. She pulled the rustling fabric upward, over her head, moving as quickly as she dared because she did not trust Colin to fail to take advantage of her momentary blindness. But when she emerged from the stiff silk folds, he had not moved. Fern laid the skirt aside and began untying her petticoats, first the one of lace-edged silk, then the light linen one beneath. She took both layers at once and dragged them swiftly over her head, adding them to the growing pile of clothes. Her bare arms prickled in the slight draft from the open window—she knew the breeze was not cold, but her skin seemed superheated. Without waiting for Colin's next order, she untied the tapes on her crinoline and let the steel contraption clatter to the ground. Now she stood in nothing but her corset, her pantaloons, and her stockings and shoes.

"I think I like you just like that," Colin said. "Pink against white, softness and hardness together." He stepped forward.

Fern backed away, stepping on her crinoline, the light in his eyes making her uneasy. "I need to bathe, Colin," she said. "I am tired; my clothes are not fresh, and neither am I."

Colin did not react to her words. "Did you know that some husbands have such admiration of their wives' wedding corsets that they do not allow them to be unlaced for the duration of the honeymoon?"

He was making fun again. She knew he was, and yet there was no hint of humor in his face, and Fern's heart began thudding hard against her chest. Who was this man? she wondered yet again. They were at least a mile from the nearest living soul, and no one but a coach driver knew where they were. . . . What could he do, this man who laughingly helped her wrestle a mattress though the doorway and then, a mere hour later, threatened her for his own amusement?

Fern scrambled for something to say, something to break the farce. *Pretend you are Elizabeth or Mary*, she told herself, fixing upon the image of her brash, fearless friends for an appearance of strength. The words came to her. "Those wives must have been very uncomfortable, and those husbands must have had a very poor sense of smell."

Something flared in the depths of Colin's eyes, but it was gone too quickly for Fern to identify it. She retreated another step—and sat hard as the back of her knees struck against the bed.

Before she could react, he was on top of her, pressing her into the musty mattress, his mouth coming down hard on hers. Cornered, she felt panic well up in her throat, and she swung out automatically, striking him in the temple with all her strength. He pulled back, breathing hard, his weight still pinning her to the bed.

"Make me release you from your corset, then, Fern," he said, his eyes as dark as windows into another world. "Hurt me."

Hot with lust and ire, she put both hands against his chest and pushed—not straight up, but to the side. He rolled off of her, and she followed, so that he was lying beneath her. She could feel the hard muscles of his stomach against her thighs, and the harder, hotter weight between them.

"Stop it," she said through clenched teeth. "Stop these stupid games. We're not playing at anything here. This is real! As real and as important as anything in our lives, and we don't even know what we're doing yet. If you need this"—she tweaked the skin over his bicep hard, digging in her nails—"then you need it, and I will not demand a reason. But I will not allow you to make this into a joke."

Colin looked at her steadily. "Sometimes, earnestness is dangerous."

"It is real," Fern insisted.

"And some things are hard to ask for."

That quiet addendum silenced Fern, the anger flowing out of her at once. "Then do not ask again," she said gently. "There is no need. I already know."

"Give it to me." The words ground out of his throat.

Fern leaned over him, the busk of her corset digging into her abdomen. She found the sensitive place just behind his jaw and kissed it gently. "If you wish me to be cruel," she whispered with a boldness that came from that unruly corner of her mind, "you should deal more generously with me." And she took a piece of skin between her teeth and nipped it sharply, crushing the delicate layers.

Colin grunted, his pelvis lifting hard against her as his hands clamped down on her thighs. His erection slid between her pantaloons. She steeled herself and moved deliberately downward along his throat and bit him again, and he came hard into her. The sudden heat of him sheathed fully inside her made her gasp, clutching the bedclothes on either side of his head as her body accepted him. For several seconds, she could only hold on as he thrust under her. Then, with a shudder that shook her whole being, she gripped his shoulders hard, her fingernails digging into his flesh, and seized the rhythm from him. She felt the tightness building within her, winding into a taut ball of anticipation, and she steered him closer, pushing toward it as the roar of blood grew louder and louder in her ears. She felt the impossible edge, the one that she had tripped over almost by accident the night before, and she *reached*. . . .

Her body tightened in waves of jagged-edged pleasure that jolted through her brain, until it seemed as if
her mind were attached directly to sea of raw nerve
endings. Distantly, she heard a noise that she knew
must be Colin, calling out a command, but she could
understand no words. Her senses blazed, blinded and
alive. She couldn't breathe—the corset was suffocating
her—her brain was going to explode, and she couldn't
hold on. . . .

Gradually, the sensation receded, the waves drawing back, ebbing away. She was left hollow and spent,
just like the first time.

Except that it wasn't like the first time. She was hollow, yes, yet it wasn't the vacuum left where something had been stolen but the emptiness after
something had escaped, bursting into freedom.

Fern opened her eyes. She was slumped against
Colin's chest, his scent still making her head spin.
They were both panting, out of rhythm now, that in-
credible unity shattered.

He shifted, rolling them both so that they lay one
next to the other. "A considerate lover," he said breathlessly, "does not smother her partner."

"Oh," Fern said. For a long moment she said nothing else, staring at his throat, unwilling to look at his
eyes and see the intimacy that she knew must still be
there—knowing that hers would be the same. *Coward*,
a corner of her mind whispered. But another warned
more loudly: *Do not trust this man until he's shown himself worthy of your faith.* So she kept her eyes down and
her soul locked inside her own skin.

The fire snapped on the hearth.

"I think our water is ready," Fern said.

Her voice roused Colin from his half stupor. "I only

hope that it has not boiled dry." He disengaged himself from their embrace with a gut-deep reluctance that disturbed him, leaving his wife's loose-limbed form sprawled upon the bed.

Ignoring his unexpected reaction, he wrapped his hand around his discarded undershirt—with a silent apology to his valet, who would have been highly aggrieved—and lifted the kettle from its hook. He blew as much dust from the nearest washbasin as he could before pouring half the kettle's water into it. He returned the kettle to its hook and added a generous measure of cool well water from the wooden bucket, sending up a thick cloud of steam.

"I found some washcloths and towels in the linen press."

Colin's lungs pinched around his breath as he turned to look at his wife. Fern had pushed upright and was now sitting on the bed, her light brown hair voluptuously tumbled and her eyes still smudged with passion. The complete lack of seductive content in her words somehow made it worse, and he wanted to take her all over again with a strength that made him ache—a desire that went far beyond the physical joining into something else that he did not care to examine. He pushed down that feeling.

"I see," was all he said. "I suppose you could not have told me that before I ruined my shirt?"

The high color of her cheeks deepened even more. "I was distracted."

Colin hid a private twist of his lips as he retrieved the towels from the linen press. Distracted, she called it. She was driving him to distraction, for certain, and beyond. . . . Driving him to stubbornness, foolishness, ridiculousness, to find himself in an empty, half-rotten manor house with her when they should both still be in Brighton.

This place was proving as intractable a problem as she was. Wrexmere. The name itself was becoming a bane to him. His father, never loquacious, had been particularly taciturn about their ancestral home, shuffling it off to Colin as a part of his allowance with almost unseemly eagerness when Colin reached his majority. The income was paltry, after the quantity set aside for the maintenance of the place, so absurdly small that it had bothered him since he'd been given control. He'd asked his solicitor to look into it, unleashing an abrupt flood of incomprehensible, half-literate, and menacing letters from the steward's wife that had made the situation intolerable.

Perhaps it was not the best solution for him to have compounded one difficulty with another, however logical it had seemed at the time. The ravings scrawled across the walls of the servant's chamber, however ancient they were, seemed a stark insult to whatever it was that he and Fern were working out between each other, puncturing his hope for an easy solution. And yet, he felt as if he was coming very close to learning something extremely important—about himself, about Fern, and about everything.

Putting those thoughts from his mind, he set the towels next to the basin. "Come here, Fern. I will help you with your corset."

Her expression had an edge of wariness. "You are through playing games?"

"Through with the last game, at least," he said, privately amused at how any woman who looked so wanton could be so reticent.

She slid off the bed and stepped forward cautiously,

stopping in front of him and regarding him with her frank gray eyes for a moment before turning her back and pulling her tumbled hair out of the way.

He untied the bow at the bottom of the corset and began feeding the laces back through the metal eyelets inch by inch to loosen the garment. He could feel her breathing through the corset's rigid boning. Following a sudden impulse, he kissed her neck lightly, and she shivered.

"Why did you marry me, Fern?" he asked.

She stiffened. "What a queer question to ask a woman!"

"It is the same question you asked me only two days ago," he pointed out.

"You never did answer it." Her response carried no bite.

"Will you answer mine?"

She paused for a long moment, seeming to consider it, and he continued to feed the laces back through the corset. "Yes," she finally said. "I will. I married because I am meant to be married. I married you because you are going to be a peer, you were a respected gentleman, I was deeply flattered by your attention—and because you asked."

"You married my title, then," he concluded, obscurely disappointed.

"It sounds so cold when you say it like that." The protest was halfhearted. "I would not have agreed if there had been an indecorous difference in age or you had been a boor."

"As much as it stings my pride to hear you, I was no more passionate in my choice," he said. "You were pretty, quiet, inoffensive, kind, and had connections to the right families. What more could I want?" The words had a bitterness he had not intended to express.

"How about love?" she asked softly.

Colin stopped, then put his hands on her shoulders and turned her gently around. "Love was not anything I had aspirations to enjoy."

"Why not?" she asked seriously. "Your parents seem happy enough together."

"They are good partners," Colin conceded. "But love? It is not something that would occur to them to miss."

"Your mother was not sufficiently affectionate, and so you did not look for love?" Fern asked skeptically.

"No. My brother Christopher looked for—and found—his love match, as unlikely as it was for an Edgington daughter to agree to marry a man of the cloth." Colin's smile was wry. "And Peter has cut a wide and passionate swath through the debutantes for three years running. My lack was not caused by my parents, but it was, perhaps, allowed by their example to persist. Why did you not look for love, if you are such a romantic?"

"I thought it came automatically upon marriage, with the wedding ring," Fern said simply.

"The more fool you?" Colin asked, the words causing a pang he had no right to feel.

"Not a fool," she said evenly. "Merely naive. Though I fear sometimes that you are a madman, I haven't given up hope for us having something that is worthwhile."

"Even love?"

She shrugged, seeming a little helpless. "I don't think I know what it is anymore." She dropped her eyes, as if to escape the conversation, and began unfastening the hidden hooks of her busk. "Right now, all I know for certain is that I want to be clean."

Colin took the mass of hair from her shoulder and lifted it out of the way, letting it slide across her back. "It is so strange to me that we grew up in the same circles and never really knew each other."

Fern shrugged out of her corset. "What was there to know? I was the middle sister. Faith was ethereal, Flora clever, and I . . . I was dependable. I envied Elizabeth and Mary Hamilton's brazenness—I still do— and I became their shadow at all the summer house parties. But I could not be like them, and when I was with them, I seemed to fade even more, so that no one noticed me at all. Whereas you . . . you simply stood apart—apart from your brothers, apart even from young Hamilton, for all that he will be an earl. I remember you as a solemn shadow at the edge of the children's games, and I remember thinking even then, How can someone so young be so grave? So, no, I did not know you, for all that we spent many summers of our youth in the same houses. No one did, I think. You weren't a boy who could be known."

Colin took in her unusually voluble speech in silence. What could he say? There were no secret motivations, no deep and burning wound that caused the distance that she observed. "I think, perhaps, that I was simply born with a character not easily moved toward amusement or pleasure, greed or fear. Fine feeling was something that was never sought in me by my nurses and tutors nor valued by my parents. I developed only those virtues that were desired of me—circumspection, dignity, deliberation, and an awareness of my place and duty."

"It sounds like such a sad fate for a little boy," Fern said.

Her observation took him unawares. "Sad? I was not sad. I was not happy, either. I was simply there. That was the sum of it."

Fern lifted a hand to the place on his neck where she had bitten him. "And now you do feel."

"It is like waking from a long dream," Colin said quietly, "confused and uncertain."

Understanding dawned in her eyes, clouded still but there. "That is what you meant by your talk of facades and escape. You wanted to discover what it was like being awake without the world looking on." She gave him a delicately reproachful look. "You did not explain it very well."

"I am not accustomed to explaining my actions to anyone."

"I don't think you're accustomed to having actions that need to be explained," Fern countered, though softly. She sighed, looking lost. "Where are we going, Colin?"

"I don't know," he answered. "But I think we shall both know when we get there."

"I suppose that is enough to hope for right now," she said.

Colin raised a corner of his mouth and turned toward the basin, wetting and wringing out a cloth. He washed his face, then moved to his shoulders. He could feel Fern's eyes on him, and a rustle of cloth told him that she was finishing the process of undressing. He did not turn around, as much as he wanted to feast himself upon the sight of her bare flesh; he knew she would still be uncomfortable, and somehow, that now mattered to him for reasons other than how it would make her treat him.

He finished washing—Fern made a startled noise when he quickly scrubbed his genitals, and he knew that she had been watching—and wrung out the cloth and dried himself briskly. He took the washbasin and turned to empty it out the window.

Fern was standing with her back firmly to him, the soft, narrowing curve of her waist flaring to ample hips and buttocks brushed by the ends of her hair, her skin pink-tinged white except for the two red pressure spots that her corset had left high on her hips. He dumped the water out the window, and holding the dripping basin in one hand, he came up behind her. She stiffened as he approached, and he could feel the carnal tension running through her.

"Now it's your turn," he said.

She turned to face him, and he stepped forward again, pinning her between him and a dresser. Her nipples brushed his chest even as she tried to lean away. "No games?" she said, frowning at him.

"None that you won't enjoy as much as I do," he promised.

"I doubt that," she said even as her breath quickened.

He smiled. "I will take that as a challenge, *mon ange*." He backed away, taking the kettle from the fire again and pouring its contents into the basin, adding the rest of the cold water from the bucket. He wet a fresh cloth. "Sit down," he commanded her, nodding to the nearest chair.

She obeyed, wariness and expectation warring in her eyes. He wrung out the cloth and bent over her. She looked up at him. He caught her chin, holding it against her automatic recoil, and gently washed her face, pausing to smooth out the creases of surprise that furrowed her forehead.

"Why?" she asked as he dropped the cloth back into the basin.

"Because it pleases me. I promise that it will please you."

She bit her lip but said nothing more.

Colin rinsed and wrung out the cloth again, turning his attention to her neck but stopping, decorously, at the point where her breastbone met her clavicle. Then he lifted her silky mass of hair.

"Bend over," he said. She did, and he let her hair slide so that it streamed across the back and top of her head down between her knees, exposing the elegant line of her neck and back. He washed them slowly, thoroughly. Her skin pinkened in the trail of the steaming rag as he followed the delicate arch of her spine down to where it met her tailbone and traced the curves of her ribs, hard under the sweetly soft padding of her flesh. At first, she held stiff and motionless under his ministrations, but slowly, the knots of muscle on either side of her spine loosened, and her breathing began to match the slow, even strokes of the soft cloth across her skin. She gave a small shiver as he lightened his touch, moving into his hand, then sighed as he deepened the pressure, rubbing the muscles beneath her skin.

When he finally turned to rinse out the rag, Fern straightened slowly, her eyes half-lidded and her face flushed under the cascade of curls that clung to it damply. Her hair divided, covering her breasts in its brunette waves.

Colin looked consideringly down at her. "You look like a painting of Eve made for delicate tastes."

"More like Susanna and the Elders," Fern countered, her voice slightly hoarse.

"Am I an elder, then?" he asked. "How about Bathsheba instead?"

"Bathsheba must have been exotically beautiful to catch the notice of the king. I'm better fit to be ogled by a handful of dirty old men," Fern said.

"You may not be exotic, but you are the near ideal of English maidenhood," Colin said bluntly, raising an eyebrow.

She blushed even harder. "I am no maiden."

He chuckled darkly. "No, you are not that." He knelt and took one soft, warm foot into his hand and began to wash it. She gave a gasping giggle and jerked away.

"That tickles!"

"I'll be more careful," he promised, recapturing it. He washed slowly but more deeply, rubbing from her heel across the softness of the arch to the firmer ball, then took the other one and repeated the procedure.

"That feels amazing," Fern said. "All of it. I thought—I thought it would just be strange, but this . . ." She laughed a little breathily. "You may bathe me any time you choose."

"I might just do that," Colin said.

Another rinse, and he moved to her calves, following their curve out from her small ankles and then back in again at her dimpled knees, first firmly and then softly, titillating. She had stopped smiling by then, her face drawn in concentration, and she gripped the arms of her chair with expectation as he refreshed the cloth and moved higher. He could feel the muscles tighten under the translucent skin of her inner thigh, and her reaction made his own pulse speed up in sympathy. But he stopped where her hair cascaded into her lap, mingling with the short curls at the juncture of her legs, and paused to get a fresh cloth.

When he turned back to her, her eyes were wide and deep in expectation and apprehension. He fed off it, bathed himself in the responses he invoked in her. Mutely, he pushed her hair back, first one side and then the other, revealing her generous breasts.

He pressed her back against the chair so that she was still sitting on the edge but leaning fully against the back. She resisted only a moment before giving in. He started at her collarbone and moved downward, slowly, thoroughly, teasingly. She stiffened as he neared her breasts, her hands tightening on the arms of the chair, but he made a pass of the cloth down her breastbone first, across the soft roundness of her stomach to the top of the dark curls that began below. He worked his way up, and even though his touch stayed light, she was now too taut with desire to find his touch ticklish. He skimmed up her rib cage and cupped one of her breasts in his hand, holding it there as she gazed at him, a mute plea in her eyes.

Slowly, slowly, he raised his cloth-wrapped hand toward her nipple, rasping it across the delicate flesh. Fern's head tilted back, exposing the smooth line of her throat as her hips and back arched toward him. He did it again, and she moaned. He rubbed it then, gently, between his thumb and forefinger.

Her legs pressed hard against the arms of the chair, and he could not help himself any longer—he bent down and took her other breast in his mouth, enveloping it in heat. It was hard against his tongue, and he sucked it against the roof of his mouth. Fern's hips pressed against his belly, her head thrown back, and he had to swallow a groan as he pulled himself away from her with a shudder.

"Don't," she said, her eyes wide with desire. "Don't stop."

"I am not done yet," he said.

He dipped the cloth once more into the water and pressed it against her belly. He slid it downward steadily, moving between her legs.

"No," he said when she started to straighten, putting a restraining hand on her knee. "Don't move." He took the cloth and passed it with deliberation across her flesh from the base of her tailbone and in between her folds to the hard nub at the front of her opening. She shook when the textured cloth passed across it, and he paused to rinse it one last time.

"No more," she said, the words a low plea. "I need it now. I need you now."

Colin simply smiled and took the cloth, still dripping with steaming water, and rubbed across the nub at her entrance again, with deliberation. She wriggled hard against the chair, but he used his weight against her leg to pin her against its arm. He rubbed her there again, and then again, until she was panting with the need for the release that he was denying her.

Only then did he move downward between her already slick folds. She made a choking gasp as the rough cloth met her swollen flesh. He passed over once lightly, and then again, the second time pressing deeper so that she whimpered. And then he shifted his grip so that it was not the cloth that was pressing against her but his water-slick fingers, and he pushed.

Her body opened for him as she cried out, clasping his fingers tightly, hotly. Her hips came up against his hand hard. Eyes screwed shut, she gasped for breath, her lips parted as she strained with the strokes of his hand. She shuddered once, her breath catching, and then again, and then her entire body began to move with the rhythm of his hand, and his own surged in sympathy.

She made another choked noise, and he knew that she was on the edge. He seized both of her thighs and, still kneeling, plunged into her, pulling her hips toward him. She cried out, but he was already half gone and scarcely heard her.

Alive, alive, I am alive. The words matched the rhythm of his thrusts, his heartbeat, his being. Without the pain, he was still alive, alive with her. Then Fern's fingernails scored hot lines of pain across his shoulders, and he welcomed that, too. *Alive, alive . . .* He felt her peak a moment before he lost control, plunging through the deadening entanglements of his body into a realm of pure sensation as surges wracked it, pulling it apart.

He clung in that place as long as he could, but all too soon, it was over, and he returned to his ordinary senses. He slid back to his haunches, blinking the sweat out of his eyes. He could still feel that tingling sense of here-and-now, only muffled somehow in the background, and he nursed it like the first fire. It was over, and he was still . . . alive.

Fern lay collapsed and panting on the chair, her gray eyes dark with lovemaking. She opened her mouth to say something, shook her head, and then shut it, closing her eyes as she did so. Colin took the moment to discreetly clean himself before rinsing out the rag to hand to Fern when she opened them again. She gave him an uninterpretable look, and he did not know whether she understood the gesture until she stood and turned from him. He looked away, respecting her privacy, until he heard the splash of the rag in the basin.

When he looked back, Fern was already slithering into her nightdress. Colin took the hint somewhat reluctantly, finding his nightclothes and pulling them over his head.

Without looking at him, Fern padded across the carpet and slid into the bed. A distant roll of thunder rumbled across the countryside, and Colin realized that the plaster around the open casement was now being spattered with rain.

"Shall I close the window? The storm seems to be getting worse."

"Whatever you wish," Fern said with lingering traces of stiff formality, a contrary reaction to the intimacy they had just shared. "I wouldn't mind some coolness even if it is a little damp. The fire has made the room into a steam bath."

He left it open, slipping between the covers next to his wife. The heavy curtains above were gray with dust. He blew out the lamp, setting it on the seat of a chair. Darkness swallowed the room, except for the dull fire in the grate and the occasional spear of lightning from the storm.

"You were right." Fern's voice drifted out of the darkness, taking him unawares.

"About what?"

"I do think that I enjoyed your teasing at least as much as you."

"Mmm," Colin replied, thinking, *I sincerely doubt*

that you did. Still, that small recognition of what had passed between them loosened a knot deep in his gut that he hadn't realized was there, and he relaxed into the dusty pillows. The only sound was the rain washing down the walls of the house and pattering more sharply against the open windowpane.

"What is your favorite color?" Fern's question roused him from semisomnolence.

"What?" he asked.

"What is your favorite color? I just realized that I don't know."

He paused. "I don't think I've ever thought of it."

"Mine is red. I almost never wear it because I am afraid it isn't a good color for young girls, and I haven't got the kind of dramatic coloring that makes it look right, but I still like it."

"I shall buy you a dress of scarlet velvet, then," Colin said. "You aren't a girl any longer, so you should wear what you like."

"What if it caused talk?" Fern asked. "I've never been one to wear bright colors before. Wouldn't that matter to you?"

That made Colin think. A few days ago, the answer would have been a firm, *Of course.* But now things didn't seem as simple as they once had. He . . . cared. It was not enough simply to follow the path of expectations. He found that he had his own opinions, coming from a part of himself that had atrophied with disuse. "I believe that I like red, too," was all he said.

He felt Fern move before her hand snaking through the covers found his. "How will you know that it is time to return to society?"

"I don't know, Fern," he said. "Just have a little faith."

"And you shall keep me here with you until then?" Her voice was even softer, but the hand that held his grew tight.

"You are no prisoner," he replied.

"I am your wife." She said those words as if they explained everything.

"Abide for a few days, a few weeks, Fern," Colin said wearily. "Just abide."

She gave a hiccoughing kind of laugh. "I don't know where else I would go."

Her words were not exactly a declaration of unconditional devotion, and yet Colin felt his heart unaccountably lightened. She wanted to stay. Given a choice, she would choose him.

Colin stared at the invisible canopy somewhere above his head, listening to the thunder rumble over the tors. After a while, Fern's hand went limp.

A while later, his did, too.

Chapter Twelve

Fern jerked awake to darkness, sitting up so quickly that she sent a cloud of dust into the room. Instantly, she began fighting a sneeze as Colin surged into a sitting position beside her, coughing violently.

"What was that?" he demanded between wracking coughs.

"I'm sorry," she said, scrubbing at her nose with a corner of her nightdress. "I thought I heard something."

"So did I," Colin said. "The crash—what was that?"

"I don't know," she said, hugging herself. She didn't want to know.

"I will go see." Colin pushed out of bed and, after many muttered imprecations, struck a match and put it to the lamp wick. The oil burned sluggishly, casting a dull orange glow. "I think it came from out there." He nodded at the door, holding the lamp out in front of him as he headed for it.

He was going to leave her alone. Fern's heart jumped, and she untangled herself from the bedclothes and scrambled out of bed behind him. He turned at the noise and gave her an inquisitive look, but she just stared at him, making no declaration that he might be able to contradict. He shrugged and turned away.

He opened the door to the hallway and stepped through, Fern close on his heels. At first, she did not see anything amiss in the dull and guttering light of the lamp. But then she realized that a portion of the floor was catching the light wrong. She frowned. It looked as if it was wet. . . .

Colin advanced, and Fern followed. In the lamplight, the puddle glowed like mercury. Another peal of thunder rolled distantly, and almost in answer came a deep, house-shaking groan from directly above their heads.

Fern bunched her fingers into fists to keep from seizing Colin's arm in fear. He raised the lamp higher and looked up, and, dreading what she would see, Fern followed his gaze. The ceiling above was dark with moisture, and part of the plaster had fallen away. There was something black in the center of the wettest part, but between dimness and the unsteadiness of the light, Fern's eyes could make no sense of it.

"Upstairs," Colin said tersely, turning back toward the staircase. Then tension in his voice made Fern's heart beat even faster. She followed him up the stairs, spiraling up into the darkness, and emerged on the attic level.

Colin froze, and she looked around him and blinked. She couldn't seem to see anything. A drop of water fell on her cheek, and then another. The floorboards were wet beneath her feet. She peered into the gloom as her brain tried to decipher the tangled shapes that her eyes were reporting.

A distant flash of lightning gilded the boiling clouds

and cast everything into sudden silvery illumination before plunging it into darkness again. It was all the time that Fern needed, for what she had seen in that instant had etched itself upon her eyeballs.

The roof was gone. Just half a dozen feet in front of them, the timbers had given way, dropping the ceiling onto the floor in a pile of mangled slate and timber and opening the rooms to the sky and wind. One of those beams had even been driven by the power of its own weight through the floorboards, and the confused object on the ceiling below suddenly made horrible sense.

A gust of wind crossed the fractured gable. The beams groaned again, low and menacing. Fern's breath froze in her chest as she mentally saw the half timbered tracery of the old walls, how each timber fit so snugly into the next, how they leaned on one another to keep the house upright. How a dozen of those timbers were now lying rotten and shattered on the attic floor.

"Go downstairs." Colin's voice was eerily calm. "Down to the ground floor. Quickly."

Fern gulped, nodding mutely, and spun on her heel to flee down the stairs. Her bare feet slid on the slick, wet wood, and Colin's lamplight was lost after the first turn, but she didn't dare slow until she had passed the first floor and emerged, gasping, in the corridor that led between the parlor and the dining room.

She could see nothing, and the only sounds in the darkness were the wind-driven rain against the windows and the harsh panting of her own breath. Her heart thundering in her chest, she turned back toward the staircase.

Nothing. Where was Colin? A choking panic began

to rise in her throat. Perhaps he had fallen, or perhaps the collapsing house had shifted to trap him. What was she going to do?

I have to find him, she thought, staring at the black, blind hole of the stair in dismay. *I must.* She groped her way forward and swallowed a cry of pain as she stubbed her toe on the first riser.

A light appeared in the stairwell, no more than a faint glimmer, but enough to make her pause. It grew stronger, sending shadows dancing across the wainscoting. Then Colin came around the corner, laden with their hand luggage and the lamp.

"I thought you'd been hurt!" Fern blurted.

"It took me a moment to find our shoes and your corset," Colin said. He looked at her askance. "Were you coming back upstairs to rescue me?"

"I didn't know what had happened," Fern said, glad that the darkness could not betray her blush as she delivered the nonanswer.

Colin didn't seem to notice. "We should go to the keep. If the rest of the house hasn't collapsed by tomorrow, I'll get our trunks then."

"I'll take the lamp," Fern offered, determined not to be separated from a light source again.

Mutely, Colin handed it over. Its cool cut-glass base felt good in Fern's hands. She led the way through the dining room and the hole in the thick, ancient stone wall into the kitchens on the ground floor of the keep.

"There should be a great hall and perhaps some bedrooms above," Colin said.

Fern's bare feet were silent on the wide flags, but even her breath seemed to echo in the dim, vaulted recesses of the cavernous room. She held out the lamp like a talisman as she passed between the fat square pillars that supported the upper floors, dividing the great space into a series of artificially foreshortened views.

The stairs finally came into view, and Fern kept her eyes firmly averted from the door behind which the hateful message lay. She could not shake the feeling that the house itself was chasing her into these rooms, where the cold stone walls could close in and swallow them both.

Don't be silly, she told herself, mounting the stairs. The wooden treads creaked under her feet, and Fern climbed with mincing gingerness, nightmares of dry rot clamoring through her brain. She glanced behind and caught Colin's eye. His expression did not change, but somehow, she felt better.

They reached the first floor. Fern's lamp revealed only more blackness ahead of them, and she advanced cautiously.

"The great hall," Colin said.

"It must be," Fern agreed. She could make out high stone walls as she penetrated farther into the room, tattered tapestries flapping in the draft like slow, leathery wings.

"This room is sound, at least," Colin said. "If it weren't, the tapestries would have disintegrated long ago."

"I don't like this place," Fern said.

Colin made a grunting noise. Fern kept going.

Slowly, a group of shadowy forms took shape in front of her, their outlines growing clearer with every step. It was a tight grouping of furniture, huddled under the shelter of an enormous fireplace hood on the farthest wall as if someone had risen from dinner two hundred years ago and never returned. There, near them, was the angular shape of another flight of stairs leading up into darkness.

Fern led the way to the foot of the staircase, which was cut from the same stone as the walls. Her stomach clenched. It was dizzyingly steep and narrow, the precipitous drop over the edge unguarded by any balustrade.

"There should be bedchambers above," Colin said, the calm normality of his voice doing nothing to mitigate the fear that welled up in Fern's belly to make her head light and her legs wobbly.

Fern took a deep breath and began to climb, holding the hem of her nightdress up with her free hand and pressing her shoulder against the wall. Each stair looked like the next, and Fern tried to trick herself into imagining that she was not progressing at all, that each step was no higher than the one before. It didn't work, for her imagination was only too eager to supply her with images of the depths of the black void to her right. The hand that held the lamp trembled, making the shadows jump and dance on the stairs.

Finally, the last stair approached. Fern kept her eyes fixed upon the edge of the riser until she stepped upon the second floor. Only then did she look around, moving aside so that Colin could join her.

There was scarcely room at the stair's terminus for both Fern and Colin to stand together, just a small landing as a new staircase, turning the corner, continued into the upper reaches of the keep. A single iron-banded oak door barred the way into the rooms of the second floor.

Fern's constitution could not take leading the way any longer. She tightened her grip on the lamp and invited Colin to open the door with a nod. "Go ahead."

Colin lifted the latch and pushed, and the door swung wide. Fern braced herself, but there was only a perfectly ordinary if ancient bedroom, its furniture sparse and massive, covered with dark, heavy carvings that were scaled with age. A wave of stale air met them, thick with the stench of rotting feathers. A second door stood opposite the first, and Colin opened it.

"Another bedroom," he reported tersely, standing to the side so that the lamplight could pass within. He should have looked foolish or at least a little weak, standing there in his nightshirt with sleep-tousled hair and bare feet. But his sheer physicality was in no way diminished by his attire; if anything, the lack of extraneous accoutrements drew attention to the long, hard lines of his physique. He looked very real—more real even than the stone walls around him, laden as they were with the ghosts of memory.

Now that the rush of adrenaline was beginning to wear off, Fern realized how exhausted she was. The lamp began to shake again in her hands, her muscles struggling to hold it steady, and a wave of dizziness overtook her, making the room swim threateningly. Colin was a still point in the center of it, and Fern drew strength from the sight of him as she forced herself to speak in normal tones.

"I think the stink is coming from the mattress," she said.

"I wouldn't want to sleep in the other room, either," Colin reported. "Let's look above."

Colin led the way upward this time. The next flight of stairs passed between two reassuringly thick stone walls, but Fern's neck still prickled at the memory of the previous climb even as she kept her eyes fixed upon Colin's broad, strong back, his shoulders slightly tensed with the weight of their hand luggage.

The stairs ended at another landing, and this time, only an ancient, rickety ladder continued up. Fern held up the lamp, and the orange light revealed a dark trapdoor above, the ancient planks dark with seeping rainwater.

Another door confronted them, and Colin stepped through without hesitation before Fern had lowered the lamp again. The bedroom was almost a mirror of the one below, including another door in the opposite wall leading to a fourth and final bedroom.

"These beds are no better," Colin observed, a detachment in his voice that reminded Fern, chillingly, of the man of her wedding night. A quick look confirmed that he was right, and the discovery sent a sense of despair through her sleep-deprived body that was completely out of proportion to its import.

"Perhaps we can sleep in a chair," Fern offered without much hope. There were only two chairs, pulled up to a table before the cold fireplace, and they were stiff, thronelike affairs. "Or if I can find some better blankets, perhaps on the floor."

She set the lamp on the table and opened the massive press at the foot of the bed, hoping to run into the same luck with bed linens that she had earlier in the Tudor wing. Instead, there were only a few pieces of clothing, brittle with age, and a packet of documents secured with a ribbon. Fern picked up the papers automatically before shutting the lid again.

"It is either one of these beds or nothing," she reported unhappily. "And I don't think I could sleep in any of the beds no matter how tired I was."

"Then I suppose we might as well sit," Colin said,

nodding at the chairs. "First, though—your dressing gown. This place is clammy. You'll catch a chill."

Fern had forgotten that she was wearing nothing but a nightdress, which offered no protection against the damp air that had penetrated it. Now that Colin called attention to it, she realized that she was shivering slightly, in short bursts. Gratefully, she set down the bundle of papers and allowed him to drape the folds of her dressing gown over her. "The night is not cold, but I am," she admitted as she buttoned the front of the garment, sitting in one of the stiff, high chairs.

Colin found his own dressing gown and threw it swiftly across his shoulders, tying it with a quick tug of the tasseled sash. He took the chair opposite her.

She stared at him numbly. "I want you to promise me something," she said, the words slow and heavy with weariness.

"What is that?" His face, tired though unnaturally handsome still, drew into cautious lines.

"When we leave here, promise me that we shall never come back."

Colin cocked an eyebrow. "Is it really as bad as all that?"

"Bad?" Fern gaped at him. "The place is filthy and moldy, there are no servants, it is the former abode of a madman or madmen unknown, and the roof tried to fall on our heads!"

"But it missed," Colin pointed out.

Fern opened her mouth to retort, then shut it, biting her lip. "You're teasing me," she accused.

"I am," he agreed. "You are such a curious woman. You bear up with remarkable stoicism under a dozen novel travails, and then when you make an explicit request for the first time, it is merely that I do not inflict any of them upon you again. Rest assured, *mon ange*, that none of this is part of a diabolical plan to drive you to insanity. If you wish to see no more of this place, then you may have that request, and welcome, in return for the forbearance that you have demonstrated thus far."

Fern sighed. "Thank you." Her shoulders slumped slightly, and she rubbed her forehead, where a pounding headache was beginning to form. "I am so tired that my vision is blurring, but I don't think I'll be able to sleep in these chairs."

Colin nodded at the bundle on the center of the table, where she had dropped it several minutes before. "What did you find?"

Fern pulled the ribbon off and spread the documents across the table. The sheepskin was brittle, but the sheets did not crumble. "They look like letters," she said. She examined half a dozen cursorily—to her relief, the handwriting looked nothing like the spidery scrawl in the room downstairs. "All to the same person and from the same person."

"They should distract you well enough. Are they love letters?" Colin speculated, his mouth quirking wearily.

"No. Not love letters," she said, slowing down to read a few of the passages. "A friend, perhaps? 'I entreat thee to keep constant mind on the service I have done thee, and to always maintain th' affection between ourselvs that thy mother and I once shared.' They are dated, but the signatures are all initials. From E to JR." She looked up. "Do you think that these may have been written by one of your ancestors?"

"More likely to one," he said, "seeing as they were found here."

A rumble of thunder shook the windows in their frames. The old, angular script blurred before her eyes. Fern rubbed her face. Her headache had increased to a dull throb. "I am so tired that I am dizzy. Do you think I would catch something dreadful if I slept in the bed?" The words were wistful but hopeless.

"I doubt you'd sleep at all, even if you didn't catch anything." Colin's face was haggard in the lamplight. "They all smelled foul to me."

Fern sighed. "You are right, of course." For want of any better occupation, she went back to scanning through the letters as Colin watched her broodingly from across the table. She tried to ignore the prickling of her neck under his attention, the slow stirring deep in her center that seemed oblivious to her body's exhaustion.

"I apologize, Fern."

The words came from nowhere, taking Fern by surprise. "You do?" she blurted.

"I did not imagine that our arrival would be anything like this," he continued, his voice subdued. "I had pictured a neat, modest old manor with a steward and warm food prepared by his wife."

"Food," Fern echoed. "I hope we will be able to find breakfast in the morning. I hope it will be morning soon," she added.

"Any normal woman would be filling my ears with blame and complaints right now," Colin said. "And I cannot say that I do not deserve it."

Fern sighed. "Would it do any good?"

"Not in the least. But that rarely stops complaints," he said with a trace of humor.

Fern shook her head. "I am not pleased that we left Brighton for this place, and I am even less pleased that we might have been crushed by a collapsing roof, but I understand your motivations even if I do not agree with your decisions." She cocked her head to the side slightly. "I can forgive decisions I do not agree with. If I did not, how could I hope that you would extend the same courtesy to me?"

Colin looked at her steadily in the lamplight. "I am not used to people making decisions that I do not agree with. I do not know how I would react. I can only hope that it would be with as much restraint as you have shown."

"Consider yourself indebted to me, if it will help," she said lightly. "I do understand that there is a great difference in expectations between being an eldest son and a middle daughter. But as we must be married to each other, you shall have to learn to yield a little, too, if we are to hope for harmony."

"Yield." Colin's expression was wry. "Marriage is not what I imagined it to be."

Fern looked around the grim, shadowed room and laughed without humor. "I should hope not, or your imagination should be morbid enough to quite frighten me."

At that, he gave her one of his rare sincere smiles, and Fern warmed in response. "There is that," he agreed.

They lapsed into silence. The rain was soundless on the thick stone walls, but short bursts of it would patter against the narrow windows as gusts of wind caught the falling drops and dashed them against the side of the keep.

Finally, Colin spoke again. "Why don't you read the letters, for as long as the oil lasts?"

"It would certainly be easier than trying to talk to

each other." Fern regretted her words instantly, but it was too late to take them back.

"What do you wish to speak about?" Colin's response was coolly measured.

"Nothing," Fern said. "I am just tired. It makes me waspish, and I am sorry for that. I will read." She fanned the letters out on the table. They were jumbled, the dates confused. She deciphered the Roman numerals on one of them: 1604. More than two and a half centuries ago. She picked one of the letters up at random. " 'I write again to thee, to vouchsafe the news of my safe delivery from child-bed. I have been delivered of a boy child, and my lord is pleased with me. He is not the only one with an heir. Thou also hast one to follow after thee anon. Keep this little one in thy heart, and think not ill of him, for as he is of my blood, so is he of yours.' " Fern paused, rubbing her head. "That doesn't make any sense. If the writer and the recipient are related, and the writer is a woman, how can she produce the recipient's heir? Unless she and her husband were cousins . . ."

"There are a few titles in England that could be passed down through the distaff line," Colin said. "This manor, though, wasn't one of them, because there is no title attached. It was a fiefdom controlled by a baron who chose the wrong side when Margaret of France invaded, and he lost his life and cost his heirs much of their lands. The warden of Wrexmere, who had betrayed his master to Margaret's forces, became a landholder in his own right. As he had no sons and no brothers, he requested and was granted a fee tail that was not restricted to the male line."

Fern digested this. She had heard often enough the stories told by her parents of their respective families, but they tended to be tales of heroism in battle or amusing anecdotes, divorced from real history. "You seem to know a great deal about this place, for never having been here," she said.

"Only the most salient points relevant to the inheritance," Colin said dryly. "And, of course, as much about its current state as my solicitor has been able to wrestle from the ledgers. I know the story of the initial granting of the fief, its independence and the granting of distaff inheritance, the marriage of a Radcliffe to an eldest daughter and mistress, and the reversion of the Radcliffe barony to my own cadet branch of the family." He paused. "JR would probably be John Radcliffe. All the Radcliffe masters of Wrexmere were named John."

"So then the author, E, must have been writing to the current master, or perhaps his heir," Fern said. "She could have been his sister, or his cousin, or his aunt." She picked up another letter. "'Be thou not swayed by any soft words. Jane Reston's brat is a snake in the garden, which will bite thee when she can. She knows all, and will not forgive her bastardy.' How queer. I should sort them. . . . " She put actions to her words, arranging the letters in chronological order. She frowned as she scanned over the first ones. Jane Reston. The name sounded familiar, but she could not remember why. "It starts in the middle. I am afraid that none of this makes any sense."

"An ancient mystery," Colin supplied, settling back in his chair. "If you can't rest, trying to put it together shall give you something to do until morning."

"What are you going to do?" Fern asked.

"Sleep, if at all possible." And with that, he closed his eyes.

Fern looked at him for a long moment, but he did not move, and after a while, she concluded that he truly was asleep. They had eaten an inadequate dinner, they might have died in the roof collapse, and now they were sitting in hard and uncomfortable chairs. Yet he could simply close his eyes, shut it all away, and go somewhere else. Perhaps that somewhere else was where he usually was, though: a place where there was neither fear nor passion, a great, bright, empty plain that stretched from horizon to horizon in his brain.

So he had come here—to escape the nothingness or to regain it? He had never said for certain, and the thought chilled Fern. Whatever he would become, she hoped it would not be the cold, polite mannequin she had been joined with on her wedding day. It would be exactly what she deserved, exactly the path she had chosen, so wrongly, to take. But the thought of living with such emptiness forever was now more than she could bear. He had changed too much to go back now, she reassured herself. And so, she realized, had she.

Determinedly, Fern shoved those thoughts from her mind and began to read through the letters. Their tone was strange—veering from beseeching to dark hints at blackmail, from friendly confidence to portentous warnings. Their content was even stranger, for the writer scarcely ever said anything in a straightforward manner, writing in convoluted allusions and strange riddles that made Fern wonder if she were entirely sane.

Fern studied the pages until the words swam in front of her exhausted eyes. But she learned very little. E was certainly JR's aunt; there was a woman named

Jane Reston who had a son and daughter who were a great danger to him, the son also, confusingly, named John, making three separate JRs in the correspondence; the recipient's mother had died at some point in the letters; and there was another woman named Lettice who knew something important, as well. Other than that, Fern could make out nothing but a vague sense that the danger was related to the property of Wrexmere itself.

The more she stared at the words on the page, the more they seemed to multiply, dancing like motes of light before her eyes. She seemed to hear the writer's voice, worried and querulous one moment, hissing with threat the next, and as her eyes began to sag, a woman's hard and bitter face rose before her in a foggy vision. Fern slipped into confused dreams in which she was stumbling through the darkness, searching for something—sometimes Colin, sometimes the unknown answer to everything—while a woman's voice droned on and on in her head.

Chapter Thirteen

Sunlight on his face brought Colin awake. He stood—and winced as his muscles and joints simultaneously protested. He was not as limber as he had been when he used to sneak into the library as a small boy after his bedtime to fall asleep with a book in one of the chairs.

Working out the crick in his neck, he looked down at his wife. She was slumped over the table, a little crease between her eyebrows as she slept. Her usually rosy cheeks had a wan cast, and Colin shuddered a little inside to remember their precipitous flight from the Tudor wing the night before. Whenever he looked at her now, he had that same strange stirring of life inside him, and it seemed to have a lingering effect on his perception of the world. Colors seemed brighter, scents stronger, and he was beginning to feel that this was the way the world should be.

He stood and went to the window. He could not make out the position of the sun behind the even gray blanket of clouds, which diffused the light into a flat, pale uniformity, but he sensed that it was late in the morning. The narrowness of the windows had restricted the light so that the gradual change from blackness to dim shadow had not awoken him until the sun had reached an angle behind the clouds to cast a slightly lighter bar across his face as he slept.

Colin looked around the room. In daylight, it was perhaps less eerie than it had been the night before, but it was more forlorn, the musty bed hangings dangling limp and faded from the canopy and the chest riddled with beetle holes.

He pulled off his dressing gown and nightclothes and dug in his hand luggage for the clothes he had worn the day before. Wadded inside his valise, they were now a mass of wrinkles. Surveying the mess of his shirt, he thought for a moment about venturing into the Tudor wing to find fresh clothing, but he decided that he'd much rather be clothed and have a hearty meal in him when he faced a half-collapsed building. A coat might not provide much protection, but at least he'd die with some dignity.

He was pulling on his boots when Fern stirred. Scraping her hair out of her face, she sat up and blinked at him with an expression of profound confusion. Then memory spread across her face, and she blanched.

"I can't believe . . ." She paused. "I can't believe that any of this happened."

"I can assure you that it has," Colin said dryly, stepping toward the door.

Fern stood up swiftly. "Don't leave without me!"

He paused. "I was going to try to find breakfast for us in the village."

"Looking like that?" Fern's expression was appalled.

"Perhaps they shall think me an ogre, and I can loot their larders with impunity," Colin said, shrugging.

"But you have never looked like that. Never . . ." She searched his face, as if expecting to discover that he had been possessed.

Colin considered her statement for a moment. "I suppose you are right. It is not that the thought of looking shabby disgusted me; it is simply that it is not done, and so I had no reason to do it. However, now I find myself without a valet or a clean change of clothing within easy reach, and so I have ample reason to break with custom. I am also hungry enough that I have no desire to wait half an hour to lay and light a fire to heat water so that I can shave."

"I hope my clothes aren't as wrinkled as yours," Fern said, without displaying much hope. "Please help me get dressed. If I can just brush my hair, I will be ready to go soon."

"You are not ashamed to be seen with me like this?" he asked with some amusement.

"Right now, I should not mind if you were a real ogre. I don't want to stay here alone," she said firmly, her small jaw setting. "Besides, I greatly fear that I shall not look much better."

He raised no further protest, helping her into her corset. There was a small, erogenous thrill in re-forming Fern's waist to its circumference, but any libidinous thoughts were overruled by the increasingly insistent demands of his belly.

"I did not retrieve your crinoline," he admitted as he held out her first petticoat.

"I wouldn't dare try to wear it on those stairs," Fern said. "My small one is five feet wide, and the stairs can be no broader than two and a half. We're in a rustic lodge of sorts anyhow, aren't we? I don't need a crinoline for country sports."

Once her dress was buttoned, she bent and fiddled with some ties on her skirts. When she straightened, they were no longer dragging the ground but were hiked up several inches above the colored silk hem of her uppermost petticoat.

"Clever," Colin said.

"It's my country walking dress," she explained gravely. "It lifts so that the dew can't stain it."

Her arranging of her hair was less swift. She appeared to decide upon a simple twisted braid, but her plait kept coming out off center and her twist crooked. Finally, red-faced with irritation, she stabbed it ruthlessly with a dozen hairpins as Colin watched.

"I want a maid," she said flatly, turning to look at him as she finished.

Something similar to his own transformation was occurring to Fern, he realized, for he could not have imagined that the meek little thing he had wooed in her mama's parlor would state her desires—almost demands—so flatly.

"Of course," Colin said. He had deprived her out of thoughtlessness, not design. He was simply unaccustomed to thinking of the needs of another person. Tenants and servants were provided for automatically, without particular accommodation for their individual wants and needs. A wife, though, was different, he was coming to discover—not an appurtenance like a carriage or a housekeeper but something else, something far more intimate that lay uneasily in his mind and that demanded special care.

With that disturbing thought, he led the way out of the door and down the narrow stairs. When they reached the unguarded staircase leading from the second floor to the first, Colin slowed, turning slightly so that his back was angled toward the wall, his empty stomach clenching.

The flagstones of the floor below looked very distant and very hard. How long a fall was it? Twenty feet? More? The next inevitable question rose unstoppably in his mind: How far would it have to be to kill him? He had never given heights a second thought before, but he had never experienced them so directly, either. He was preternaturally conscious of the texture of the stairs through the soles of his boots as he stared down at the clutch of furniture below.

He made the last step to the floor with a palpable sense of relief. He turned as Fern joined him, her normally rosy face pallid and drawn.

"I do not like that," she said distinctly.

"I couldn't imagine that anyone would."

She nodded toward a pair of vast double doors, centered on the long wall. They had been invisible in the darkness the night before. "Can't we get out there?"

"No," Colin said. "I saw them when we arrived. There would have been a staircase that led up to them from the ground level at some point, but it's long gone. The doors open up over thin air."

Fern shuddered. "I've had enough thin air for a long while."

They took the back stairs down into the kitchens, and Colin led Fern to a small, battered door hidden in the shadow of one of the columns. It had been cut through the wall of the keep several centuries after it had been built, the stone that formed the frame and lintel a slightly different color than the rest.

He pushed it open and stood aside to let Fern pass

into the pump yard that he had discovered the night before.

"It's on the far side of the keep from the village, so it's a longer walk than through the front, but this way, we won't have to go through the Tudor wing," Colin said in answer to Fern's questioning look. "Speaking of which, I wonder how it held up in the night." He backed away from the keep's wall and squinted up at the adjoining wing. "From this angle, one can't even see that half the roof is gone. At least the outer walls are still standing."

"I will gladly take a longer walk rather than risking a house falling on my head," Fern said fervently. "Even if it seems sound now."

"I think the village is no more than a mile away," Colin said, extending his arm toward her.

She took it. "All this land is yours? A square mile is three hundred sixty acres."

"Around a thousand acres are ours, perhaps a little more," he answered. "Though nothing in the old village proper belongs to my family."

Fern frowned. "That is a great deal of land to be so neglected."

Colin looked around the boggy terrain consideringly. "I had thought so, too, though how much more can be done with this without extensive—and expensive—modifications, I can't say. I had begun with the intention of introducing some better sheep strains and breeding practices, but when I asked my solicitor to look into the fiscal situation in preparation for such investments, he met nothing but confusion in the records and got no help from the steward. When I reached my majority, Father simply handed the books and the small profit to me. After the two hundred

pounds per annum that I spend on maintenance, such
as it is, there is usually scarcely any surplus to be had.
I assume that the probable lack of return is the reason
it was allowed to fall into such a state. Father is usually contentious about his landholdings to the point of
fussiness, but he has always avoided this place."

As they circled to the front of the manor house, the
track that the coach had taken came into sight, overgrown and frost-heaved cobbles giving way to a slight
double depression in the turf that wound down the
long slope of the tor toward the village.

The overcast sun had not yet burned away the fog
below, and white tendrils curled through the village
lanes and around the steeple of the church. The air had
only the slightest hint of chill, but it was heavy with
water.

"Are you sure that someone lives there?" Fern
asked.

From somewhere over the fens came the distant,
lonely clank of a bellwether's bell, as if in answer to
her question. "Where there are sheep, there are people," Colin assured her, but the village below lay in unnatural stillness.

"Let us try the vicarage first," Fern said. "I should
not like to go rapping arbitrarily on the doors of
strangers. Besides, it shall be hard enough to convince
the vicar of your identity in our current state. I
shouldn't imagine that we would have any luck with
a suspicious peasant at all."

Colin nodded and fixed his eyes on the church. He
led them the long way down the road, ignoring the
temptation to take a shortcut across the bog. Colin
knew that tussocks of grass and even entire bushes
that looked anchored on firm land could be merely

floating on top of a quagmire that would readily suck down an unwary trespasser.

As they walked, Colin found that he felt surprisingly good. He was tired, he was hungry, and, despite his wash the night before, he still felt somewhat gritty, and he had a kink in his back from how he had slept. Yet a sense of vigor coursed through his usually sluggish veins. The light and warmth of it seemed to find a focus in Fern, even as she trudged stolidly beside him, a look of faint worry on her face. She did not have to smile at him or touch him to make him feel this way, and her effect gladdened him and disturbed him at the same time. What if the color fled, and he was left again in a gray world? Would he care? Or—and this was the most disturbing thought of all—would he lack the depth of feeling needed for caring to be possible?

As they approached the village, the wind blew an eddy of fog toward them, and Colin caught the tang of wood smoke. A few scrawny chickens scratched aimlessly in the central lane, wandering among the collapsed foundations.

"There is someone here," Fern said with audible relief.

"Yes," Colin agreed. The block of the church squatted in front of the road at the edge of the village, the half-sunken headstones of the cemetery merging into the bog. He followed an overgrown path toward the back of the structure, where a small cottage in the same stone sat in its shadow.

Colin smoothed his hair—an utterly pointless gesture, considering the rest of his appearance—and knocked on the peeling paint of the door.

It was a long moment before he heard the sounds of someone approaching. There was a slow scrape as the bolt was drawn back, and then a small, wizened face appeared in the crack.

"May I help you?" The voice was surprisingly mellifluous despite its tremor.

Colin cleared his throat and pressed his calling card through the crack in the door. "I am Colin Radcliffe, and this is my wife," he said coolly. "We arrived yesterday to review Wrexmere Manor, but there were no servants and no food when we arrived, and half the roof collapsed on us in the night."

"Oh," the man said. He blinked at the card for several seconds. And then he shut the door in their faces.

Chapter Fourteen

Colin stared at the door in mounting irritation before the scratching sound of a chain being removed made him realize what the old man was doing. A moment later, the door was swung wide.

"Come in, sir, madam," the man said in the same resonant, cultured voice. "Mrs. Willis has just put a kettle on. It has been a very long time since I have seen a Radcliffe in these parts." With that, the man turned away and hobbled into the depths of the house, leaving them to follow.

Fern glanced up at Colin, her expression uneasy. He simply shrugged and stepped inside, and, still linked to his arm, she came with him. He shut the door, and the narrow hallway was instantly swallowed in shadow.

The little old man's silhouette disappeared as he turned into a room. Colin followed, squeezing past a narrow stair to find the doorway through which the man had gone. Fern clung to his arm. The elderly gentleman was seated on a wing-backed chair that dated from the middle of the reigns of the Georges—as the old man did himself. As they entered, he rocked forward and began to rise creakily.

With a quiet noise of pity, Fern released Colin's arm and all but lunged for the nearest chair, sitting before the old man was halfway to his feet. The man gave a sigh and sank back again.

"Thank you, young lady," he said. "I am not quite as spry as I once was."

Colin looked at his wife, who had an expression of deep concern on her face. Just a moment before, she had been half-terrified of their host, all but cutting the circulation off in Colin's arm as she gripped it. Now she seemed to have forgotten her fear in her care for the old man's frailty. Colin found the switch obscurely charming.

He had to climb over Fern's legs to take the remaining chair. The back parlor was scarcely larger than a cupboard, made even smaller a tiny brick fireplace on one wall and the tall, musty bookcases that crowded the narrow window.

"I don't believe I introduced myself," the old man said, putting his tassel-slippered feet on the ottoman before him with audible effort. "I am unaccustomed to meeting anyone who does not already know very well who I am. I am Reverend Biggs, the vicar." He paused and blinked owlishly at Colin. "Well, I don't suppose you've ever heard of me, but I was in your grandfather's college at Oxford. He was kind enough to offer me the living here when I graduated."

Something of Colin's aversion must have shown on his face, because Rev. Biggs chuckled. "I suppose you think it a poor kindness. But I was a scholarship student, without connections and without expectations. I was happier as the vicar here than as a subdeacon in a larger town. I like my independence."

"I am surprised you believed me when I told you who we are," Colin said.

The vicar gave a papery chuckle. "Believed you? I was expecting you. The vicarage is also the village post office, of sorts, as we have no other. I was given quite a turn this morning when I received a letter addressed to the Honorable Mr. Colin Radcliffe at Wrexmere Manor, but I deduced that it would be only a matter of time before you appeared at my door."

The man pulled a letter from the pocket of his dressing gown and extended it to Colin, who slid it into his coat. He turned at the sound of footsteps in the hall. A large woman appeared in the doorway, a tea tray between her meaty hands. She looked at Fern and Colin with a flat expression, as if she were incapable of surprise.

"Your tea, sir," she said curtly, squeezing in to place the tray on a small, rickety table. "Ye didn't say ye'd be inviting over no guests. I suppose I'd best start making them viddly little sandwiches." With that, she gave Fern and Colin a look of dislike and backed out of the room.

"That was Mrs. Willis," Rev. Biggs said unnecessarily. "She has done for me for twenty-seven years, ever since her mother died."

"How nice," Fern said faintly.

Colin cleared his throat pointedly. "We came to see you in hopes that you might provide us some direction. I have been paying a man and his wife by the name of Reston to maintain the manor house in my name."

The vicar's face clouded. "Yes. That would be Mrs. Willis' girl, Dorcas, and her husband, Joseph."

"Seeing as how the house was covered in several years' worth of dust and the roof collapsed only hours after our arrival, I cannot say that I am impressed by their attention to duty," Colin said coolly.

"Yes . . ." The vicar peered at him, his rheumy eyes piercing. "The Restons and the Radcliffes have never been easy with one another."

"Reston," Fern repeated, looking startled. "That's it. Jane Reston was the name of the woman in the letters whom the writer did not like."

The vicar's interest sharpened. "Letters?"

"Yes," Fern said. "I found a bundle of old letters in the keep last night—from the late sixteenth and early seventeenth centuries."

"Jane Reston," the reverend said thoughtfully. "I can't say for certain that I know who she is. But the Restons have worked at Wrexmere since before the first Radcliffe came, so I daresay that whoever the girl was, I'm not surprised she was in the letters."

"That was quite some time ago," Fern said.

"Oh, my, yes," the man said. "In fact, your letters must be from around the time when the cadet branch of the Radcliffes married the current heiress. Now, what was her name?" The man thought for a moment. "Charlotte. Yes, I am sure that it was Charlotte Gorsing. She had a sister named Elizabeth who married a baronet from the neighborhood and another named Lettice who never married anyone at all."

"I think you may be right," Fern said. "There was a Lettice mentioned in the letters, and they were signed with an E."

"I daresay they are one and the same as Lettice

Gorsing and Elizabeth Fitzhugh, then, because that must have been at the very end of the sixteenth century," Rev. Biggs said. "Charlotte Gorsing married John Radcliffe and gave birth to his heir several months after he died, whom she also named John. It was the first John Radcliffe's son who made the addition to the manor house and his great-grandson who inherited the barony and was raised by the king to the title of viscount."

"Did ye say Radcliffe?" The growling voice jerked Colin's attention away from the old man. Mrs. Willis was standing in the doorway with a tray containing more cups and a stack of scones and sandwiches. She fixed Colin with a glare. "Do ye be the new Radcliffe, then?"

"I am a Radcliffe," he said, narrowing his eyes at the unfriendly expression on her face.

The woman grunted and set the tray upon the table hard enough that the spoons clattered, then turned and pushed out of the room.

After a moment of awkward silence, Fern cleared her throat and began serving tea, her shaking hands rattling the cups slightly against the saucers. Colin's stomach rumbled impatiently. To distract it, he said, "I don't mean to imply that my family history is anything but fascinating, but I am rather concerned about the present—and future—at the moment. We need a cook, a valet, a housekeeper, and a lady's maid at the very least, as well as the services of a greengrocer and a butcher, never mind workers to repair the roof. I assume that, however lax they have been, Mr. and Mrs. Reston will be eager to make up for the past." He took his tea, scones, and sandwich from Fern gratefully.

Rev. Biggs hemmed and hawed for a moment before finally saying, "I suppose that they might, at that."

"Why would they not?" Colin frowned at the vicar, forcing himself not to snap.

The man's reserve was clear. "I may have had this living for nigh on sixty years, but there are some things in this village that one shall always be too much of an outsider to know unless one happens to be born into the right local family. So I cannot say anything with the confidence of full knowledge. However, it does not take being family to know that the Restons do not like the Radcliffes, and the Radcliffes . . . give them room, as it were."

"Why would my father—any of my relatives—do that?" Colin demanded. "The Restons are meant to be caretakers, but they have clearly taken care of nothing at all. Why were they not sacked years ago?"

Rev. Biggs shook his hoary head. "I have told you all I know. I will have Mrs. Willis arrange for provisions to be sent to the manor for you. If you wish, you can speak with Joseph Reston yourself to try to find domestics for your stay. His cottage is just down the lane, the only one with a green door." And with that, the vicar took a sip of his tea and rang a bell at his elbow, effectively closing that line of discussion.

Fern cleared her throat, darting Colin an uncertain look. "So tell me, Reverend Biggs, what do you like most about living here?"

The old man's face instantly lit up. "Butterflies," he said firmly, and that topic, sustained by Fern's questions and the vicar's eager answers, filled half an hour, until all the sandwiches and scones were eaten and the last drops of tea had grown cold.

Finally, Rev. Biggs looked at his empty plate and

said, "Goodness! I did not mean to keep you here so long. Mrs. Willis never did come, did she? She must be out. Or perhaps she is in the cellar. She was in the cellar when you called, and she never can hear anything from in there. I will see you to the door, then." He began to lever himself out of the chair.

"Oh, no, sir, you mustn't," Fern said quickly. "We remember the way. Thank you for your kindness—and the tea. Both were very welcome."

"Yes, thank you," said Colin, rising. "Now we must find Mr. Reston."

"Good luck," the vicar called from his chair. "And please, come see me again."

"I would like that," Fern said, with every appearance of sincerity, and they left.

Out on the front walk again, Colin looked down at the neat figure of his wife. He had known before that she was a kind woman and a good hostess, but he had seen those qualities only in the context of his usual society, which was a flat kind of place to display any virtue. He had not truly considered what they meant, how she could use them to put someone at ease and draw them, almost unconsciously, into her friendship, and he found that he was touched by the generosity of the woman who was his wife.

Fern gave Colin a frowning sideways look. "That was queer."

"What, his interest in butterflies?" Colin said lightly. "Most men have a mania, if only you can find it."

"Not you," Fern said instantly. "It is not a requirement of gentlemanly behavior. No, what I mean was all this talk about the Restons and the Radcliffes not liking one another. The Radcliffes are peers, and the

Restons . . . well, they marry housekeepers' daughters. They are not from the same world, so why would a Radcliffe even know what a Reston thought about him, much less care?"

Colin shrugged, uncomfortable with his uncertainty. "I understood what you meant, and in all honesty, I have no idea. My father has certainly never spoken of the Restons to me, and I don't even know if he would be familiar with the name."

"Yet they clearly haven't done their job in years, and no one has sacked them. Do you think there might be something in what the vicar said?"

"We will find out soon enough." Colin nodded to a small cottage with a shiny green door. "This is where they live."

Given the general dilapidation of the village and the utter collapse of the manor house, Colin had expected a slatternly little hut. But the cottage was orderly and in good repair, with a burgeoning flower garden in front, new paint on the door, and the raw, red wood of recent repairs on two of the silvery shutters. The incongruity of the neat little home in such a village was almost disturbing. Colin knew where the money for the pretty green paint came from, and his jaw set.

Colin opened the gate and stood aside to let Fern through. He followed her up the short path and knocked crisply on the door.

After a moment, it opened. A young woman with rolled-up sleeves and a gray work apron stood there. Her features echoed those of the stocky Mrs. Willis, but that matron's ruddy face and heavy jowls were replaced here by the flush and roundness of youth. The woman smiled, but her eyes stayed tight.

"Ye must be Mr. and Mrs. Radcliffe, then," she said. "My mum told me you had come. I be Dorcas Reston. Come in."

She stood aside, and they stepped into a tidy little parlor, slightly crowded with chintz furniture and little china figurines.

"My Joseph's helping old Abner vind a lost sheep," she explained, her hands knotting in her apron. "But he should be coming here any moment."

"I believe that some of my business can be handled more directly by you," Colin said bluntly. "Mrs. Reston, my wife and I came to Wrexmere for our honeymoon, in hopes of escaping the unpleasant crowd at Brighton. We had no expectations that there would be rooms prepared for us when we arrived, but we were nonplussed to find the manor entirely abandoned. We had to go without food and sleep in a filthy room last night, and, far more gravely, the house has been so neglected that the ridgepole of the wing gave way in the rainstorm and came crashing through the attic, nearly killing us both."

Mrs. Reston's smile hardened, and the hands in her apron twisted harder. "My Joseph never did expect to do much vor that place because of the papers," she said, pronouncing the last word as if it were a proper noun. "But he didn't know about no ridgepole being near rotted through. He had another beam brought for the new hall and he were going to vix it next week— he didn't know nothing about it being so bad."

"It must be fixed today," Colin said flatly.

Mrs. Reston nodded convulsively, then froze as if she were afraid that she had made an error.

"We also need a cook, a housekeeper, a lady's maid,

and, if at all possible, several other maids as well," he added.

The woman looked relieved. "If ye'll pay them, I can have half a dozen girls up there in two hours."

"They will be paid," said Colin coolly. "We need rooms cleaned for us, a fire laid, and a hot supper."

"Why don't . . . why don't I arrange vor that now?" the woman said, and before Colin could respond, she swung the front door open and fled, leaving Colin and Fern alone.

"Does she feel guilty?" Fern asked, staring after her.

"She seemed more frightened to me," said Colin. His neck prickled with suspicion, but he could not say whether it was merely a reaction to meeting the wife of the man who had clearly stolen so much of his money or whether it had a more profound cause.

"And what kind of papers was she talking about?" she added. She looked around the room. She was beginning to dislike it, with the chintz and doilies and the dozens of cheap china figurines haphazardly leering at her from every surface.

"I haven't any idea." Colin chose a seat. "We might as well make ourselves comfortable while we wait for her husband, though."

Fern hesitated, as if afraid to seem rude, before choosing another chair and perching on the edge. "I hope it doesn't take him too long. This entire day has been as strange in its way as last night."

No sooner had she said those words than an interior door opened and a man stepped through. He wore rough woolen trousers, a matching jacket, and a cap pulled low over his forehead. His face was weathered but not old, and when he saw Colin and Fern, his creased eyes widened in surprise.

"Mr. Radcliffe. Mrs. Radcliffe." His tone was neither welcoming nor hostile. "Our boy came and told me ye were here. I didn't credit it."

"I hope that now you do," Colin said, leaning back in the man's chair. The action was a veiled insult in the man's own home, but at this point, he was too irritated to care—the only thing keeping him from sacking the steward on the spot was the knowledge that he needed local cooperation if their stay in the manor was to be bearable. "Your son likely failed to tell you that the rotted ridgepole in the manor house collapsed last night and nearly killed us."

An expression flickered across Mr. Reston's face, almost like a grimace. It was gone too fast for Colin to identify it, but it disturbed him.

"I were going to vix it next week," the man said. "I keep my end of the bargain, ye know. I have papers."

Colin looked disapprovingly at the man. "Yes, your wife mentioned that. You shall find some men and fix it tonight, before it brings the rest of the wing down."

The man nodded curtly. "I can start on it today, sir, but seeing as it's already past noon, it will probably be two, three days before the slate's ready to be put back on."

"As long as the work is started immediately and with enough laborers, I will be satisfied," Colin said. It would have been more accurate to say, *I will be less angry with you*, but he could see nothing productive in that. "Your wife has already gone to find women to help clean the place for our visit. If you can gather the men to work on the roof, my wife and I would like to return to the house."

"Yes, sir," the man muttered, and with that, he pivoted abruptly and pushed through the front door and out of the house.

"Now they have both run away," Fern observed, standing.

Colin rose, too. "Let us hope that they will be true to their word this time," he said darkly. "Each of these pretty little trinkets represents several shillings of my money that did not go toward the manor house. Our presence and my disapproval should be enough to keep them from shirking their duties for the time that we are here. I will send them notice as soon as we leave. Surely there is someone in the village who would be better suited—with proper supervision—to caring for the manor house."

Colin opened the front door for Fern, then offered her his elbow. She took it, holding on a little more tightly than was necessary for politeness' sake.

"We have company," Colin murmured. The village was no longer deserted. A heavyset woman hoed dully at the patch of weeds in front of her house as she watched them, and a youth lounged in the doorway of a house across the street. A small gaggle of dirty little children hung, wide-eyed, on a fence rail.

Fern gripped his arm more tightly. "Why are they all staring at us?"

"They're here to see the circus."

"Circus!" Fern objected.

"The closest that they will ever come to it, if they stay here," Colin replied.

The villagers stared mutely at their future lord, and he felt their steady gazes changing him, shaping him back into the insensible mold of a viscount's heir. He put a gloved hand over Fern's, and the warmth in it reassured him, thawing the coldness that he felt creeping through him.

"What is it?" she asked, her face thrown into lines of concern.

"I am a viscount's son again," he said.

She frowned. "You are always a viscount's son."

"Not for the past two days. Then I've been... someone else. Someone real."

Colin knew the words were inadequate, but he saw understanding in her eyes. "Can't you stay real and be a viscount's son, as well?" she asked.

He shrugged. "I do not yet know."

She put on a tremulous smile. "I am glad that you are trying, at least."

The side of Colin's mouth tilted upward. "It is good to know that it matters to you."

By the time they reached the manor house, there was already a hum of activity in the pump yard as women crossed to and from the keep kitchen, carrying buckets sloshing with suds.

Colin slowed as they neared the back door, not wanting to plunge so soon into the dim, dank keep. But he followed the damp trail inside and up the stairs to the great hall, Fern at his side. Dorcas Reston stood in the center of the vast room, directing several other women as they scrubbed the table and dusted the chairs clustered at one end of the hall. Two women were already mopping the floor. Someone had tried to move one of the great tapestries, for it dangled in tatters from its rod high upon the wall down to form a pile of disintegrating cloth on the floor.

"Abby vound your bags on the third floor, sir," Mrs. Reston said with her tight little smile as they approached. "We'll be cleaning those rooms next."

"Thank you," Colin said. "Tell your husband that our trunks are still on the first floor of the Tudor wing and need to be brought up."

"I'll do that. Be careful on your way up," Mrs. Reston added as they moved toward the foot of the staircase. "They say the first John Radcliffe fell from the top step and split his head like a melon." She nodded toward a spot on the limestone, a wide blotch that was darker than the rest. Next to him, Fern recoiled, and Mrs. Reston's hard little smile widened slightly.

Colin paused at the foot of the stairs to allow Fern to start up first. She did, setting one foot carefully in front of the next.

"I do not like Mrs. Reston," Fern said with feeling when they were halfway up, suspended a queasy dozen feet above the cold stone floor.

"She seems a bit . . . tetched, as my nurse used to call it," Colin said.

"Tetched," Fern repeated. "Yes, I think so."

They emerged onto the third floor, and Fern opened the door to the bedroom in which they had spent the night. The familiarity of it was almost welcoming to her, as inhospitable as it was. She sat in one of the chairs before the table, picking up a letter at random and leafing through it. The angular writing seemed almost to crawl across the page, filled with Elizabeth Fitzhugh's bile and cunning. Fern shivered, setting it down. Elizabeth had written to her nephew John Radcliffe to warn him of Jane Reston's brood and to . . . what? To bind him to her? How and for what purpose? Her letters flattered him one minute and made dark hints of extortion the next. What did she want, and what could a married aunt who didn't even live in the manor house have possibly known?

Colin walked over to one of the windows and looked out over the gray bog. "This must have been the lord's solar once," he said. "The other room would have been the bedroom."

"And what about downstairs?" Fern asked, more to distract herself than because she cared.

"The second floor?" Colin said. "One room was probably for the ladies-in-waiting and the daughters of the house. The other, perhaps for the seneschal and his wife, or maybe the knights and the sons of the family. Or it could have been a cabinet or an armory, any number of things."

"I don't like this place," Fern said. "Last night, it seemed sad to me, all neglected and forgotten. Today, though, it just seems angry."

"It's only your meeting with the Restons that has changed the way you look at it," Colin said. "You should forget them."

"I can't. I don't know why I feel this way, and I don't particularly care," Fern retorted, her nerves fraying. "I just don't like it."

Colin did not reply to that, merely looking at her expressionlessly. After a moment, Fern sighed and pushed to her feet.

"Perhaps I just need an occupation. Or a nap," she added, looking longingly at the musty bed. "I truly ought to be a good housemistress and direct the work, but the thought of being so near Dorcas Reston makes my stomach turn." She rubbed her temples, trying to regain her frayed composure. "I'll pull off these bed linens, at least—perhaps that shall add a little more speed to the process of cleaning."

Fern went to the head of the bed and flipped the heavily quilted coverlet down, taking one of the pillows and pulling off its case. Her fingers went through the linen, and she tossed it aside. Colin watched her for a moment, then reached and took the other. Something crinkled, and as the case came free, a package fell out and dropped to the floor with a light thud. Colin stooped. When he straightened, he was holding a bundle of papers in his hands.

"It looks like more letters," he said, extending it to Fern.

She was strangely loath to accept it, wanting suddenly to distance herself from the ancient Radcliffes and Gorsings, the current Restons, and everything to do with the lichenous manor. But telling herself that she was being silly, she forced herself to walk around the bed and accept the package. She looked at the top letter. The handwriting was the same as the ones on the table. She slipped the packet into her pocket, where it hung heavily against her thigh. "Thank you," she said belatedly.

She went back to the head of the bed, and, taking hold of the counterpane, she pulled it off briskly and dropped it in a pile for the laundry, in the unlikely case it survived a scrubbing. She began pulling off the quilts beneath, one at a time. Reaching for the fourth and final quilt, Fern paused. All of the other bedcoverings had been dusty and half rotted with the damp, yet they had been otherwise unmarked. But this one had a large black circle in the center of it, as if someone had spilled a glass of dark molasses and had simply covered it up.

"What is it?" Colin asked.

"I don't know," she said. Frowning, Fern reached out to brush at the cloth. The substance crackled at her touch, some of it rising in a fine dust. The faint coppery smell of it triggered a distant recognition in Fern's mind. Puzzled, she raised her dust-covered fingertips to her nose and sniffed.

Realization and horror dawned simultaneously. Her stomach lurching, Fern scrubbed her hand against her skirts and backed away.

"What is it?" Colin repeated again.

"It's blood," Fern said, barely managing to say the words without her gut rebelling. "It's blood, Colin. We sat here all night next to a bed that was covered in blood!" Exhaustion, fear, and disgust threatened to overwhelm her, and she shoved them down mercilessly to keep the tears at bay. "I cannot stay in this place. Not one more second!" And with that, the floodgates burst.

Chapter Fifteen

Fern whirled away from Colin so he would not see her weakness and threw herself blindly through the door and onto the stair landing. But that was only an instant's reprieve. He would follow her—she knew he would—and she couldn't talk to him now, not with tears turning her face blotchy and her nose running and her mind racing in circles and not making any sense. The massive stone walls seemed to close in, crushing her, and Fern had the urge simply to run away from everything. But she quashed it firmly and took the stairs with jerky care, slowing still further when she reached the unguarded flight that ran from the second floor down to the first.

With her eyes fixed determinedly on the path in front of her, she nearly barreled into Dorcas Reston as she took the final step down to the flagstones of the hall. Mrs. Reston's expression moved swiftly from surprise to smugness as she took in Fern's tearstained face, and her reaction sparked a sudden ire in Fern. She shouldered the woman aside and dashed for the stairs to the kitchens, ignoring the woman's outraged gasp. Fern hurried down the stairs and to the door to the pump yard—and out into the clammy air. A girl looked up from filling her bucket at the pump, her eyes widening with alarm as she took in Fern's condition. Fern ignored her and cast about for a direction to take. She wouldn't take the road—that led right back toward the village and more people, which was exactly what she wanted to avoid. She knew better than to try to walk straight across the boggy moor. But there—there was a path that wandered off from the corner of the overgrown courtyard, moving away from the village. A sheep track.

Sniffing now, Fern headed toward it. She felt ridiculous and ashamed for crying, but she still wanted nothing better than to curl up into a ball and sob and hide until the world went away. The low bracken caught at her hem as she moved farther from the keep, but she ignored it. Around her, the land sloped down into a boggy maze, stretching out toward a gray horizon that was foreshortened by the dull humps of a ridge of low tors, the moor's granite skeleton thrusting through at their crests. The path took the highest way, dry and firm despite the rains the night before. Hiccoughing now, her brief fit of exhausted tears subsiding as quickly as it had overcome her, Fern walked until the keep was out of sight and hearing. She found a hillock in a small, sheltered curve in the path, where three boulders cut the wind. Disregarding her silk skirts, she sat.

From such a vantage, the moors seemed to grow smaller, drawing tight to wrap her in a nest of heather and tangled grasses. It was almost comforting, the rustling of the undergrowth in the faint wind, the gray sky low overhead like a ceiling. She sank the fingers of the hand that still had blood stench on it into the thick, tannin-rich earth until all trace was gone.

What am I doing here? Fern thought, but she pushed that thought from her, closed her mind, and tried to find that internal balance point that she had maintained automatically for most of her life and that only now seemed to elude her.

Gradually, she came to realize that the rustle in the heather was more than the wind. She opened her eyes reluctantly to see Colin striding toward her, his face hard.

"Are you hurt?" he demanded.

"No," Fern said, brushing the last traces of tears from her cheeks—and realizing too late that this would leave smudges of dirt instead. She wiped her hand on her skirt; it was surely ruined now, anyway. "I was resting."

The tenseness in his face shifted, darkening. "What were you thinking?" he demanded. "You might have stumbled into a mire and been sucked under. Or you might have fallen into a pond that was obscured by weeds and scum and drowned."

Fern looked at him calmly. "I was following a sheep track. Unless entire herds have plunged repeatedly into a boggy pit and died, I should be perfectly safe."

Colin stood over her, still fulminating but mute, the perfect lines of his face cast into a hard expression. He was so beautiful that he made her heart squeeze.

"Why are you really angry?" Fern asked softly.

He froze, surprise flickering across his face. "What do you mean?"

"Just what I said," she responded. "Why are you really angry? It isn't because I ran, is it? You knew that

I was in no danger as soon as you began following the track."

Colin sighed, and all the pent-up tension seemed to go out of him at once. He sat on the grass beside her, folding up his lean form. His presence warmed her; she could sense the heat of the spirit that flamed inside him, and she was glad for it.

"I am not used to this, you know," he said. "This . . . feeling, all the time. Sometimes, I feel like my nerves will burn through my skin."

"I know," said Fern. "So do I."

"How do you live with it, day after day?" he demanded.

"I am not sure," she said, dropping her eyes to a tiny orchid that was growing beside her booted heel. "It isn't always like this, you know. It isn't usually like this. But since our wedding night . . ." She trailed off. "I suppose I shall have to wait and find out, just as you shall."

That silenced him for a long moment. "I thought this would work," he said finally. "I thought that we would come here and I would discover . . . something . . . and everything would fall into place."

"Something certainly fell," Fern said, giving him a tentative smile. "Though I doubt you meant the roof."

Colin snorted, but softly, his green eyes remaining intent. "I thought I had begun to discover something, at least, but then we went out among people, and nothing was as I had expected it to be. Everything had changed, yet nothing had changed. And I am not used to anything being contrary to my expectations."

"What did you discover?" Fern asked.

Colin shrugged. "What I'd had all along. I found you, and I found myself, but I still don't know what to do with either one of us. The world here seems wrong, out of key, out of step, out of tune."

"Out of time," Fern said, more vehemently than she intended. "It's the detritus of other people's lives. Worn-out furniture, a house that no one wants anymore, old, bitter letters, and mad ravings from another age. I don't like it here, Colin. There's no room for me among all these memories. Time is all used up—there's none left to make anything new."

"But where is our place right now, Fern?" Colin asked, frowning. "Give me—give us—a little more time. A week, no more."

"A week," she repeated. "This is not how I imagined spending my honeymoon. But then again, I never imagined myself married to a man with whom I would *talk*." She spread her hands, indicating everything she meant in that word. "Certainly not you. I never imagined that it was important. Which now seems quite odd to me, that I would not care if I could talk to the man with whom I would spend the rest of my life. When I did realize that it was important, I was afraid that it was too late, that our choice was an impossible one for such a simple exchange." She shook her head. "But it seems that what we really needed was something to talk about."

Colin's lips quirked upward, and a hint of a smile crept into his eyes. "What would you like to talk about now, then?"

"I still think we should get to know each other better," Fern said gravely.

"And how do we go about doing that?" he asked.

"Well," she said, taking his teasing question in earnest, "usually, two people first get to know things *about* each other, before they can really *know* each other."

"I think we already have known each other, in the biblical sense, multiple times," Colin said blandly.

Fern stared: "Is *that* what that phrase means?"

He chuckled. "It is easy to forget how naive you still are."

"They talk about such things in the Bible?" she repeated, scandalized.

"'Let him kiss me with the kisses of his mouth: for thy love is better than wine,'" he agreed, and he put action to his words and pulled her into his lap, planting his lips over hers and moving his mouth slowly, luxuriantly across her own, the stubble of his beard rough against her skin. Her body came alive with a jolt of delicious sensation that shivered up her spine and deep into her center.

When he broke off, she gave him a light shove, even though her breath came fast. "You are trying to provoke me again, aren't you?"

"Honestly, no," he said, the words a rumble in his chest. "It is only that I have wanted to kiss you ever so badly since I found you here, and I had not found an excuse to do so until now. It seemed inappropriate earlier." He shifted so that she sat with her head against his chest, her legs stretching out between his own.

"I thought we were going to fight," she confessed.

"So did I," he said. "That is one new thing we now know about each other: We are not as good at fighting as we think we are."

Fern laughed. "I am glad of that!"

"And well you should be. What else do you want to know about me?" he asked.

"Well, I already know that you have no favorite color," Fern said.

"I was wrong. I do have a favorite color: the color of your eyes."

"Liar," Fern said without rancor.

She felt his shrug. "I tried."

"If you could go anywhere in the world, where would you go?" she asked after a pause.

"I don't—" He broke off. "I have already been to France, Switzerland, and Italy. I suppose that if I could go anywhere at all, it would be back to Rome again, but in the time of the Romans."

"Would you be a martyr thrown to the lions?" she asked. "Or a barbarian gladiator, captured in desperate battle against the Roman oppressors?"

"Neither. I would have a supper of dormice and flamingo tongues and then go warn Caesar—in much clearer terms than the mad old soothsayer managed—what exactly lay in store for him in the Senate on the Ides of March. And then, while he was slaughtering the conspirators, I would sneak into the house where he was keeping Cleopatra and convince her to run away with me."

"You're not serious," Fern chided.

"No, I am not," he agreed. "Where would I go? In a very real sense, I could go anywhere if I cared enough to, but a combination of habit and my dislike for the unpleasantness and mortal danger of much travel keeps me at home. Suspending the possibility of danger for one moment, I would like to be the first man to see something. The first to climb a great mountain, perhaps, or the first to reach the poles."

Fern said, "I know I should like to see Paris again, but I should also very much like to see Spain."

"Why Spain?" Colin asked.

"Because it has touched England's history so often," she explained. "I always wondered what kind of a place it took to create a man like Philip the Second or a woman like Isabella of Castile."

"That is logical enough," Colin conceded. Fern felt his fingers twisting gently around one of the locks of hair that had slid from her braided bun. "I should have made arrangements for you to have a lady's maid accompany you to Wrexmere. It was not an intentional omission—I simply did not think of it."

She cocked her head slightly so that she could see his face out of the corner of her eye. "Is that an apology?"

He looked rueful. "It was meant to be. Apparently it was less successful than I had hoped."

"So why did you give up your own valet rather than replacing my maid?"

Colin shook his head. "You saw that public house. There was no one suitable."

"And you were too proud to admit your mistake."

"Too irritated by your cheekiness," he corrected.

"Cheekiness!" She tried to sound incensed but ruined it by laughing. "That sounds like a way to describe a squirrel. Anyhow, you redeemed yourself, however oddly, by choosing to become as bedraggled as I. You are usually such a precise dresser."

"No. I merely hired a very good valet. Who would have a fit if he saw me sitting on the ground in my good gray trousers."

Fern just smiled. After a moment, she said, with some surprise, "I have just thought something curious."

"What is that?"

"I thought that you would make a rather nice friend."

"A friend?" Colin's voice was skeptical.

"Yes, a friend," she said staunchly. "You are some-one I should like to talk to often. I didn't expect it in a husband, and I am glad."

Colin grew very still, feeling those words imprint into his soul. "So am I." He raised his hand to his lips and kissed the lock of her hair still tangled around it. Then he pushed her half off his lap so that he could turn her around enough to kiss her squarely on the lips. They were so hot, those lips, so small, sweet, and soft. They continually surprised him—with her pas-sion and her words, both. She responded to him ea-gerly, tangling her fingers in his hair, pulling him down so that he was above her as she lay on her back in the bracken. His body tightened, the surge starting in his groin and moving outward through all his mus-cles. Finally, he pulled away.

Fern lay for a moment with her eyes closed, her lids shaded delicately and her brows drawn in that way of hers that made her look so innocently intent. Slowly, she opened her eyes, their gray depths flickering with desire.

"That is not very friendlike," she said.

"I didn't mean it to be," he replied.

She looked at him, unblinking. "Do it here," she or-dered, but with a shyness that made her voice small. "Away from that odious house and the odious Res-tons. I want you here."

"You can have me," Colin swore. He kissed her again, more deeply, tasting her, glorying in the slick-ness of her small mouth. His body drank it in, pulling tighter in anticipation. Her fingers tightened in his hair, and he shuddered, moving down to kiss her jaw, her neck, the line of her dress. Her knees slid up to clasp his hips.

"Now. Please," she said.

With a muttered oath, he unfastened the buttons of his fly and pulled his erection free. She hiked her skirts up, and he took the invitation, finding the opening in her pantaloons and the hot slit of her entrance. She was already wet with wanting him, and he thrust inside in one stroke. She gasped, pushing back against him, and it was all he could do not to lose control right then. He shifted his position, lifting her pelvis upward against the constriction of her corset.

"What—" she started to ask, but the question was broken off with a hiss of pleasure as he thrust into her again. "Oh, my," she said with wide eyes.

Colin chuckled through clenched teeth and thrust again, and her hands tightened convulsively. He built up a rhythm, responding to her reactions as he found the pace that would send her breathing spiraling out of control, her body arching hard into him and finally a strangled cry of release escaping her as she tightened convulsively around him. He let himself go, and for one glorious instant, fire tore through his body in a pulsating wave. Then it was gone, and a slow, warm lassitude overtook him in its wake. He rolled to the side, straightening his clothes even as he tried to regain his breath.

"Short . . . can be good . . . too," Fern observed, sprawled bonelessly against him. "'Specially . . . since I think . . . I felt rain."

Colin turned his face to the sky. The clouds had got lower and darker since they had set out from the manor house. He groaned and shoved himself to his feet. "Let's go."

"I am fine," Fern said, not moving and still slightly breathless. "I should not mind a little rain just now."

"You shall if it makes you ill," Colin said. He held out his hand.

Fern looked at it reluctantly for a moment before taking it and allowing him to lever her to her feet. "How far away do you think the house is?" she asked.

Thunder rumbled overhead. "Too far," Colin said firmly. "Look over there—there's a hut or a shed of some sort." It sat on a slight rise only a hundred yards away, a small, windowless stone building half-hidden in a tangle of overgrown shrubbery.

Fern looked. "Are you certain it has a roof?"

"It's close. Let's find out." Colin began walking toward the building, and since he still held her hand, Fern had no choice but to follow.

The hut looked more dilapidated the closer they got. The door hung slightly askew, silver with age, and there were visible cracks in the mortar of the stones. But Colin pressed on, going up to the door and pushing it aside.

Instead of the bare lambing hut that he had expected, Colin found himself in the center of a crowded and well-used little room. It was dominated by a square deal desk, piled high with neat stacks of paper, and shelves of jars lined the walls.

"How queer," Fern said, freeing herself from his grip and circling the table. "It looks like someone simply took all the paper he could find and saved it here. Newspapers . . . shopping lists . . . business correspondence. Some of these are a scant dozen years old, but others . . ." She held up a scrap of paper. "I'm sure no one has written like this in a century."

Colin joined her, putting a hand on the small of her back. She leaned into the touch, and he was momentarily taken aback by his surge of proteciveness that resulted from that display of trust. He cleared his head. She was right: There seemed to be no design behind the stacks, no purpose in them.

"Whatever could he have been doing?" Fern mused.

"I don't know," Colin said. "I'm just glad the roof is sound." He inspected the jars. "They are all food. Jellies, meats, and vegetables."

"I wonder how old they must be," Fern said, looking at the dusty labels.

Shrugging, Colin sat on one of the chairs.

With a sigh, Fern took the other. A puzzled expression passed over her face, and she pulled a bundle of papers out of her skirt. "I had forgotten about this," she said. She turned it over in her hands.

"Would you like to read them?" Colin offered. "We seem to be doing a great deal of reading during rainstorms."

"I don't think so," Fern said. "They're rather unpleasant, and even if everyone is long dead, it feels like spying to read their correspondence." She pushed them back into her pocket again.

Just then, the door swung open. In the doorway stood Joseph Reston, water streaming from his mackintosh and down his creased face. His eyes narrowed at Fern's hand, still in her pocket. She pulled it out quickly, paling.

"My woman said ye had left. I thought it best to vind ye before the water starts to rise and the bog gets treacherous," the man said. "I brought these vor ye." He thrust out his arm. Draped across were two rubberized cloaks.

Fern didn't move, but Colin took them, instinctively interposing himself between the man and his wife. "Thank you," he said coldly, meeting the man's gaze with challenge in his eyes.

At his look, Fern rose, and Colin wrapped one across her shoulders. Parts of the lining had got wet in the rain, leaving dark spots on the light gray taffeta of her walking dress. He threw his own on. A damp spot rubbed against the bare skin at the back of his neck.

Joseph Reston was still looking suspiciously around the room, his gaze flitting from one pile of papers to the next. "Ye didn't touch nothing." The growl was half statement, half question.

"We only looked," Fern said. "Is this your . . . cottage?" She asked the question tentatively from the shelter of Colin's shadow.

"Belongs to the manor," the man answered. "But my pa used to stay here sometimes, when he got tired of all of us. Died here, too. No one comes here but me now, sure enough."

"Died?" Fern echoed, her eyes going wide, but Reston's face closed up, and he merely grunted in reply.

"Ye'd best hurry. The water is rising."

Colin offered Fern his arm, and she took it, pulling the hood over her bare head. He pulled his up, too, as he stepped out into the steady rain. His boots sank into three-inch-deep mud, and as he began to stride after Mr. Reston with Fern struggling behind him, he could feel the water seeping through the fine stitching on the uppers to soak his feet.

There was no thunder; this was not a repeat of the

storm from the night before. Still, the rain came down in a steady, even wash that showed no sign of remittance. The water chilled him through the rubberized cloth, creeping in around the opening of his hood to soak his collar.

Colin held Fern close, shielding her as well as he could with his body. Her face was wet with rain, and a dark stain was spreading across her skirts where the cloak separated whenever she took a step. He wished that Reston had thought to bring an umbrella, too.

It was not as far back to the manor house as it had seemed when Colin was in pursuit of Fern—in less than ten minutes, they were passing through the side door into the kitchens. Joseph Reston gave them both a flat look.

"I've got to help the men clear the attic," he said. "The ground floor is safe enough, but don't ye go upstairs if ye can help it till we're done."

With that, he turned toward the Tudor wing, leaving Fern and Colin alone in the shadowed kitchen. From behind the thick square columns came the clatter of pots and pans—somewhere in the kitchen, someone was cooking or cleaning. Cooking, Colin hoped earnestly.

"His father died in the hut?" Fern said, her expression divided between confusion and revulsion.

Colin shrugged. "Everyone must die somewhere, I suppose."

"Why did he tell us that?" she demanded in a bewildered tone.

Colin gave her a sardonic look. "He doesn't much like us, and he truly didn't like us being in that hut. Did you see the way he looked at those papers, making sure we hadn't disturbed them?"

"But they didn't mean anything," Fern protested. "They were trash."

"People have funny ways. Anyway, his father just as likely as not died at home in bed. Reston was only trying to keep us away."

Fern shook her head, offering no resistance as Colin led her to the foot of the stairs. "It doesn't make any sense."

"You expect too much out of people," Colin said dryly.

They reached the great hall, and Fern gave a cry of surprised gladness. "A fire!"

On the far side of the room, a small fire had been lit on the vast hearth. Its size was almost ridiculously out of proportion with the vast chimney hood, but Fern hurried down to kneel beside it, holding her hands over its modest flames.

"Are you chilled?" Colin asked, following her to the hearth at a more moderate pace.

"No," Fern said. "I just like the fire. This room hasn't had a fire in a very long time." She straightened and surveyed the rest of the changes. "It seems less frightening, now," she said.

Colin followed her gaze. The remnants of the disintegrated tapestry still clung high on the walls, but the moldy pile of cloth below had been cleared away. The other tapestries had been left alone. The floor had been swept, the chairs polished, and the tabletop scrubbed, with service laid out for two. He looked back at his wife, but her expression had turned troubled.

"I should have directed the cleaning," she said, looking at the heavy earthenware plates. "I shouldn't have hidden from Dorcas Reston, and I certainly shouldn't have run away."

"You were tired," Colin said quietly. "And this is not in the usual line of duty for a gentleman's wife."

Fern's laugh was unsteady. "I am tired. Dorcas Reston frightens me a little, as silly as that sounds, and when I touched that blood . . . " She shuddered at the memory. "I don't like this place. I am beginning to sound like a parrot, I know, but I mean it with every fiber of my being."

"I don't care much for it myself," he said. "We'll leave soon. I promise."

"A week, you said."

He reached out, pushing back a stray lock of her hair. "Sooner than that, I hope."

Fern smiled, her gray eyes warming.

"Mr. Radcliffe! Mrs. Radcliffe!"

Chapter Sixteen

Colin turned to see Dorcas Reston descending the stairs, her pale hair frizzing around her face.

"I've prepared a room for ye," she called, pausing far enough down from the top that she did not have to stoop past the floor above to look down upon them. "The third vloor were vilthy, so I had ye moved to the vront room on the second." With that, she turned and went back up the stairs.

"I'm glad we aren't staying here much longer," Fern confided. "I should feel obligated to try to take Mrs. Reston in hand, and I don't think I have the constitution for it. Please tell me that I shan't be terrorized by any of your other servants."

Colin's lips twitched despite himself. "Perhaps the chef, but he terrorizes everyone. Do you wish to go above?"

"I wish to have a proper hot meal," Fern said stoutly. "A light tea is no substitute for a skipped breakfast and luncheon with only half a cold dinner the night before. But since food does not yet seem to be forthcoming, I wouldn't mind getting into fresh clothes."

"Lead on," Colin invited, waving to the staircase. Fern did, edging up the vertigo-inducing stairs. Colin stayed close, protectively behind her, watching the back of her downturned head, her frizzing braid affixed lopsidedly to it. It amazed him how frail and yet how strong she was. She had faced the collapse of the roof in stalwart silence, but she could not even arrange her own hair. Somehow those contradictions made her seem more precious to him, her strange admixture of courage and helplessness stirring an unfamiliar sort of tenderness in him.

When she got to the top of the staircase, she sighed. "I don't think I could ever get used to that," she confessed.

Colin snorted. "I should hope not. Getting used to something like that would show a suicidal degree of complacency."

He reached past her and pushed open the door to the front room. Inside was Dorcas Reston, scowling over a woman who was polishing the heavy oaken table and chairs. A fire burned on the hearth, a kettle hanging over the flames.

Mrs. Reston looked up as they entered, her expression changing to a pasted-on smile, her hands fluttering as she spoke.

"I had a new mattress and clean linen brought, even though I had to buy them vrom Mrs. Poll," she said. "That's vour pounds at your convenience, Mr. Radcliffe. I brought down your valises vrom above, and my man had your trunks a-carried up, too."

Colin imagined the procedure involved in getting their two substantial steamer trunks up the narrow stairs and suppressed a shudder. "Thank you, Mrs. Reston," he said, with some sincerity, for once.

Mrs. Reston made a noise that was half snort, half sigh. "That's Abby," she said, nodding to the other woman. "She's to be Mrs. Radcliffe's lady's maid vor now. She ain't done no lady's maid work, but she once worked vor a big house in Lincolnshire, and so she's seen it. Old Jim will be the valet, but he's working with the men until my husband sends him to you. He used to be a batman in the cavalry."

"Thank you," Colin repeated.

Mrs. Reston paused, then said to Colin in a much lower tone, "I heard vrom my ma that ye didn't know about our arrangement."

Colin looked at her in distaste, unable to bear her hints and posturing any longer. "There is only one arrangement between us, Mrs. Reston," he said, at his chilliest. "I am to pay you and your husband a substantial sum every year, and you are to use it to maintain my property. Since I have come, I have discovered neglect, filth, and disrepair to the point of catastrophic structural failure. That arrangement, therefore, has been abrogated, and badly. All I want is a forthright relationship between a master and his dependent staff. But you—you didn't even stay on the premises you had been hired to watch."

The woman's face grew even tighter. "Ye should know that there were an arrangement," she repeated. "Another arrangement, one that ye'd best continue, if ye know what's good vor ye. My man and me, we weren't asked to do much of anything until ye showed up. After a spring bubbled up under a corner of the little lodge and made the side of it sink, we thought it'd be best to stay in my ma's old house in the village." She paused. "We've done everything that was asked of us. We haven't broken our end of the agreement."

"You are trying to assert that my family have knowingly paid you for nothing for generations. Why would any sane person do that?" Colin demanded.

She shook her head, looking frustrated, and dropped her voice even more. "It's the papers, Mr. Radcliffe," she said. "We have the papers."

Fern shook her head, her expression baffled. "The papers in the hut? But they were all rubbish."

The woman looked offended. "Not the *papers*," she said, as if that answered any objection.

"What is in these papers?" Colin tried to steer the conversation in a more rational direction.

"Everything," she said darkly; then she pressed her lips together and left.

Fern gaped after her, giving Colin a look of complete astonishment, but he just shrugged and went to the bed, pulling back the blankets.

"It's clean now, just as she said," he announced, waving to the white sheets.

Fern came up beside him. "Thank you for checking," she said. "I don't think I would have had the nerve to pull the blankets down myself. I still have the chills from the last surprise."

The woman that Dorcas Reston had called Abby looked up quickly at that, then down again at her work.

Fern exchanged glances full of significance with Colin. Abby knew something about it, Fern was certain of that, and she was equally certain that the woman would have to be questioned if any answer were to be had of her.

Colin raised his eyebrows and nodded toward the door. "I will leave you to freshen up and change, shall I?"

"That would be nice," Fern said. She cleared her throat. "Abby, would you attend me, please?"

"Of course, m'm," Abby said, while Colin left the room, shutting the door behind him.

Fern's heart beat a little faster despite herself—she was not used to even the most harmless of dissimulations. She unbuttoned the front of her bodice rapidly. "I suppose you must have been the one to take those sheets away upstairs," Fern said, attempting to sound casual. "Do you have any idea what caused such a mess?"

"No, m'm, not for sure," Abby said slowly. "But there be a story. . . ."

"What is it?" Fern asked, curiosity winning out over delicacy.

"Well, m'm, it had to have happened a bit before the second John Radcliffe built the new manor," Abby said, beginning to loosen Fern's skirts. "The old hall were shut up then, and nobody used the upper vloors ever again. People still talk about how much he hated that old place. He ran away when he were a boy of sixteen to join the Royal Navy and didn't come back till his mother were dead."

"Yet this was two and a half centuries ago, was it not?" Fern asked.

"Near enough, m'm."

"But you know all this?" The casual way with which people in Wrexmere referenced ancient events was a little hard to become accustomed to.

Abby's efficient hands slowed on the tapes to the last petticoat. "Wrexmere's an old village with an old memory. We have stories going back to the time of the Conqueror. There's certain times that stick in the mind, times when things go strange and everything changes.

When the virst John Radcliffe came and married Charlotte Gorsing were one of them, and everything that came after. When the vourth John Radcliffe became a viscount and left the estate vorever—well, that were another."

"I see," Fern said. "What happened, then, that could account for the ... the stain upstairs?" she asked, stumbling slightly over the words. Abby stepped back, and Fern began to pull her taffeta skirt over her head.

"Well, m'm," Abby continued, more freely now, "after the second John Radcliffe had left the manor, a girl came to the hall, all secret-like. No one was supposed to know she were there, but Charlotte Radcliffe—the second John's mother—and Lettice Gorsing, his spinster aunt, had a cook, and the cook told the village." Abby sniffed, probably at the futility of secrecy in such a close-knit community, as she helped Fern pull the second petticoat over her head. "The girl were carrying a brat, and she'd been sent out to Wrexmere to give birth to it."

"Who was she?" Fern asked, despite feeling that this story was going to turn very unpleasant very rapidly.

"Neither Charlotte Radcliffe nor Lettice Gorsing ever said her name, but no one but family would send a girl out to them to be delivered of a bastard, and the Gorsing-Radcliffes had only one other relative."

"Their sister Elizabeth," said Fern, remembering the name from their visit with the vicar.

"She were Elizabeth Fitzhugh by then," Abby said, showing no surprise that Fern knew who it was. "Everyone thinks it must have been her girl what came."

"Did the girl die?" Fern couldn't help the question.

"No. No, after a vew months, she left—without a baby," Abby said seriously as she took the last petticoat and set it aside. "And none were left behind, neither. There were a vresh grave, though—my grandmother said her mother once showed her where it were—and though the vicar would only look sad when people asked about it, we think the baby must have died soon after it were born."

"Murdered?" Fern gasped.

Abby shrugged. "Some say aye, others nay. I don't think the poor scared girl killed nobody. No, I reckon it must have been a very hard birth for a girl so young." She began to work on Fern's corset laces. "If that were the birthing room up there, well, 'twere a miracle that it didn't take the girl, too."

"But the room was just left . . . " Fern said, bracing against Abby's brisk unlacing.

"You have to understand, m'm, that Charlotte Radcliffe and Lettice Gorsing were old women by then, and they hadn't been quite right in the head since the second John up and left. For all they knew, he was dead. Elizabeth had been the youngest, and if the girl were hers, she were a child of her middle age. I don't reckon the sisters ever climbed they stairs to the top vloor after the girl what had the baby came."

"There was a cook," Fern said doubtfully.

"One of the Restons, sure enough," Abby said. She paused. "That's the other odd thing, why that time sticks so in everyone's minds here. The Restons have worked at the manor house vor as long as anyone can remember, but something happened in they years that made them change. After the virst John Radcliffe came, the Restons became more and more airy in their ways and held themselves apart, and the Radcliffes seemed afraid to stop them."

"Because of the papers," Fern murmured.

Abby shrugged. "So I hear them muttering to each other now and then. I ain't seen any papers, though, m'm, not in all my years here."

Fern undid her busk and slid the corset off, her mind in turmoil but with no more answers than she'd had before. Did the papers have something to do with the girl? If so, what? Perhaps she wasn't a relative at all but someone despoiled by the second John Radcliffe. Perhaps the cook found out, and since then, they had held the Radcliffes hostage with threats of blackmail. But over generations? Perhaps a son would pay to keep his father's name unblemished, or a grandson would pay to preserve his grandfather's name, but it scarcely seemed likely that a tarnish any more distant than that might sway a family to permit the level of freedom that the Restons had been taking for over two hundred years. Fern looked at the pile of discarded clothing, where her pocket lay tangled among her petticoats. Perhaps the answer lay in those letters. Even knowing that, though, she did not want to pick them up and hear the voice of Elizabeth Gorsing Fitzhugh again.

Abby had begun to hum under her breath as she mixed hot water from the kettle with cold water from a pitcher in a basin, as if the maid had already forgotten the macabre story she had just told. Fern reminded herself that these were legends to the villagers, the fireside stories they had grown up with, their strangeness having grown hackneyed long ago.

Without seeing any other profitable line of questioning, Fern finished undressing and took the clean cloth that Abby offered. Determined to fix her mind on less morbid things, she said, "What I wouldn't give for even a hip bath now!"

"There must be some hip baths in the new hall somewhere, m'm," Abby said seriously. "Except my man Sterne said that they'd only got so var as to take out some of the bits of roof that were holding the rest steady, so it's best to stay away."

"I wouldn't ask you to go inside," Fern said. "Not until the men have firmed things up a bit, at least. I was merely wishing. I haven't had a proper bath in four days." *Since the night before my wedding*, she added silently. Had it truly been only four days? It seemed like a lifetime.

Fern scrubbed the sweat and peaty dirt from her body, her tired muscles relishing the heat of the wet cloth even as the memories from last night's wash played in her brain. Abby gave her fresh underclothes and laced her corset. Fern pulled on her dressing gown and sat at an angle on one of her tall chairs to have her hair brushed.

"Can you dress hair?" Fern asked. Her question was almost pathetic—she knew it was, and she wished that she were less helpless. But wishing did not solve anything, and though she resolved to have her new lady's maid, whoever she might be, teach her how to arrange her own hair, she had no time, energy, or patience for it now.

"I can't do nothing vancy, but I can do good enough vor the likes of me," Abby replied stolidly.

"It will be plenty well enough for me, too," Fern assured her.

Abby was putting the last pins in her hair—which was smooth and even for the first time in two days—

when the door opened and Colin came in. He looked subtly different, and it took Fern a moment to realize that his chin was clean-shaven again.

"I found my valet," he said. "He was bringing in peat blocks. I stopped him long enough to get a shave and then told him to carry on. I'd rather have a good fire than a straight necktie." Despite the emptiness of his speech, the gaze he swept the room with was keen, and Fern felt the undercurrent of words left unsaid.

"Thank you, Abby," she said. "If you will have dinner sent up, I believe we will eat here tonight. I won't need any more assistance until morning."

"Yes, m'm," Abby said, and she left, picking up the thread of the song she had been humming earlier, the haunting tune floating wisplike up the stairs as she descended.

Fern looked at Colin expectantly.

He blew out a gust of air. "Dorcas Reston didn't say the batman was her husband's cousin. I did think you were perhaps being a trifle hasty in your dislike of that family, but I tell you, with that man's razor just a fraction of an inch from opening my neck, I began to share your judgment."

"Did he say anything?" Fern asked, her heart beating fast.

"Nothing at all," he said. "I hope that you at least had the conversation you were hoping for." He rubbed his hand across his chin and grimaced. "Tomorrow, I will be shaving myself."

Fern briefly related what Abby had said. Colin just shook his head.

"I think this place must drive people to madness. Papers, bastards, secrets, madwomen—none of it makes the slightest sense."

Fern sighed, rubbing her forehead. "I know. I just wish that I could forget about all of it."

Colin smiled slowly, predatorily. "I believe I might be able to arrange that, at least temporarily."

"After dinner," Fern said firmly, even as her stomach fluttered in reaction. "I'm light-headed with hunger and exhaustion, and I must fix at least one of the two first."

He began unbuttoning his coat. "In that case, I hope you will pardon me as I get clean." His movements were economical, his undressing rapid and businesslike, and yet Fern felt a slow, sullen heat stir deep in her midsection as the lean shape of his body was uncovered layer by layer.

He paused as he dropped his shirt upon his coat and something crinkled. He retrieved the coat again and pulled a letter out of its pocket.

"I had forgotten about this." He grimaced at the handwriting on the front. "A neat, impersonal legal hand." He opened it and scanned its contents as Fern watched, then dropped it with a bark of laughter. "It is in my solicitor's name, but most of the words are my parents'. It seems that my actions have shocked them, and they fear for my mental well-being. My solicitor only reiterates his ignorance of all Wrexmere affairs." He gave her a look of suppressed irony. "I am afraid that when we return, you will be treated with some suspicion by my family, for it seems that my mother thinks your wiles have driven me out of my senses."

"Oh, dear," Fern said with a surge of dismay.

"Don't worry. My parents recover quickly from any small trauma. If things appear as they expect them to, they will not question what happened."

Fern nodded, but her mind was elsewhere. She

wondered, for the first time, what her own family would be thinking. She had never imagined that they would consider that she might be anywhere other than in Brighton, but if Colin's parents knew, it was only a matter of time before hers found out. How they would worry . . . "I must send my family a letter. They will be mad with concern."

"You can send it when we fetch the mail tomorrow," Colin said. He finished undressing, emptied the basin into the waste bucket and poured more water from the jug and the kettle, sending up a billow of steam. He scrubbed himself briskly as Fern watched, then rummaged in his trunk for new trousers, a shirt, and his dressing gown. He had just shoved his feet into his slippers when a knock on the door interrupted him.

"Dinner. Finally," Fern said, dragging her eyes away from her husband's body with some effort.

Colin opened the door, but instead of a village woman bearing a dinner tray, Joseph Reston stood in the doorway, his brow lowered in anger as he dripped puddles onto the wide board floor.

Chapter Seventeen

Out of the corner of his eye, Colin saw Fern jerk to her feet, her chair scraping noisily out of the way. He reacted more subtly, shifting his weight to the balls of his feet as he angled his body to simultaneously put himself between the man and Fern and block his entrance.

"Where did you find those letters?" Joseph Reston snarled, his face purpling. "Tell me!"

For an instant, Colin thought the man must mean his correspondence.

"The old letters?" Fern echoed the words. "They were in the bedroom—"

"It is no concern of yours where we found documents belonging to my family," Colin cut in, easily overriding Fern's answer. He narrowed his eyes at the burly man, bracing himself in the doorway. "You have no business here, man. Leave—at once. I do not want you see you again until morning."

But Reston's gaze had grown distant as soon as Fern had said the word *bedroom*. "The bedroom, the bedroom!" he muttered. "Why would the old man have put papers in the bedroom? He kept nothing in bedrooms." Looking dazed, he blinked several times before he focused on Colin again. "Good night," he said roughly, then bolted for the stairs—lumbering up to the third floor rather than down.

"Ought I follow him?" Colin asked himself aloud, staring at the empty landing.

"Please don't," Fern said. "He's gone mad. He's left now—that's all that matters."

With a suppressed snort, Colin shut the door and slid the bar across to secure it. He turned to deliver a retort to his wife, but he was interrupted by sudden heavy footfalls from above. He paused where he stood and stared up at the ceiling—which doubled as the bottom side of the floorboards of the third floor, lying across the thick, blackened rafters above their heads.

The footsteps paused, the silence as loud as any noise. Then came a deep thud that made Fern jump and Colin's heart race with adrenaline, followed by a series of scrapes and thuds.

"He's tearing the room apart," Fern whispered. He looked at her—her eyes were huge, her face unnaturally pale.

Colin lifted his hand to take the bar from across the door. "I will send him away."

Fern shook her head vigorously. "No, please don't. I fear that he has lost his mind. No one could say what he might do, nor do we know whether he is armed."

That idea had not occurred to Colin, and the thought of an armed man in his house so close to his wife caused a hot, angry ball to form deep in his gut. "What do you think he is doing? Searching for more papers?"

Fern looked helpless. "He must be. The man is mad for papers. But none of them are worth anything."

The thuds turned to the sharp sound of tearing cloth. A single feather drifted down through the cracks in the floorboards.

"He's shredding the pillows and the mattress," Fern said, a hand fluttering uneasily over her stomach.

Colin's jaw clenched, his hand straying once more to the door's bar. He couldn't countenance the idea of the man rampaging with impunity through his property. Yet he was stayed again—stayed by Fern's warning and the knowledge that it would be foolish to confront Reston without a weapon, which their bedchamber did not afford him. It didn't even have a set of fireplace tools.

"I should like to have a knife, at the least," he said.

Fern shivered. "So should I. We had best not tell Mr. Reston about the second packet of letters."

Colin snorted. "I had best not tell him I have calling cards. The man is a maniac."

There was a pause in the noise above, and Colin and Fern both froze automatically. The silence was soon broken, however, by a thin, piercing scream, the sound so inhuman at first that it raised the hairs on the back of Colin's neck. Slowly, it descended the register, ending in a snarling growl that sounded like it was half a sob.

"Is that Mr. Reston?" Fern whispered.

"It must be." Colin's eyes were riveted to the ceiling as heavy, trudging footsteps crossed the floor above. He heard the door open, then held his breath as the man started down the stone stairs. Reston's boots crunched on the gritty landing. Colin stared at the planks of the oak door that were all that barred Reston's way, his heart speeding up with a surge of bitter anticipation. Then, after a moment that seemed to stretch into an hour, the footsteps continued, slowly, down the stairs.

Gradually, Colin relaxed, his heart still racing. He realized that he had automatically tensed to spring for the nearest weapon, in case Reston had thrown himself at the door and the old iron bolts securing the bar hadn't held—a bench, its boards darkened with age and smoke. "I must get a knife," he repeated to himself.

Fern took a shaky breath. "The man is a lunatic," she said.

Colin turned toward her. She was pressed into the corner farthest from the door, her arms wrapped tightly around herself. "We are not staying a week," he said flatly. "I will make arrangements tomorrow for us to leave as soon as possible."

"Please don't let the Restons know," Fern said intently. "You can't tell what they might do."

"I don't intend upon it," Colin said crisply.

"Where will we go next?" Fern's voice was small. "After we leave here, I mean."

Colin grimaced. "I don't know. Perhaps we can stay unannounced in my town house for a while." He paused. "Or perhaps we can go to a quiet hotel in one of the more distant social orbits, rather than trying to obtain complete obscurity. Avoiding society is only a secondary concern right now. My primary one is to leave here as soon as possible, before we are murdered in our bed."

Fern shuddered, and Colin instantly regretted the last addition. "Thank you," she breathed. She came out of the corner, moving like a spooked animal, and returned to her chair at the table. "I loathe this place," she said with great feeling.

Colin's eyes strayed back to the door. "It is not the place I am worried about," he said.

Another knock made them both jump.

"Who is it?" Colin called though the barred door.

"It's Abby, m'm, sir," came a light female voice.

Colin lifted the bar and opened the door cautiously. Sure enough, there was Abby, alone with a tray in her arms. He stepped back.

She bustled efficiently inside and set the tray on the table. "That should be everything, m'm," she told Fern. "Even a lamp vor ye. Will ye be needing anything else tonight? My babies and Sterne are waiting vor me at home, and everyone else has already left the manor house."

"No, Abby," Fern said, her voice remarkably steady despite her continuing pallor. "Are you sure you're quite fine? Going home alone, I mean."

"Oh, la, m'm," she said, "I can't see why I wouldn't be. Night's not even vull come yet."

"I mean, with Mr. Reston," Fern said.

Abby shrugged, her cheerful expression unchanging. "Meg said she thought he raised a ghost. She heard the strangest sound, then saw him running down the stairs like his pants were afire. He's back at the village by now, vor sure."

Fern shook her head in a helpless kind of way. "Well enough, then. You may collect the plates in the morning."

"Thank you, m'm," Abby said, and with an awkward, old-fashioned curtsy, she saluted them both and left the room.

"She isn't mad, at least," Fern observed as Colin barred the door again. "At least, not the same kind of mad that Mr. Reston is. Taking ghosts as a matter of course might be another kind of illness."

"Reverend Biggs doesn't seem too mad, either," he pointed out. "It's just those deuced Restons and their relatives."

Fern gave a quick laugh that had only the slightest edge of hysteria. "Perhaps that is why the village is so empty—the Restons have been driving people away for generations." She lifted the lid off the tray and gave a genuine cry of delight. "A crown roast! And fresh rolls. Sit, Colin, for I shan't wait politely tonight."

With a final glance at the door, Colin joined her at the table. Steam rose from the roast, and his stomach growled loudly enough that Fern looked up at the noise and tittered slightly.

"This must have been intended for someone else's table," he said. "There hasn't been enough time to cook it. And there aren't any ovens that I've seen in the kitchens, either."

"It was probably the Restons'," Fern said. "Who else in this village has enough money for a Tuesday roast?"

Colin paused with a forkful of food halfway to his mouth. "You don't suppose they might have poisoned it?" he said.

Fern looked at him and took a defiant bite of a roll. "I wouldn't think so, but at this point, I don't care if they have," she said around the mouthful of food. "I shall at least die after a hearty last meal."

Colin ate the food on his fork. "I can't imagine that they really would, either, but for half a moment . . . well, I think I am just a bit jumpy after Joseph Reston's appearance at our door."

"Understandably so," Fern said, making a moue of distaste.

They lapsed into silence as they ate their dinner. Fern devoured hers with a single-minded concentration that Colin found covertly amusing—though his wife was far from a glutton, he doubted that she'd ever had a meal delayed for so much as the space of two hours before. For that matter, neither had he. The recognizable, appetizing, familiar meal seemed to be a thread of normality connecting them to the rest of the world in the midst of the chaos of the past several days, and it was with reluctance that Colin pushed his plate away.

Fern primly dabbed her mouth with the napkin, then stretched luxuriantly. "I am clean, I am full, and I have a bed that I can use," she said. "I feel almost civilized again."

Colin nodded at the picked-over bones. "It is a good thing you are sated, for we've nothing left to eat."

Fern rose and went over to the basin, her movements more relaxed than Colin had seen in a long time. She began washing her hands. "You have your knife now," she said, pointing a damp hand to the meat knives upon the table. "And I have mine."

He picked them up, casting around for a good place of concealment before sliding them under the mattress. "Now there shall be no awkward questions in the morning when the dishes are cleared away."

"Good idea," Fern said, drying her hands on a towel.

Colin washed his own hands as she stepped aside. Fern watched him from a perch on the edge of the bed, a small thoughtful crease between her brows. After a moment, she laughed.

"What is it?" he asked.

She said, "I have realized that I am now decidedly more frightened by the Restons than I am of you."

He paused in drying his hands. "You are frightened of me—still?"

"Of course," she said flatly. "Though this afternoon . . . not so much."

"Why?" he asked, feeling a slow, unfamiliar stirring of curiosity. And a more familiar sense of satisfaction, though he wasn't sure it was caused by her fear of him or the lessening of it. Perhaps both.

"Because you scare yourself," she said. "I would be a fool not to be frightened of a man who is frightened of himself."

Colin dropped the towel next to the basin. "That is an odd way to choose whom to fear. I doubt Joseph Reston is scared of himself."

Fern's expression was wry. "I did not say that I am not also frightened of raving lunatics."

Colin leaned back against the edge of the table. "Scared." He tried the word out. "You think that I am scared of myself."

She looked awkward then, shrugging and dropping her eyes. "So it seems to me," she said in a small voice.

"I wouldn't say scared," Colin said. "Uncertain, definitely. Perhaps a little angry, as well. Lost? Maybe. I do not think, though, that it even occurred to me to be afraid."

"Then perhaps I am just not very brave," Fern confessed. "I find it hard to face your confusion, as you call it, especially as the outcome of your struggle shall have such drastic ramifications upon every aspect of my life." She looked at him, her gray eyes clear in her soft face. "I have ever been dependent upon others.

My father's house was a gentle tyranny, the yoke so light that I scarcely noticed it, especially as it was one I was born into. I listened to what he, my mother, my governess, and my nurses told me, and I accepted that dependence was to ever be my lot in life. Except a part of me couldn't accept it, couldn't believe it, chafing against a destiny of always being a daughter-sister-wife and no more."

"And then you married me," Colin said, awake to the irony of it.

Fern's expression was troubled. "For the most wrongheaded and deluded of reasons."

"Which were no worse than my own," he reminded her.

"Even so," she said. "I discovered, swiftly, that the life of a wife is much more circumscribed than that of an indulged daughter. I might throw parties, choose charities, pick out flowers and dresses, and even turn your household staff upside down . . . but it is freedom inside the cage of your will. Whatever you allow, I may do. Whatever you do not, I cannot. It is only sane, then, that I fear your desires and your whims and what they might do to my small freedoms."

Colin digested this, feeling his mind turn sideways to understand a world in which such a view made sense. "Fern," he said, and stopped.

"You want the control," she said softly. "I know you must. It is yours by every legal and social right. Why should you relinquish it, even if you could? I know that I shouldn't care to, were I in your place."

Colin looked at his wife, seeing the sinew under the softness, the clarity under her kindness. "There are social requirements that are outside of either one of us," he said.

She sighed. "Yes. You must be a good viscount and I a good viscountess. I am not saying that I do not want to be. I like parties and pretty dresses, babies and charity subscriptions. They are so much a part of my world that I would not know what to do with a life without them. What I am frightened of is . . . stiflement, if that is even a word. I am frightened of swallowing dissatisfaction until it chokes me. I am frightened of not being able to speak—or worse, not being heard."

"I hear you, Fern," he said gravely.

"You begin to hear me now," she agreed. "You did not before, but over the past two days . . . Even before Mr. Reston's rampage, you promised me a week here, no more. But when we leave—will you still hear me then? When you have your solicitor's meetings and your fox hunts and political clubs again, will you still listen?"

Colin thought of his life as it had been before—self-directed, independent. . . . And yet, in a very real sense, it had been none of those things. It had been directed not by a father or a master but by nothing more than social expectations. He had possessed the self-determination that Fern longed for, and he had done nothing with it.

His automatic reaction was to reject what she asked for out of hand, soothing her with meaningless assurances. Yet how much freer would he be if he chose to let her have the voice that she longed for than he had been before, when all of his choices had been made by default? It would a kind of circumscription that he was unaccustomed to, but it would be one taken upon himself consciously, out of care for his wife, rather than one stumbled into by chance. That consciousness would be in itself an exertion of control.

"Is a freedom deliberately not exercised more or less real than one that is never seized?" he mused aloud.

"What?" Fern asked, shaking her head.

"It is a strange thought, that," Colin said. "Particularly for one like me, who is not accustomed to thinking at all. What I mean to say is that I will hear you, Fern. I will not always agree with you, nor will my decision always be the one that best pleases you, but I will hear you. Even if your freedoms are to be defined by my indulgence—by law and custom, as you say—I will still respect them."

Fern sat in silence for a long moment, looking at him. He knew her well enough to know that her placid exterior concealed a tumult of thought as she weighed what he said. Finally, slowly, she nodded, her eyes intent and liquid as they fixed upon his face. She slid to her feet and padded softly across the room toward him. "That is as much as I could dream of in this world. Thank you, Colin." Tentatively she rose to her tiptoes and closed the space between them with a kiss, her lips moving across his with a timidity that stirred him and then, with more confidence, ending in a sharp nip upon his bottom lip, sending a jolt of reaction through his limbs.

She pulled away, looking up at him shyly.

Colin raised a hand to his lip. "I do not need this anymore, Fern," he said. "But I still want it."

She shivered a little, her hooded eyes fixed upon the mark she had made. "So do I."

She reached for the belt of his dressing gown, untying the slick silk, and pushed the fabric off his shoulders. She worked quickly down the buttons of his shirt, as if afraid of thinking about what she was doing, loosening each. Pausing as she saw that he wore no vest beneath, she looked up at him, pressing the cool flat of her hand against the bare flesh of his chest.

"You prepared," she said, her expression conflicted, as if she were not certain whether she was pleased or disturbed. "I had not noticed."

He put his hand on top of hers. "I expected."

"Expected this?" Her tone was skeptical.

"Expected something," he answered. He lifted her hand to his lips and kissed her palm, running his tongue and teeth across her soft flesh. She made a noise deep in her throat, half closing her eyes in pleasure, but after a moment, she shut her fingers and pulled away.

"It is my turn," she insisted.

She finished the last buttons down the front of his shirt and loosened his cuffs, pulling the fabric down over his wrists. He was naked to the waist, and she looked at him consideringly for a moment before lacing her fingers behind his neck and pulling his mouth down to hers.

Her mouth was sweetly gentle under his, her tongue teasing him, her teeth catching at his lips just on the threshold of pain. He had to fight the urge to crush her against him, gripping the edge of the table behind him in both hands. He wanted to pull her into his arms, but even more badly, he wanted to find out what she would do next if he did not.

What she did was slide downward, moving under his jawline and across his neck as her fingers traced delicately, teasingly down the muscles of his back. Her nipples, pressed against him, brushed his chest through the fabric of her dressing gown. Her kisses grew harder, nips turning to bites, and Colin's breath sped up involuntarily. Her shoulders shook, first slightly, then harder, and with a start, Colin realized that she was giggling.

"Now, that is enough," he growled, wrapping his arms around her and using his weight to bear her to the bed.

She went without resistance, collapsing upon the bed as her silent giggles erupted into a burst of laughter. She lay half pinned under him, clutching her sides helplessly as peal after peal seized her. Looking down at her, Colin could not help but chuckle, too, though not a little befuddled at what she found so very funny. Finally, she regained control of herself, though she still gasped for breath, wiping her streaming eyes.

"I hope you intend to let me know how exactly I was so unintentionally hilarious."

"Oh, it was not you," she said, still slightly breathless. "Or rather, it was at first, because I could hardly believe that I was making you . . . well, want me like that. It was so incredible, and I felt so silly that I began to laugh, and once I started, it felt so good. . . ." She shook her head, rocking it back and forth across the counterpane. "I don't think that I have laughed like that or felt like that in years." Her expression turned rueful. "But I suppose I still make a terrible seductress."

"There are certainly worse vices in a wife," Colin said. "But perhaps you should leave the initiation of lovemaking in my hands, at least for now. However satisfying a fit of giggles might be, *mon ange*, it leaves much to be desired for the purpose of beginning an intimate encounter."

"You are quite right," she said, still smiling. "Please, then, exercise your superior abilities and sweep away my better self in the heady surge of your passionate embrace."

Colin snorted. "Your better self?" he asked, looking down at her. Her hair, for once, was not in a state of collapse. That was swiftly rectified, however. Colin's arms were on either side of her, pinning her to the bed, the back of her head even with his hands. He reached under her head and began pulling out her hairpins one by one.

"My better self," she repeated airily. "Every woman is an ethereal spirit, unconcerned by fleshly matters unless dragged down by a degenerate male." She grimaced. "Why are you taking down my hair? This is the first time it's been properly arranged in days."

"Because I am a degenerate male who much prefers the way you look when your hair is fallen like the worst kind of slattern," Colin said firmly.

She laughed, this time without the edge of hysteria, and threaded her fingers behind his neck. "Thank you," she said, her voice scarcely louder than a whisper.

"For what?" Colin asked, pausing in puzzlement.

"For liking it when I look slatternly," she said. "For not shunning my failings."

"Imperfections," Colin corrected. "Imperfections and differences. They are what make you interesting." He kissed the tip of her nose lightly. "They are why I discovered what it is like to be alive."

The words hit Fern in the gut, causing a strange, sideways lurch that she couldn't identify. She started to say something but could think of nothing that would express what she felt—nor was she even entirely sure exactly what it was that she did feel. So instead, she pulled his mouth down to hers and kissed it hard.

Colin kissed her back thoroughly, devastatingly, his mouth moving hard over her own as he unfastened her dressing gown with one hand, holding her head still with the other. At his urging, she sat up, wriggling so that he could pull her dressing gown and nightdress off. His mouth moved to her body, teasing and tasting with increasing insistence. Her hands urged him on, her nails digging into the flesh of his back, which was still faintly marked from their previous two nights together. Unpredictably, his mouth moved across her skin, never letting her body find its rhythm, challenging her with a new touch, a new sensation every time she began to adjust so that her nerves quivered with reaction, raw and discordant.

His lips followed the line of her collarbone down, then moved across to circle the delicate skin of her breasts. Anticipation formed a hard, hot knot in her center, dimming her vision and making her head light as everything became sensation. Her hands tightened on his shoulders, and he took her nipple in his mouth, the sudden damp heat of it sending a coil of need through her frame. She gasped, her hips tilting hard against his stomach, her thighs lifting to clasp him. His tongue rasped across the sensitive tip, once, twice, and she shivered hard, her breath growing raw in her throat. Leaving that breast abruptly, the sudden chill almost as shocking as the heat, he went to the other, rolling her nipple in his teeth as it rose up in a hard nub. Sensation radiated out through her at each movement, curling though her body and leaving it suffused with need. He closed his lips and began to suck, and the sensation gained a new urgency, a new demand.

"Hurry," she urged him hoarsely.

He did not reply but released her, leaving her nerves tingling as he moved across her belly in a way that should have been ticklish but was now anything but. He moved up again, between her breasts and up her throat to her mouth.

"Roll over," he murmured against her lips.

"What?" The dazed word escaped, for she could make no sense of his demand.

"Over," he repeated, putting action to word as he urged her to turn.

Her head swimming, Fern obeyed as he pushed off her to give her room. He grasped her hips and pulled downward, sliding to the edge of the bed until her legs hung off. Breathing the musty counterpane, she fought the confusion and anticipation that rose within her.

"What are you doing?" she asked, feeling his muscled flanks between her legs.

"This," he replied.

His hands on her hips lifted slightly, angling them up off the bed. Before she could respond, she felt the hard tip of his erection pressing against her, entering her and filling up the aching hollow inside. She gasped against the pressure as it pushed against new parts of her, her hands bunching in the covers. He moved, and the novel sensations again took her unawares.

"Good?" The breathless word had a ragged edge of laughter in it.

"Yes," she said, and he thrust again. "Oh, *yes*."

He built up a rhythm then, fast and insistent, driving her to the edge and over in a sharp, blazing climax. Her body burned with it, the surge taking her and pulling her apart. Before the sensation had fully receded, he withdrew and urged her to turn back over, joining her on the bed.

She scarcely registered what he was doing until he entered her, his air-chilled erection sending a shock through her body—already she was on the edge again. She pulled him against her hard as he began moving with slow thoroughness inside of her, kissing and biting him in a near-frantic counterpoint to his slow movements. But he would not be urged to greater speed, and she felt the heaviness build up, higher and higher, inside of her, until it collapsed into a release under its own weight. The sensation was marrow-deep, shaking her soul with every wave, as heavy and inexorable as the sea. Her breath left her as she sank into it, darkness closing over her eyes. It rolled again and again across her, until the only things in the world were herself, those inky depths, and Colin, moving against her.

Gradually, she rose up again, and gradually, she realized that Colin was now lying beside her, his arms still holding her against him. He radiated heat into the shadowed room, and though she was not cold, Fern basked in it.

She did not say anything. Nothing needed to be said.

Chapter Eighteen

Colin woke to darkness and the sense that there had been a noise. He tensed as a flood of memories of his abrupt awakening the night before shot through him, but the noise came again—muffled, and from the blankets beside him.

He rolled over. The coals from the fireplace cast just enough light for him to be able to make out Fern's face, creased in a troubled frown. He kissed her forehead, pulling her toward him. Her frown deepened and she shook her head, but then her body changed subtly to wakeful tension, and she opened her eyes, blinking blearily.

"It's you," she said, and her frown cleared instantly, replaced with such relaxation that it jerked something inside him.

"Always," he said, not even sure himself what that meant, yet meaning it completely.

She snuggled against him, and he stared into the darkness for a long time after she had slipped back into sleep.

* * *

A knock on the door roused Colin. Dull gray daylight seeped in the window overlooking the bog. He was about to call for whomever it was to enter when he remembered that the door was still barred, and that recollection brought back the whole of what had happened the night before—Reston's fit as well as the long, entirely satisfying night that followed.

Fern did not stir, her face as still and smooth as porcelain. He swung his legs out of bed as the knock repeated, slightly louder. He cast around for some clothing and found a fresh pair of drawers and his sporting trousers and got them on and loosely fastened, reaching the door as the third knock patiently came.

He lifted the bar and cracked the door cautiously, his shoulder braced to block any precipitous entry. Abby stood there, a bucket and kettle hooked over one arm and the other raised to knock again.

"Come in," Colin said softly, opening the door to allow her admittance. "Mrs. Radcliffe is still asleep."

"No," came a groggy voice from the blankets. "I am awake, Colin, but thank you."

"Where is my valet?" Colin asked as he retrieved a clean vest and pulled it on, buttoning a fresh shirt over it.

Abby placed the bucket beside the basin, pouring the fresh, steaming water into the ewer and pouring the used water into the bucket. "Old Jim's below in the kitchens still, sir," she said. "His gimpy leg's bothering him today, so he's working out the kinks over a pot of tea before trying the stairs." She began to gather up the dirty dishes from the night before.

Colin was not glad that the man was in pain, but he couldn't help but feel a certain gratitude for the fact that he wouldn't have to face the man—and his razor—first thing upon waking.

Fern sat up with a suppressed groan, holding the blankets over her body with one hand. Though Abby had taken in his bare chest with equanimity, she now blushed and rattled the dishes a little louder. Fern caught her reaction and reddened as well. Colin supposed that Abby had assumed that he had been caught in the middle of dressing, while Fern's nakedness left no doubt about what their states had been before the maid had knocked on the door.

To spare them both, Colin found Fern's nightdress and tossed it to her. With a look of gratefulness, Fern pulled it on over her head before dropping the covers and slipping out of bed. She picked her dressing gown up from its pile of froth on the floor and pulled it on, primly fastening the buttons as her blush subsided to mere pinkness.

"What is for breakfast, Abby?" she asked, studiously ignoring all reference to her appearance when the maid arrived.

"Toast, eggs, rashers, ham, and tea, m'm," Abby said, seeming glad for the omission. "It shall be ready any moment. I'll go check on it now, shall I? And then bring up some more peat vor the fire." With that, she took the slop bucket and the dishes and ducked out of the room.

"I am afraid you embarrassed her," Colin said.

"I embarrassed myself," Fern returned, making a face. "And your chest . . . I hope she thought you fell through a thicket!"

"I think that she very carefully failed to look at it," Colin said. He tucked in his shirt and fastened his trousers all the way. "I don't think I care for old Jim's help today. I'd much rather shave myself."

Fern shuddered. "I cannot find fault with that sentiment. You have a stronger nerve than I to have borne it the first time."

Colin didn't answer, shrugging on a tweed waistcoat to match his trousers and fastening the top button.

"Are we being rustic today?" Fern asked.

"I doubt we will succeed at looking refined," Colin countered. He paused, remembering the knives under the mattress, and slipped a hand beneath, sliding the length of steel into his coat pocket.

Fern's expression turned shy. "Will you help me dress? I know that Abby is here now, but . . . "

An involuntary reaction stirred at her request. "I prefer to undress you, but given the choice of putting your clothes on or allowing someone else to do it, I will help you gladly."

She colored slightly again. "I am glad."

By the time Abby returned with breakfast, both Colin and Fern were washed and fully clothed. Their conversation was subdued over their meal in the presence of the maid, full of allusions and significant looks. When Abby finally finished dressing Fern's hair and left, Colin said, "I plan to watch Reston work today— and to arrange for a coach to come as soon as possible to pick us up."

"I cannot wait to leave," Fern said. She put her hand on her pocket. "I have the letters here for safekeeping." Her face grew troubled. "I never wrote my family last night. I need to do so this morning, to get the letters out in today's post."

"I shall have an eye on Reston, so you shall be safe

enough going to the vicarage alone," Colin said. "I'll
leave you to your writing. I doubt you want a husband
hanging over your shoulder."

"You wouldn't be a bother," Fern said, but Colin
could tell that she was glad enough to have some privacy for the task.

"I shall see you before luncheon?" he said.

"Certainly," Fern said, then amended, "If Reverend
Biggs does not end up keeping me for a long tea."

Colin bent down and kissed his wife softly on the
lips. "Until then, *mon ange.*"

Then he left the room with a feeling, despite everything, that was bordering on cheer.

Colin edged carefully down the long staircase and
then passed though the kitchens, which echoed with
the activity of washing up from breakfast. Reston and
his crew of village men were already at work in the
Tudor wing. Colin could hear them as he reached the
first floor. A glance down the corridor revealed that
more of the ceiling had given way in one of the two
rains, half a dozen timbers now protruding through
the stained plaster. He frowned, wondering how much
more rot was concealed in the walls.

At the top of the attic stairs, he emerged into daylight. The collapsed rafters, with the heavy slate roof
now mostly pulled off, looked like tangled ribs against
the gray sky, the freshening wind blowing through
them. Reston stood braced on two of the timbers,
shouting orders down to the men below. To Colin, he
looked haggard, with blotchy purple circles under his
eyes and a sallow cast to his skin.

When he saw Colin, he stretched his mouth in an
expression that was more of a grimace than a smile.

"Good morning, sir," he said.

"Good morning," Colin returned coolly.

"Have care of the vloor up here—it's none too solid. Charlie already vell through and broke his wrist. He a-went home." The man continued to show far too many teeth.

Colin simply grunted, leaning against the corner of the wall for the stairs. He wasn't exactly sure what he had been anticipating with Reston—wild-eyed mania, perhaps, with a full-scale looting of the Tudor wing. Whatever it was, it certainly wasn't this. However surly, the man appeared in full charge of his reasoning faculties, such as they were. Then again, there was also notably little paper in the attic to set him off.

Colin resigned himself to a dull morning of watching the men work. After a few minutes, he let his gaze wander out over the moor and bog to the horizon, where darker clouds were massing, and down to the village. A spot of violet caught his attention among the grays and greens of the fens, and he watched as Fern came around the corner of the building with an umbrella hooked over her arm and a bonnet perched upon her hair. Colin had the sudden foolish urge to call down to her, but he suppressed it, watching instead as those swaying violet skirts slowly traversed the distance to the church, disappearing around its side as she went back to the vicarage.

With a grimace, he returned his attention to the work of Reston's crew.

It had taken Fern no small amount of effort to devise something appropriate to write to her parents. Faith's letter had taken a mere matter of moments—it would not occur to her sister to question the motives behind any action one's husband took. But Fern's parents and most especially her sister Flora were less blindly trusting. They would fear the worst, and the strangeness of Colin's sudden retirement could not be hidden from them. But Fern did her best, explaining that the social pressures of Brighton had proved excessive for her and that Colin had therefore decided to move to a "country retreat." It was a retreat, indeed, in the sense of fleeing Brighton—Fern hoped that the word would also carry the implication of a sanctuary, as well, without her explicitly stating such a falsehood. She carefully refrained from telling her parents not to worry, for that was the surest way to convince them that there might be something worth being concerned about.

She had slipped the letters into her pocket next to the packet of antique documents and had taken an umbrella—as the sky was ominous out over the distant tors—and strolled around the manor house and down the road toward the village.

The vicarage looked almost welcoming, which was, Fern decided, more of an indictment of the manor house than a virtue of the comfort of Rev. Biggs' home. She knocked, and this time, a scowling Mrs. Willis answered, her sleeves rolled up and dark smears of blacking across her apron.

"It ain't time vor tea," she said ungraciously, opening the door just wide enough for Fern to pass through.

Fern suppressed a surge of irritation as she edged inside. She was growing tired of these Reston relations, all of them. "Please show me to Reverend

Biggs," she said, not deigning to argue with the house-keeper.

The woman sniffed and closed the door. Her wide hips all but brushed against the wall and staircase as the two of them passed down the narrow corridor on their way to the back of the house.

Rev. Biggs was in his tiny study again, the remains of his breakfast sitting at his elbow and his shabby slippers propped upon his ottoman as he perused a journal by the light of the narrow window. He looked up as Fern entered, unannounced by Mrs. Willis, who disappeared into the kitchen. Fern sat quickly before he could do more than swing his legs down in preparation for trying to rise.

"My dear Mrs. Radcliffe!" the old man said in his curiously sonorous voice as he settled back in his chair. "What a pleasure to see you again."

"The pleasure is mine," Fern said, smiling with genuine warmth. "It is so nice to see a friendly face and to have a pleasant conversation in Wrexmere."

Rev. Biggs chuckled, blinking owlishly at her. "You have had a dose of the Restons, I understand?"

Fern made a noncommittal sound, embarrassed at being so transparent, and the vicar chuckled again.

"After our last conversation, I looked through some documents that I have here—my predecessor was quite mad for the village's history and wrote a number of monographs for the shire's historical society and even had two hundred copies of a book about it printed up, for one pound apiece." He looked wry. "There are still one hundred seventy-four in the attic—I counted when I first arrived, and have since sold three. Anyhow, he goes into quite a bit of detail about the time period surrounding the unification of the Radcliffes and the Gorsings."

Fern had heard quite enough of Radcliffes, Gorsings, and Restons, but there was no polite way to tell the vicar, nor would it repay his kindness in searching out the information for her to let him know that she simply no longer cared. So instead, she put on an interested expression and said, "Oh?"

"Yes," the old man continued. "There are a swirl of rumors surrounding that time. John Radcliffe was known in the village to be quite a monster. He was married to his wife for eleven years, and after two miscarriages, she never showed another sign of being with child until after he was dead. It was said that he beat her almost nightly, and he had two bastards by his cook, Jane Reston." The man paused, looking chagrined. "I forget that young ladies are more delicate these days than in my youth. I do apologize if I have offended your sensibilities—"

"Nonsense," Fern said firmly, hiding her slight shock at his bluntness. "Please, go ahead."

Rev. Biggs settled back in his chair, looking up at the ceiling as if reading it. "Anyhow, John Radcliffe flaunted these natural children of his to shame his wife, and it is said that she had already gone a little odd in the head by his death. His death, of course, is the most interesting thing of all. It seems that he fell—"

"I know," Fern said hurriedly.

"Well, it was said that he was drunk and was making a visit to Jane Reston's room in the kitchens when it happened. But the most interesting thing was not that he . . . died," the vicar said delicately, "but the circumstances surrounding it. Sir Thomas Fitzhugh was visiting then, to woo the middle daughter, Lettice. It had become evident—or so everyone thought—that Charlotte would produce no heir, and so any child borne by Lettice would have become the next master or mistress of Wrexmere. But John Radcliffe had refused to allow either Lettice or the youngest daughter, Elizabeth, to wed, perhaps determined that if a child of his did not inherit the estate, no one else would, either. And yet he let Sir Thomas visit, and when the baronet left one week later, Radcliffe was dead and Sir Thomas was betrothed to the youngest daughter, Elizabeth, rather than Lettice."

Fern shuddered, and the weight of the bundled documents in her pocket seemed to grow heavier. "Do you think Sir Thomas killed him?" she asked.

Rev. Biggs gazed at her through the heavy lenses of his reading glasses. "No one knows. Some say that it was Sir Thomas. Others claim that Charlotte Gorsing did it in a fit of madness. And still others claim that Jane Reston killed him, for she was the only other one inside the house when it happened besides John Radcliffe, the Gorsings, and Sir Thomas. Though the whole village knew she cleaned the floor and laid out the body as the stable hand went to get the vicar, she never said anything about what she had seen that night."

"But why would she kill him?" Fern asked.

Rev. Briggs hesitated. "John Radcliffe was a very harsh man. She might have become his mistress, but before she bore his children, she had been 'walking out,' as they say, with a very decent farmer's son."

Fern took in everything that meant. "How horrible," she said softly.

The vicar nodded. "Unfortunately, there is little of

Charlotte Gorsing's period as mistress of Wrexmere that is not horrible." He lapsed into a contemplative silence, and Fern, determined to change the subject to less dire matters, cleared her throat.

"I brought two letters to mail," she said, pulling them out of her pocket.

"Did you now?" The vicar extended a hand, took them, and put them on a clear spot beside the table. "I will have Mrs. Willis add them to the mailbag. Which reminds me. I also have two letters for you." He lifted the breakfast tray slightly, slid a hand beneath the edge, and emerged with two letters that were rather worse for the wear, their pages rumpled and wax seals cracked. "They came this morning. I am afraid that yours shall not be able to be sent off until tomorrow."

"That is fine," Fern said absently, distracted by her own name—*The Hon. Mrs. Colin Radcliffe*—prominently displayed on one of the envelopes in her sister Faith's large but delicate hand. Her stomach sank. If Faith already knew where she was, then so did her parents, and they would all be wild that she had not told them what was happening. The second letter, in even worse shape than Faith's, was addressed to Colin, at least. She put them both in her pocket.

She smiled at the old man and mentioned a butterfly that she had seen on the way to the vicarage, and that peaceful subject occupied them for quite a while, leading naturally from the realm of insects to other fauna and flora of the moor and bog and the dangers to be found therein for the unwary. Finally, Fern bade Rev. Biggs good-bye and rose from her chair, assuring the man she was quite capable of showing herself out and that there was no need for him to rise or to summon Mrs. Willis.

She stepped out of the vicarage into a dull gray drizzle. She raised her umbrella under the scant protection of the eaves. She started down the overgrown walk toward the lane, casting an uneasy glance at the sky. The ceiling of clouds above had darkened to slate, the brisk wind driving the rain to wet her skirts. The umbrella bucked and tossed a little in her hand, and she tightened her grip on it as she began to walk up the lane toward the drive to the manor.

An unexpected movement among the cottages caught her eye, and she paused. It came again—the flutter of a skirt in the wind halfway behind one of the little huts, just visible behind the bulk of the small outbuilding. Before Fern could move on, the woman changed position, revealing the broad face of Abby, wearing a man's mackintosh open down the front and holding her apron up as if she was supporting something inside.

"Hullo, Mrs. Radcliffe!" she called, her sturdy boots squelching along a damp track as she came out to the road.

"Good morning, Abby," Fern said, glad that it was her that she was meeting.

"Why, 'tis almost afternoon now," Abby said. "Dorcas Reston said she'd buy some eggs off me vor her tea, as she used all hers vor your breakfast, and bless me if my hens hadn't lain six." She nodded to her apron, where the eggs nestled against one another. "My big hen's gone broody, but I'm leaving her—I've got a rooster, and I could use a few more chicks."

"That will be nice," Fern said, realizing that she

knew nothing about the raising of chickens. She continued up the lane, Abby at her side.

The woman nodded vehemently. "It will, indeed, m'm. I could do with some fat fryers, a few broilers."

"It sounds lovely," Fern said. She wished they could talk about butterflies—she now felt quite capable of holding a halfway intelligent conversation upon that subject.

"I suppose you don't have much use for chickens, m'm," Abby said with surprising insight.

"Oh, I have a use for them," Fern said. "I quite like them on my dinner plate, and I do enjoy a good egg for breakfast. It's only that I don't know much about them in the time before they arrive at my table except that they scratch and flutter about the garden and the cocks can make quite a racket when they care to."

Abby laughed. "I'd like to know so little, m'm!" They walked side by side in silence for a moment, and then Abby said, "Has Dorcas Reston asked ye about they papers today?"

Fern stopped, and after taking another uncertain step, so did Abby. "Papers!" she said, with rather more heat than she intended. "I am sick to death of papers."

Abby looked confused. "M'm?"

Fern paused for a moment, deciding what to tell the maid. "Joseph Reston came to our room last night before you brought dinner, going on unintelligibly about papers, and then he ran upstairs and tore apart the bedroom above us. He gave me quite a fright," she added, knowing she sounded defensive.

Abby nodded sagely. "That must've been after him and his woman had their spat and before Meg thought he woke the spirit."

"A spat about papers?" Fern said, without much hope.

"About *they* papers, m'm," Abby corrected. "It seems Dorcas Reston found some papers on the table in the bedroom ye was virst in rooms before me and Sal cleaned it, and she was real hot about it. I heard her scolding in the kitchen. She and Joseph Reston were behind a big pillar, so I couldn't see them, but I sure could hear them clear enough. She told her man that she thought he had them papers safe. He says he does, but she says, 'What's this, then?' He says they must be some other papers, but she says that they were just the papers that they should have had and starts calling him all sorts of names because he can't read, which ain't vair because hardly none of us can read here. And then he gets real mad and says, 'Which ones is it, then?' and she says that they're all it, but there has to be more because the most important ones aren't there." Abby paused, taking a breath. "So, did she ask ye about they papers yet?"

"No," Fern said, feeling the hairs rise on the back of her neck. The new bundle of letters in her pocket felt like a lead weight.

"Well, there is no doubt in my mind that she will," Abby said. She looked at the cottage with the green door, its walk only a few paces down the lane. "This is where I stop, m'm. All the men went home when the rain started—they've finished stacking up all the slate and taking the broken plaster down, and it's too slick up there for them to be trying to set any new beams. Annie Weaver made your lunch and left it on the edge of the hearth, since there ain't no hob. If ye want me to come up and serve it—"

"No, that won't be necessary," Fern said, wanting

nothing more at that moment than to find some private place to get rid of the package hidden in her skirts.

"Well, then, I'll come before dinner, m'm," Abby said, and with a little bobble of a curtsy, she headed toward the shiny green door.

Chapter Nineteen

Fern walked past quickly, wanting to put as much distance as possible between her and the Restons' house. Her mind teemed. If his wife wasn't merely slinging insults, then Joseph Reston could not read. Perhaps he was not as mad as she had thought. Perhaps he didn't care about all papers, but he couldn't tell the difference between the ones that were important and the ones that were not. He had a hut full of papers he could not read, but what he wanted hadn't been there at all. . . .

Wrexmere Manor loomed above her, and for once, Fern was glad of its gray bulk. She circled around to the pump yard and entered through the kitchen door, shaking out her umbrella and leaving it leaning against the door frame just inside.

The kitchen was empty and silent, Fern's footsteps echoing in the dim stillness as she crossed to the stairs. Blocking the memory of the scrawled messages in the cell nearby, she climbed the steps, then walked across the length of the great hall to climb the second flight that rose so dizzyingly from the stone floor. In her mind's eye, she saw the shadowy, brutish figure of a man teetering at the top of the staircase—and then was pushed?—before falling to the ugly stain on the flags below. She shuddered and pressed tighter against the wall.

She opened the door to the bedroom she shared with Colin with a surge of relief—but her burst of words died unsaid on her lips, for the room was empty. Fern stared at the bare table for a moment, her mind blank. She had planned to explain everything to Colin, and that, somehow, would have made everything safe again. Where could he be? Slowly, she sat down staring at the sullen coals of the fire.

What, exactly, had she expected him to do? she asked herself sternly. Wave a wand and whisk all their troubles away? He had already promised to send for a coach. In fact, there was every likelihood that was what he was doing right then—since Joseph Reston and the workmen had left for the village, why would he stay? There was nothing else, feasibly, that might be done.

With no other occupation at hand, Fern pulled out the contents of her pocket and set them upon the table. Faith's letter lay on top—she had almost forgotten it with the news that Abby had brought. With a feeling of gratefulness for the mundanity of the scolding she knew was enclosed within, she opened it. Five pages fell out, and Fern scanned them quickly, picking out the single paragraph's worth of content among the flood of words. Young James was teething. Sophia had scraped her knee and said a word very unsuited to a little girl that was eventually traced back to a gardener, who was threatened with dismissal but ultimately spared. Fern had been horribly unthoughtful and remiss in not telling her family where she and her husband intended to go, worrying them all terribly and causing a huge fuss until they had heard through Mrs. Christopher Radcliffe that the newlyweds had gone to one of the Radcliffe estates. And so on.

Fern dropped the letter on the table, then moved the one addressed to Colin on top of it. As she set it down, the broken seal gave way entirely, and the letter sprang open, revealing a single page. Fern had already picked up the antique bundle of documents and was deciding whether she should read them, put them back in her pocket, or throw them directly into the fire when the very last line of Colin's letter caught her eye:

Votre Ange.

Your Angel. Fern's lungs clenched. She could see Colin smiling at her, his chilly eyes thawed with warmth as he kissed her good-bye. *Until then, mon ange,* he had said. *Mon ange, mon ange.* Every time he had called her that lit up like a small, separate fire in her brain. After the dances that had left her breathless when he was courting her, at his proposal of marriage, during every intimate moment that they had ever shared since.

Mon ange. Votre ange.

Her stomach churning with dread, she pulled the letter toward her slowly, almost involuntarily, her eyes dragging across the page.

C—

I know I swore I would not resume our contact for some months after your m. to F.A., but only the most desperate straits has driven me to this. There is no easy way to write this, so I will state it bluntly: My worst fears have been confirmed. I had not wanted to worry you, but I am with child, and A. knows and has cast me out—"until I am rid of the brat," he says. I still would not have troubled you, as this burden is my own, except he has cut me off completely, even maneuvering my allowance out of my reach unless I take legal action, which would be sure to ruin even me, forever. All I ask is a small sum for support until I am delivered of the child, and another to pay a good family in Naples, or perhaps some little town in Provence to take it. Send the money through my maid—she will know where I am.

I wish I had some other way to communicate with you than a letter, for I fear the dangers of writing even this much.

    Yrs,

       Votre Ange

And that was all.

Fern stared at it for a long moment as her brain teemed with contradictory reactions, trying to make it say other than that which she feared—that which she knew it said. She imagined Colin smiling at another woman, making love to her, calling her *mon ange*. . . . Her mind shut down, and she clenched her arms around her stomach.

The door opened. Fern looked up. Colin stood there, looking painfully handsome, his hair windblown and damp.

"You're back, I see," Colin said, stripping off his hat and gloves and tossing them on the table. "I hope you're dry. I followed Reston's men down to the village and paid a boy half a guinea to walk to the next— larger—village through this mess to arrange for a post chaise so that we do not have to take the mail coach. There isn't a single horse in this hamlet, it seems."

Fern stood, her heart tight in her chest, and extended the letter to him. "This came," she said, the words scraping her throat raw. "The seal was broken. I saw the signature."

Colin scanned it rapidly, the color draining from his face before returning in an angry flush. "You read my mail?" he demanded.

"I saw the signature," she repeated quietly. Each word felt like a separate cut. "*Votre ange*, Colin. It is from your angel."

His fist bunched around the paper, crumpling it. He tossed it into the fire with an oath. The flames flared up, devouring it. "What do you want me to say, Fern? Even you must have known that you were not the first."

"I never thought of it," Fern said. "I am a stupid, ignorant girl who never even thought of it. That is what you wanted, wasn't it? And that is what you married." She laughed, the ragged edge of the sound catching in a half sob. "I know nothing at all. I don't know how to arrange my hair or raise chickens or cook a meal or clean a room. I don't know anything that I haven't been told, but the world is full of things no one ever wanted me to know. I can accept that you have had other women before me, Colin. If I had possessed the kind of experience that would even make me question it, I would have assumed that you had."

"What is the problem, then?" he said, the words crackling with ice.

"She swore not to contact you for a few months, Colin," Fern said simply. "I had no expectations of having been your first, but I would have hoped that I would have been your last. I may be ignorant, but I can count as well as any woman, and even I know how long it takes from the time that a woman is with child to the time that she knows for certain and someone might notice. You were making love to this woman even as you were courting me, and you were making plans to see her again after our marriage. A few months, Colin. Was that as long as your word was good for?"

His face darkened even more. "A few months? No. When I left my mistress' bed on the morning of our marriage"—he raised his voice over Fern's gasp—"I had every intention of returning to it as soon as our honeymoon was over. It was her idea that my fidelity should last so long, not mine. And if she had not wanted to see me again, she was replaceable enough."

The ugly words seemed chosen to hurt the most. Fern couldn't listen to this—not for a moment longer. She already felt the tears coming, and she would not, could not cry in front of him. She pushed from the table blindly and stumbled past him for the door. He grabbed her arm and pulled her to him.

"*Listen* to me, Fern," Colin said intently. "I confess this because it is what I planned when we were married. It is not what I plan now. It is not who I am anymore."

"Who are you, then?" Fern cried. "Why have you changed? Because . . ." She searched for a vulgarity and realized that she knew none to describe what she wanted. She said viciously, "Because sticking your thing in me is more exciting than sticking it between someone else's legs?"

"No, Fern," he said, gripping her more tightly. "Listen to me, *mon ange*—"

"*Don't call me that!*" Fern's shout sliced through his speech, her entire being rejecting the endearment. She jerked away—tried to jerk away, but his hand on her arm was too strong. "Don't you ever call me that again." A ringing silence followed her outburst until she spoke again. "I am not your *ange*. I am not another one of your . . . your whores."

"I am sorry," he said simply, so quietly that she stopped trying to pull away from him and just stood there. "I am sorry for what I was. I am sorry for not considering that it might hurt you—for not considering that you might have the capacity for being hurt. What I discovered, yes, in some ways, I did discover it between your legs, as you so eloquently put it, Fern. But that was only the beginning. You brought me to life, however unintentionally, and I am different now. You are different," he added. "You knew what I was when you married me—"

"How could I have known?" Fern interrupted. "I knew nothing! I might as well have been a cage-raised songbird, thrown into the woods. I knew what I was meant to know, and I was not raised to have thought to have questioned it."

"You knew enough," Colin said, his eyes glittering like ice. "You knew that I was cold. You knew I was empty."

"I did not know what it meant," she whispered, unable to accept what he proposed.

"But you knew," he repeated. "I have changed, Fern. Know it and be glad."

She shook her head. "In less than five days?"

"Sometimes a lifetime isn't enough. Sometimes five days is plenty," he returned.

Fern looked into his eyes and saw behind the chilly glitter . . . *him*, looking back out at her, earnest and true. She closed her eyes, feeling the tears slide past.

"And what of your natural child? And whatever other natural children you have left in your wake?"

"As far as I know, this is my first," Colin said evenly. "As for what is to be done with it, I will leave that up to you. In any case, I will send my mistress—my former mistress—the funds that she needs. Then you may tell me what you want done, whether the babe should be left in Naples . . . or something else."

Fern nodded, swallowing around the hardness in her throat. "Please. Let me go. I need to think. I need to be alone for a while."

Colin released her, stepping back. "Do not leave the keep," he said, "and I will let you be for a time."

She nodded. Scarcely seeing him, she pushed to the door and stumbled down the perilous staircase. She had to think. She had to cry—she was already crying now, silent tears turning into racking sobs that made her stomach clench and her body shake. Where could she go? She rejected the cold, empty great hall and sought out the stairs to the kitchens.

She cast around the vaulted dimness, but she already knew where the only private places were—the stone rooms by the stairs. She kept her eyes averted from the second one as she approached the first and opened the door. Within was the bed box, still full of ancient straw. Shunning the bed, she slid down the corner opposite and gave herself over to her tears, her mind spinning faster the harder she wept.

She hated herself for crying—twice in as many days! She couldn't remember the last time she had cried so much. She couldn't remember the last time that she had cried at all. It had been years, surely, since she'd had anything to cry about. That she'd had anything she cared so much about to cry over . . .

She bit her lip against a wracking sob. Her soul hurt. That was the only way she could think of to describe the pain that seared through her, deeper than bone, piercing her very essence. She felt betrayed, and yet she knew that, rationally, she had no right to feel that way, as she had possessed only the faintest sense of affection, scarcely returned, when she and Colin had made the decision to be joined together for life.

Yet it still hurt the same, stinging her pride, of course, but far more than that, making her doubt the meaning of what she and Colin had shared. How could it mean anything when he gave it away so easily? How could it be more than a momentary delusion when he had given all this before, to someone else, and it had meant nothing? Yet the night before had felt so real. . . .

Why couldn't she have continued through life as blithely as she had been when she agreed to marry him, untouched by any emotion deeper than a faint unease and a callow fluttering of desire? She'd forgo the dizzying euphoria of their nights in an instant if only she could be rid of this, too.

But that wasn't true, and the realization only made her cry harder—out of anger with herself and frustration with the entire mad world. That was the crux of it. The very attachment that brought a new kind of joy into her life also made her vulnerable to a new grief.

Mon ange. The hateful words reverberated through her head. He had changed, he said. He was a new man. And yet still he said *mon ange.*

How much had she changed, then? She felt as if the scales had fallen away from her eyes during these past few days, and yet a child blind from birth did not know what sunlight was like, so how could she know what she saw?

And how much could a man, however fundamentally altered, change the habits of a lifetime in the space of five days? She felt like a new person, a very different person, and yet she still could not keep chickens or arrange her hair. Perhaps changes, however true, took some time to work their full effects.

Mon ange, mon ange, that ever hateful *mon ange*! When the moment came, she could not tell him how much those words alone had hurt her. She had spoken the truth about his planned infidelity (Who was A? Alexander, Andrew, Alphonse, Albert, Arthur?), but she had not been able to spit out the heart of the matter, scared that she could not say words that would make her feelings seem other than trivialities and even more terrified of the answer if she could.

Why? That word bundled up all her pain and anger into a single neat package. Why her, why Colin, why his mistress, why everything? Why couldn't she decide to hate him or forgive him and be done with it? Why couldn't she decide the same about herself and her own weakness—like a climbing rose, her mother always said. But when the trellis bends, the rose falls, and she was revolted to see herself droop so helplessly at the actions of another.

Did she even have the right to be hurt, the privilege to forgive? She had known nothing about marriage a week ago—and nothing about this pain in her lungs and her gut that was now tearing her asunder. She had not understood what unfaithfulness even meant, much less had any idea that she might choose a husband to be true.

She bit her knuckles hard and brought her sobs

slowly under control, but her mind would not still, running ever more frantically in the same circles, over and endlessly over again. The bastard—what was she to do with it? Colin had left it up to her, but she wasn't sure whether it was out of consideration or cowardice. Didn't he care? She honestly didn't know.

She knew that a good wife—a perfect wife—would welcome the child into her house with open arms, treating it no differently from one of her own flesh. But she wasn't a good wife. She was rebellious and, yes, selfish, and she didn't know that she could look at the child and not feel a stab of bitterness toward both it and her husband. And worse, she knew that everyone else would know that the child was a Radcliffe bastard, and behind her back, there would be whispers about whether it was Colin's, Peter's, or Alexander's. Even she had known what an infant "poor relation" usually meant. It was pride, pure and simple, that rose like bile in her throat at that thought, and the discovery of it in her disgusted her almost as much as the fear of idle speculation filled her with dread.

The sins of the father were not the child's, and the babe deserved a house where it would be loved. She just didn't know whether she would be capable of that, whether she could become reconciled to her husband's old choices.

Yet . . . how horrible could it be? Fern took a shuddering breath. The child would be no Jane Reston's get, to be flaunted in front of her to shame her with her failings and her husband's infidelity. That thought stopped Fern cold, shocking her into considering a comparison.

Charlotte Radcliffe's husband had conducted a flagrant affair after his marriage in order to humiliate his wife. Colin . . . even the Colin she had first married was not that kind of man. He had not been vicious, merely absent. Indifferent, rather than unkind. That would be little consolation except that he had lost his indifference. Even at his most distant, she was certain he now cared. Did that mean that he would never stray again? She didn't know the answer to that—she did not know him well enough, still, and she wasn't even sure that he had been himself long enough to truly know himself, either. But she was certain that he would never do it to hurt her, for he was not a vindictive man. That was something. But was it enough? Could she have the faith to trust him—trust them— that they could make this marriage work between them, without destroying either one of them?

Fern found herself drawn, almost inexorably, toward the letters she still carried in her pocket and the specter of the disastrous marriage whose darkest secrets might be contained within. She pulled them out, examining the packet again. It was thinner and lighter than the other one, and the faded blue ribbon disintegrated at her tug. The letters spilled across her skirts. As she was gathering them up again, two words, scrawled in large letters in the middle of one page, caught her eye: *The Truth.*

She finished gathering the rest of the letters and slid them back into her pocket again, then picked up that one. In the light coming in through the doorway, still sniffing slightly from her fit of weeping, she unfolded the stiff, brittle sheepskin and began to read.

> . . . *for know I well The Truth of what happen'd the night of thy predecessor's death—I do not yet call him thy* <u>*pater*</u>*, knowing this—and the events that after-*

ward occurred. *Thou must knowest, too, now that thy cousin's heir has met such an untimely end and thou art but one man from the barony. For this is thy secret more than mine, to hide in thy bosom, and the bosom of thy son, and thy son's son forever more.*

'Twas in the dark of night that I heard Master Radcliffe open the door of his *chambre*, just below mine, and wishing to have privy conversation with Sir Thomas, I silent descended with the expectation of being his shadow and thus escaping detection whilst ensuring the greatest time for my dialogue with our guest. Master Radcliffe paused, as was his wont, upon the verge of descending to hurl vile oaths at my dear sister through the closed door, and above him, I paused, too. He began his descent, and I was upon the moment of following when the door to his chambers open'd again and a pallid figure emerged.

Before I could decide to retreat or call out, it glided down the stairs after Master Radcliffe, its movements so unearthly that my blood ran cold. I pursued, and just as I came into sight of Master Radcliffe, with the figure behind, I saw the ghostly shape reach out a wraithish hand—and push him from the stair! He bellowed like a bull, and for an instant I thought he had caught himself and bethought myself to flee his certain wrath, but he tottered like a nursling on leading strings, and fell—down to the floor, where his brains were instantly dashed out upon the stone. I gasped, and the figure turned, and I saw that it was mine own sister. Not yet Charlotte but Lettice, who had slid from her innermost bedchamber thru his after him in order to wright his demise. She wore nothing but her shift and her hair wild about her head, and in that thin garment I could see the swell of her belly.

"He would like to have killed me," was all she said. And I kept my tongue because I knew that it was true enough that he would kill all three of us rather than see a child not of his own flesh inherit Wrexmere— And also because I knew that, round with the stable hand's child, Lettice would not interfere with my designs to marry to Sir Thomas. I left within the week, and four months later, thou camest into the world and wert given into the hands of Charlotte and christened with the false name of Radcliffe.

Thou art no Radcliffe, my dear John. Thou art the brat of a loose woman and a stable hand, begotten in the filth of the barn, and the Restons shall forget it no more than I. I, though, am thy friend and kinswoman, ever eager to protect—

"What are ye doing?"

The rough question sliced through Elizabeth Gorsing's poisonous words.

Fern looked up, startled, her heart hammering at the sight of Joseph Reston standing in the doorway. The man scowled down at her, his eyes narrowed with suspicion. In her absorption, she had not even noticed his occlusion of the light from the kitchens, but now she was preternaturally aware of how much of his bulk filled the doorway.

"I am reading a letter from my sister," she heard her lips say, and she folded the correspondence calmly and pushed it into her pocket even as her heart began to race. *The secret of the papers—I know it now,* she thought. The second John had been a sham Radcliffe, and so his heirs' claim to the Radcliffe title was illegitimate. *Colin's* claim to the title was illegitimate. It was a hoax two and a half centuries old.

Joseph Reston was still glowering down at her. This was her chance to get back at Colin, if she chose, she realized suddenly. She could hand the letters over to Joseph Reston and give him the leverage with which to continue his family's traditional extortion of the Radcliffes. Or she could reserve them for herself and have them anonymously published and delivered over to a magistrate. Whether or not, after so much time, the title would be in danger was uncertain, but it would cause Colin more than a little consternation in return for the pain he had inflicted, however unintentionally, upon her.

But she did not want to see him disinherited, she thought with sudden, absolute clarity—with a certainty that had been rare to her since she had married him. Regardless of her own future, she did not want him hurt, as much as he had hurt her. He mattered far too much to her for that, and if his actions had caused her to discover a kind of grief she had not understood before, then it would only hurt that much more if he were harmed.

The man's face darkened. "I saw the letter. It had that old type of writing on it. Give it here."

She stood, slightly more jerkily than she intended, and wiped the tear tracks from her cheeks. "Excuse me," she said, edging out of the doorway past Mr. Reston. "It was rather sad news, and I would like to be alone."

The man caught her wrist as she went past. Gasping at the liberty of the gesture, she snatched back her hand. "My good sir!" she said crisply, backing away from him. "That is impertinent and offensive behavior."

"Give it here," he repeated, his voice growing rougher as he extended his hand peremptorily.

Fern's heart beat faster. Could she bluff? Staring at the man's set, purpling face, she knew it was impossible.

She had forgotten her knife under the mattress upstairs—and doubted it would be of much use against a man who could overpower her many times over, anyhow. Where could she run? He now stood closer than she to the stairs up to the keep. The door to the pump yard was somewhere behind her—but all that lay beyond was a rainstorm and the treacherous, flood-deep bog.

You could still give it over, part of her whispered. *It is the easy way.* But she held Colin's future in her pocket, and, she decided suddenly, her own. She would not surrender it into Joseph Reston's uncertain keeping.

"It is not yours," she said clearly, edging closer to the staircase to the great hall. "It was addressed to me. Reverend Biggs gave it to me this morning."

"No, it weren't," the man growled. "I saw it, and that weren't no letter written while ye were alive. Give it over now." He took a lumbering step toward her—and she turned and fled.

She sprinted toward the stairs, but Reston dove and caught the edge of her skirt, his yank whirling her away and jerking the fabric from his grasp simultaneously, leaving him sprawled on the ground between her and the stairs.

"*Colin!*" She screamed his name at the top of her lungs. "*Colin, help!*" He had promised her time—she prayed that his newfound impetuousness would override his word, for she had no chance of being heard if he was still in the bedchamber. "*Colin!*" She tried once more as Reston grunted and pushed to his feet, his face flushed with fury. Then she ran with all her strength, her long skirts tangling around her ankles. She ran in the only direction she dared to go—toward the Tudor hall, the image of the great oaken front door burned upon her brain. If she could only make it outside, she could try to run for the village, and perhaps Colin would see her from the window before Reston caught up with her. . . .

She flew up the two steps to the dining room and ran down its length toward the passage to the front hall, pushing her legs as hard as she could against the flags. Her corset felt like a vise around her lungs, dots appearing in front of her eyes as she struggled to suck in more air.

She could hear Reston's heavy footsteps behind her, growing closer. She wasn't going to make it. He was too close, and she could not get the air that her muscles demanded.

He grunted as he lunged for her again—she felt his fingers brush her skirt. She tried to run faster, but her body could not do it. She rounded the corner into the passageway, her smooth-soled shoes sliding on the stone. Reston came around too fast. His body slamming into hers, he knocked her into the wall as he continued past, falling through the passageway and into the hall. Fern lurched and regained her balance, her vision swimming dangerously. Reston pushed to his feet again, and she tried to dart away, back into the dining room, but he cut her off, pressing her back toward the stairway and the upper reaches of the Tudor wing.

"Give it to me," he growled.

Fern's fist tightened around the documents in her pocket. She felt the brittle parchment crumble, and she squeezed harder, willing the letters to dust.

Reston's eyes widened as he realized what she was doing. "No!" he shouted.

She turned and ran in the only direction she could go—up, thrusting her hand into her pocket and crumbling the papers in fingers numb from lack of oxygen. Reston was right behind her as she reached the first floor, but she didn't pause, pressing upward even as her body seemed to become strangely distant, as if she were looking down a long tunnel at herself. *Air*, she told her diaphragm, forcing it to move faster, faster against the hard whalebone of her corset. *I must have more air.* But the black spots in front of her eyes got bigger, and darkness closed in at the edges of her vision.

She burst out onto the roof. Rain lashed her face, bringing her to herself just in time to throw a foot out in front of her body as it began to pitch forward. She threw herself through the crumbled remains of a wall and toward the broken hole in the roof. She hit the edge, grasping a broken timber with her free hand as she pulled the other one from her pocket and flung the broken fragments of the letters into the rain. The wind snatched them, sending them whirling away into the storm.

She could keep the blackness at bay no longer, and she felt it close over her just as she heard Reston's bellow of rage. Then she heard no more.

Chapter Twenty

Colin stood staring at the empty doorway for a long moment after Fern had left, unfamiliar emotions warring within him.

First there was his reaction to the letter—a cold jolt of consequences that, however natural in respect to his actions, were out of place in his picture of the appropriate concerns of a future peer. A bastard. His bastard, without even the excuse of passion to mitigate the dire responsibility for another life that his actions had thrust upon him. It occurred to him, as it never would have before, that Emma was not a good mother for any child, not even if her husband ignored her infidelity and accepted it as his own. He had handed this unknown creature's future over to his wife on an impulse, but he was abruptly convinced that he could not have made a better decision. She had a greater heart than he, certainly, and perhaps a wiser one. The words of Emma's letter—passionless, practical—burned into his mind, and he shuddered that he had once seen that as the most desirable kind of relationship with the opposite sex.

The child, though, was not yet fully real to him—

and Fern was, with an immediacy unmatched by any future event. He had realized, when she looked at him with those hurt-filled eyes, that he could lose her. They would continue to live together, of course, and would even share the same bed with appropriate regularity, but she could still escape him. He had never thought of such a possibility—too self-centered or too short-sighted, he didn't know—and the idea chilled him down to his bones. He felt the familiar deadness stirring in his chest, cooling the blood in his veins.

It isn't my fault, he told himself. She had no right to have any expectations of him—she'd made no demands or even inquiries when they were wed. She had no right to read his correspondence, for God's sake. His sins, whatever they were, were his own.

But it didn't matter. All that mattered was that look she had given him right before she had left, the terrible sorrow that he had seen reflected in those eyes. All that mattered was that he had been the cause of her grief—and that her grief could destroy everything they had found together.

No, he thought fiercely, the force of that word driving back the coldness. He would not—could not—let that happen. He could not allow the pain to continue in those eyes, and now that he lived, he could not let himself wither away again, until her pain would stir no response in him but coldness.

He had promised her time. How much? He dreaded the decision she might come to in the depths of the bleak manor. He paced the room, staring out the window as the storm grew fiercer, until finally, he could stand it no longer. His decision made, he strode out the open doorway and down the dizzying stairs.

"Colin!"

He hesitated. The voice was so faint—was it Fern's, or was it his own disordered brain, playing tricks on him? The great hall was empty and silent below him.

"Colin, help!"

Without making a conscious decision, he began to run, the steep stairs falling away under his feet as the sheer drop yawned on one side.

"Colin!"

The last, despairing cry shot through him, and his heart jolted in his chest as it died away. Where was Reston? The question pounded through his brain. He had left the man safely in the village—had watched from the window of a neighboring cottage where he negotiated for the boy to run to the nearest town as Fern walked, alone and unmolested, up the drive to the manor house. But where was Reston now?

He had no answers as he reached the level floor, stumbling at the sudden change of stride. He ran toward the kitchen stairs, his only choice, and flung himself down them. Six feet from the bottom, he vaulted over the rough wooden handrail, landing hard enough that he felt the jolt in his joints. The kitchens were silent, the massive pillars blocking his sight. He paused for an instant, then sprinted for the door to the pump yard. When he reached it, it was shut fast, with Fern's umbrella leaning against the jamb just as it had been when he arrived.

Fern would have picked it up—or at least knocked it over—had she passed by. His fear growing, Colin ran for the Tudor wing. He dashed down the empty dining room, and after throwing open the door to the cabinet—empty—he ducked through the passageway. He was about to enter the great hall when the sound of footsteps that weren't his stopped him dead. He skidded to a halt, panting. There it was again—footsteps, coming from above.

He sprinted up the stairs, stretching his legs to take them three at a time. He reached the first floor—but the heavy treads continued farther above, and so he put on another burst of speed and pounded up the last flight.

He emerged into the attic and staggered as a gust of wind struck him. Then he saw her—Fern, standing at the edge of the gaping hole in the roof, her hand extended into the storm as something white streamed from it in tatters. Reston was charging toward her, shouting unintelligibly, and Colin's heart contracted hard with dread.

"Fern!" He shouted her name as he threw himself toward Reston. But what happened next made no sense: She swayed once and slid to the ground in a boneless puddle of skirts and outspread white arms.

He slammed into Reston then, and the two of them fell hard against the floorboards—and went through, falling amidst a shower of plaster and rotted wood.

Colin's vision went dark briefly as they struck something on the level below, but he shook his head and pushed off from Reston, knowing the danger of closing with the burlier man. Reston lay dazed across an escritoire.

Colin stumbled as debris caught between his legs. His shoulder sent a message of fire to his brain—it must have struck something as they fell. He moved his arm, and it swung freely, so he pushed the pain from his mind.

A quick glance around the room oriented him— they were in the bedchamber where he and Fern had started their first night. Reston shoved himself off the escritoire with a roar, lunging, but Colin reached behind himself and found the handle of the ewer exactly where he had remembered it. Bringing the pitcher around in a wide arc, Colin lashed out at the man with all his strength. Something cracked as it struck Reston's head. The man went down hard, sprawling at Colin's feet.

Colin blinked at Reston, then at the handle of the shattered ewer still clutched in his hand. He prodded the recumbent figure with the toe of his boot, ready to turn the prod into a kick, if necessary. The man grunted but did not move. Colin forced a deep breath through his protesting lungs and pushed out of the room, staggering up the stairs again.

As he emerged into the attic, he almost wept with relief to see Fern sitting up against the edge of the broken roof. She blinked dazedly at him as he approached.

"Thank goodness," she croaked. "Corset. Couldn't breathe."

"I thought I'd lost you," Colin said, his lungs feeling too tight for air. "Don't you ever do that again." He wanted to scoop her into his arms and kiss her, but he didn't dare, for she looked as if she were on the verge of fainting again.

"Won't. Promise," she said, still gasping for breath. She looked up at him, tendrils of hair clinging wetly to her face, her eyelashes heavy with rain. "He wanted the letters. Not papers—letters."

"Come on now," Colin said. "Get up. We'll talk about the madman later. I've incapacitated him, but I don't know for how long. Thank God I haven't killed him." He grasped her weakly extended arms and levered her to her feet, gritting his teeth at the pressure on his shoulder. He put her arm around his neck. She took two wobbly steps, and then her legs gave way entirely, and she shook her head mutely, panting.

Colin swung her into his arms, his shoulder sending out new waves of pain, and strode rapidly down the stairs as she clung feebly to his neck.

"He wanted the letters," Fern repeated, more intelligibly. "The letters in the packet. They were the papers he kept going on about."

"He said he had them," Colin objected, looking down at her wan face.

"He didn't know—couldn't read," she said. "He must have thought they were in the hut, but he didn't know which ones they were. He didn't tell his wife—too ashamed, or scared, or proud."

"My God," said Colin, taking it in. "But why those letters?"

"They had the secret. Colin—the second John Radcliffe was a bastard, and not even Charlotte Gorsing's bastard." Her forehead was knitted with concern.

"Illegitimate. Our viscountcy could be challenged," Colin said slowly.

"Yes—I don't know what the outcome would be...." Fern said.

"But even if we won, it could be a ruinously expensive victory," Colin finished. "Fern—"

"I couldn't let him do it," she said, her hands winding slightly tighter around the back of his neck. "I destroyed them. Crumpled them and threw the pieces into the rain."

"You ran from him," Colin said. "You fool. You bloody fool—you should have given them over! They were only pieces of parchment."

"They might as well have been knives to cut you

with, Colin," Fern said as they reached the ground floor. Colin carried her toward the front hall's door. "I couldn't let him have them. I love you too much."

Colin came to a dead stop as her face whitened again, even her lips growing dangerously pale. "What did you say?"

"I'm sorry," she said, the words barely a whisper. "I shouldn't have . . . I didn't mean to say that."

Colin stared down at her upturned face. "Did you mean it?"

She closed her eyes, her throat moving as she swallowed. "Yes," she whispered.

Yes. The word hit him like a thunderbolt. Only the knowledge that Reston was lying on the floor above made his legs move toward the door. "Thank all that's holy," he said, "because I am not sure what love feels like, but I'm pretty damned certain that I love you, too."

Her eyes flew open with a small cry, and after searching his face, she broke into a weak smile. "Do you mean that?"

"I still think that you're a fool for not giving over the letters, but yes, I do," Colin said.

"I shall be your fool gladly then," she said.

They reached the door. "We have to make it to the vicarage," Colin said. "We need to be well away from Reston and send some sturdy men up to get him." He grimaced. "I don't think the rest of the village is mad like the Restons."

"I don't think they like them much," Fern said flatly. "I can walk now," she added as he shifted his grip upon her to open the door one-handed.

"Are you certain?" Colin asked, though his arms were burning with the strain of holding her far-from-slight frame and the ache in his shoulder was beginning to slide from pain to agony.

"Yes," she said a little more strongly.

He let her slide gently to the floor. She stood firmly without swaying, though her face was still pale.

"Let's go," she said, and she pushed the door open and stepped out into the rain.

Colin strode after her, stripping off his coat and placing it around her shoulders. "Take this," he said in a tone that brooked no argument.

She started to open her mouth and then shook her head, walking slightly unsteadily across the uneven cobbles. He took her arm and placed it over his. She leaned on him slightly, quickening her pace.

"Was he badly injured?" Fern said. Water streamed from her face now, dripping onto his coat, but she appeared to ignore it.

Colin didn't have to ask whom she meant. "I don't know," he said shortly. "I hope not."

"Why?" she asked. It was a simple question, without viciousness.

"Because I should like to see him in gaol soon and would like to ensure that I do not join him."

"Oh," Fern said, her gray eyes widening. "Did you have your knife?"

His steps faltered. "Damnation. I did. I forgot all about it. If I'd remembered, I'd have skewered him." Colin's stomach churned at that possibility. An inquest of a death caused by a future peer, with all his father's political enemies determined that the result would be murder, and him having stabbed a man with a meat knife one hundred feet from his dinner table . . . He didn't think he'd be hanged, but it might be a near thing.

Fern slipped slightly on a wet patch of ground, and Colin tightened his grip on her arm.

"I almost forgot!" she said. With her free hand, she reached into the folds of her dress, pulling a pocket inside out through a slit in her skirt and sending a dozen fragments of parchment dancing away in the wind.

"It's all gone now," she said with satisfaction.

Their appearance in the village drew an unexpected crowd—houses that had presented nothing but blank, dark windows to them before disgorged their occupants into the stormy afternoon at the sight of Wrexmere's now-familiar master and mistress in such a bedraggled condition.

"Joseph Reston has assaulted my wife," Colin announced to the small crowd. He read their reactions—some were surprised but far more were disgusted, and at the absent Reston rather than at him. A small knot of fear inside him loosened—however unpopular the man was, he was still one of their own, and future lord or not, Colin was to all intents and purposes an outsider. He pulled Fern protectively closer against him. "I incapacitated him, but he needs to be brought into custody—and possibly needs medical attention, as well."

"I'll go," said one burly man, his face showing an almost unholy pleasure. In a moment, half a dozen more men had volunteered and began hiking up the long drive.

Dorcas Reston stood pale and speechless at the edge of the crowd. The men's departure seemed to trigger something in her, for she lifted a shaking hand and pointed it at Colin. "Murderer!" she cried shrilly. "Thief and murderer! Ye stole our papers and murdered my husband."

"God willing, your husband shall be fine, madam," Colin said coldly.

"There are no papers." Those words came, serenely, from Fern. "There is nothing but dust and mud."

"You and your husband shall be standing before the magistrate before a fortnight is out to answer for your misappropriation of funds," Colin continued implacably.

At that announcement, Dorcas Reston seemed to choke, staggering backward before whirling and fleeing into her cottage. The shiny door slammed closed and a chuckle ran through the assembled crowd. A few faces were still pulled in expressions of anger or bitterness, those of Mrs. Willis and old Jim among them, but among the rest, the chuckling grew louder until entire peals rang out, long and loud, battering against the silent green door.

"We shall seek shelter at the vicarage," Colin said as the laughter died away, "though I would greatly appreciate it if some women would go and fetch my wife some dry clothes, as I fear she might catch cold after her shock and drenching."

Instantly, there were more volunteers, and after they were dispatched, Colin bade the crowd good-bye and escorted Fern behind the church to the doorstep of the vicarage. He looked around. There was no one within sight—no one to embarrass her. He turned Fern toward him firmly then and took her chin, tilting it upward.

"I have been wanting to do this so badly that it hurts."

Then he kissed her, fully, intimately, his tongue exploring the welcoming heat of her mouth as her body melded against his. Finally, after a time that was too short by an eternity, he pulled away.

She sighed and opened her eyes. "Thank you," she said.

He gave her a crooked smile and knocked on the door.

It was a long time later before they were alone again. First, everything had to be explained to Rev. Biggs, and then someone had to be sent to the nearest village with a magistrate. Fern and Colin were each provided with attendants and dry clothing from the vicarage attic while their trunks were fetched.

Soon, Fern was ensconced in the vicarage's musty spare bedroom with Abby while Colin was sequestered in the churchman's own bedchamber. While she was grateful for the chance to change clothes, more than a small part of Fern would have chosen to stay wet if it meant that she could remain in her husband's company. They had discovered something new and precious and, she was afraid, delicate in the way that an oak seedling was delicate. There were still things that she must say to Colin, and the thought of them filled her with the dread that she might destroy what they had just found.

A commotion outside made Fern look out the window. "They're bringing in Reston," she breathed. The crowd had re-formed in the lane at the edge of the village as the men returned from the manor house, bearing Joseph Reston among them.

Abby craned her neck around Fern's head. "He's being carried. Do ye think he's— No, look at him; he's jumping like a vish on a line." Her tone carried not a hint of regret nor vicious pleasure.

"What do you think about all this, Abby?" Fern asked.

She shrugged. "The family's been setting themselves up as better'n the rest of us vor many years. Either they'd make true gentlefolk or they'd meet their comeuppance, is the way I see it, though I be glad enough that unkindly folk like them won't start going to the county gentry dances."

Fern watched until she saw Colin emerge from the vicarage. "I'm going down, too," she said in sudden decision.

"But your hair's not done—"

"Devil take my hair!" she said from the doorway, hurrying out.

The borrowed dress was made for a taller woman, and she took the stairs as quickly as she dared without risking her neck. By the time she stepped onto the walk, Colin was already at the road, his powerful figure just as remarkable in the vicar's castoffs as it was in the finest London suit. Fern hurried after.

She caught up to him just as the crowd and the men with Reston came together. "Fern," he said, giving her a smile that squeezed her heart and offering her his arm before turning his attention to Reston's arrival. Fern took it, clung to it, sure of its steadiness—for now.

Reston was lying on a makeshift stretcher made from a blanket and two brooms, muttering and thrashing blindly as the men bore up stoically under his weight.

"What's wrong with him?" Colin's voice rang out over the murmurs in the crowd.

One of the men—Fern remembered that he had called himself the local sheep doctor, with the implication that such a profession was good enough for doctoring people when the need arose—laughed shortly. "He's had a right good crack on the head and an even better dose of laudanum in him when he thought to fight us. He'll be right soon enough. Until then, he's babbling like a child, ain't he?"

"Where are you taking him?" Colin asked.

"To Rob Sterne's henhouse," said another of the men. "I told him he'd built it like a gaol, and soon enough, we'll see how right I am."

As Reston approached, his words became clearer. " . . . that damned man, crazy old granfer. Ye didn't never trust nobody, did ye, Pa? Hiding the papers, keeping me from school, beating me for trying to better myself by reading. Always the papers. 'Twere always about the papers vor you. Madman. Hiding out on the moors, hoarding every scrap of paper to trick me so I'd never be out vrom under your thumb. Got ye in the end, didn't it? Dying out there all alone, covered with your own vomit and vilth, and you'd never told your only son where the real papers were, as you'd meant to. Ha!" The man struggled upright for an instant, his eyes unfocused, before collapsing back against the stretcher again.

The stretcher bearers stolidly ignored him, carrying him away down the lane. The crowd followed, but Colin did not move, staring after the man for a long moment.

"I don't think he would have killed me," Fern offered tentatively.

Colin snorted. "You don't think, you say. You're a great bloody fool, Fern Radcliffe, and I am deuced glad that you married a man who could save you from your own good intentions."

"I am *deuced* glad I married you, too," she said, the raw honesty of the words hurting her throat.

"Let's go back inside," he offered, his green eyes warm. "If we don't retire immediately, we shall spend the entire afternoon being gawked at as half the village manufactures an excuse to drop by."

And they did, leaving assurances through the vicar that they would be at the villagers' disposal in the morning. They retreated upstairs to the vicar's spare bedroom, gently rebuffing even his attempts at getting them to take tea with him.

Fern sank onto the room's single chair with a sigh as soon as she entered. "I somehow imagined that, after such an adventure, the day would have a more dramatic conclusion than retreating to an old churchman's outmoded guest bedroom."

"For example?" Colin raised an eyebrow.

She rubbed her eyes with the heels of her hands. "For example, making a grand exit in a coach bound for civilization."

Colin chuckled at the patent longing in her voice. "Tomorrow morning, I've been promised."

"I hope the driver keeps his word." Fern lapsed into silence, staring at the fire in the grate, her mind turning over what she knew she must say. "Finally, the heat comes to an end, and it's the day that I get drenched." Those words took up space, took up time.

"Of course," Colin said, leaning against the mantel. "You aren't coming down with anything, are you?"

"Not at all."

Colin watched her knot and unknot her hands restlessly in her lap for a few moments. She knew he was watching, but she could not stop herself, nor could she make herself broach the hateful subject that she had left to consider before encountering Reston.

Eventually, Colin said, "You do not wish to speak to me about the weather, Fern."

She looked up, biting her lip. "You are quite right. I am just too much a coward or a prude or something to bring it up myself." She took a death breath, drawing herself together. "I thought about everything before Joseph Reston arrived, just like I said I would. And I came up with three points of difficulty. First, you said you have changed—sincerely believe you have changed—but how much can a man change in less than a week, especially since you were still calling me by the same name you were calling your mistress on our wedding day? Second, even if you have changed, what is to keep you from straying in the future, out of passion if not convenience, and can I trust your oaths of fidelity simply because they are earnestly meant now? Third, what is the kindest and most just thing to do with the babe?"

Colin's face froze. "And your answers?"

"I don't know," Fern confessed. "I only have questions. I do not think the first two are entirely answerable except by time, and as for the third . . . I don't know if I'm as good as I should be to do what would be best. I rather fear that I am not." She sighed with bone-deep weariness. "But just because I have no answers does not mean that the risk is not worth it. I love you, Colin, and that changes nothing and everything."

"What do you mean?" The words were tense and quiet.

"I mean that I want to pretend that we have the answers, the best possible answers, and that I want to work toward making them true." She spoke from the deepest part of her, the rebellious portion of her mind for once in harmony with everything else. "Loving you has not improved my ability to see into the future or to judge the largeness of my heart or the wisdom of trust. But in another sense—in the sense that, I hope, matters the most—loving you has made every difference in the world. It has made me choose to be an optimist, because I have realized that it is something that is worth risking everything for."

Colin just stood, swaying slightly. Even slightly disheveled, he was painfully handsome, with his perfect features and raven black hair. "I was angry that you read my private correspondence until I realized that, fundamentally, it didn't matter why there was a rift between us, only that it was there. I told you the truth— I am a changed man."

"And I believe that you meant it," Fern said.

"But flesh is weak," Colin finished. "I understand. Yet I want to share your optimism and your dreams."

"Truly?" she said, the breath catching in her lungs as she scarcely dared believe the words that her ears were reporting.

"Truly," he said.

She let out a peal of laughter and pushed to her feet, throwing herself into his arms. And Colin laughed, too, an awkward, rusty sound that she thought she could become quite accustomed to.

Then he kissed her, hard, and they said no more for a very long time.

Esmerelda is keeping a secret. Lord Varcourt is determined to know the truth. Passion and mystery turn adversaries into lovers in Lydia Joyce's next sizzling historical romance, on sale December 2008.

Turn the page for a sneak peek.

The smothering velvet curtains were shut against the night, but Thomas Hyde, Lord Varcourt, could feel the darkness pressing against the edges of the crowded parlor, tightening around the silk-shaded gaslights and dimming them from yellow flame to orange.

The coals glowed sullenly in the grate as the chill of autumn sank deep into the old stones of the city. Parliament still sat in its new limestone palace, already damp and lichenous where it crouched beside the stinking Thames, and so the Season continued, with the endless rotation of dinners, dances, operas, and soirees, accompanied as always by the constant, grating murmur of politics and gossip, marriage and legislation, secret cabals and open scandals that took place in the myriad stifling rooms which celebrated rising stars or betrayed faded glories.

Thomas stood apart in a corner of the Rushworth parlor, watching the currents in the room. Jewels glinted in the muffled lights, on swan necks, and on wrinkled wrists alike. The men moved, shadows in superfine and linen, between and among the wide

skirts of the ladies, stooping to murmur in a delicate
ear or pulling aside a hoary one for a moment's stern
exchange. The world was made and unmade in
rooms like this, and already, Thomas could begin to
read the threads that went into its making. Soon
enough, he would have enough gathered in his hands
so that he could pull them, and watch men dance. . . .

Bright laughter rose above the subdued murmurs
with the suddenness and clarity of a shattered wine-
glass. His sisters, ever oblivious to any nuance they
did not care to notice, stood by the piano with Mrs.
Christopher Radcliffe. They were a false focus in the
room, as insignificant as the bustling of the servants.
Of more interest to Thomas was the presence of Lord
Edgington in one corner of the room; the men around
him shifted uncertainly, uncomfortably, for the
staunchly Tory, if wildly libertine, family reputation
had been shattered a year ago with Edgington's de-
fection to the Whigs.

It was whispered that perhaps some portion of
Edgington's political shift was due to his marriage
two years before to the utterly unknown Margaret
King. Thomas did not discount it. That tiny woman
sat in a chair directly in front of him, her thick black
coils of hair framing her delicate face, as silent and
unreadable as an exquisite sphinx.

Only one other woman sat as quietly as she—and
more still, for Thomas at times wondered if she had
breathed since the gentlemen had rejoined the ladies
after their postprandial cigars. That day, the woman
wore a dress in a shade of red so dark that it was almost black, accompanied by a filmy veil of jet lace
cascading from a golden comb on the top of her head
to fall in folds across her face.

Esmeralda, she called herself, though God only knew who she really was or from whence she came. She was the newest accessory for the fashionable parlor, one of a thousand charlatans who now pretended unnatural powers for the credulous admiration of peasant and monarch alike, a mass continental insanity that Thomas had instantly despised and suspected. It was an unpredictable element. A corruptible element. A potentially useful element, to be sure, but far too fickle to be trusted.

Whom was she watching from behind that veil? Whose tool was she in this game of empires? And how many of the women present, in addition to his own mother, had already been drawn into her thrall? Not even Edgington, with all his spies, had been able to find out. Not even Thomas, with all his ability to coax out confidences.

Lady Hamilton passed on, rubies glittering in her ears in utter disregard to the dark lilac of her dress and her bold new necklace, which marked her captivity to this Esmeralda. Rubies guarded against harmful thoughts, the woman taught—emeralds against envy, diamonds against the spirits of the other world, and topaz against ills of the spirit. Thomas' gut clenched, but as long as his father clung to both life and title, there was nothing he could do about his mother's preoccupation with mediums and spirit guides, who promised to reunite her with the son she had lost some ten years before. The son who many in that very room thought Thomas had a hand in killing.

Lady Hamilton's hand fluttered self-consciously at her neck. She had been playing with her new necklace all evening, all but flaunting it in front of the other guests. Thomas wondered cynically what charms Esmeralda had said over it, or if her visions had led his mother to a certain jewelry shop where the spiritualist coincidentally knew the owner.

Lady James Ashcroft intercepted his mother as she passed near Thomas without acknowledging him. The countess gave the necklace a near-convulsive jerk, and Lady James' eyes obediently slid downward.

"What a brilliant new piece that is!" Lady James exclaimed, her own hand rising to the heavy jewels hanging from her neck and ears, relics of the Indian mines that had made her husband so rich. "It is so deliciously medieval. Please do tell me whom you had make it."

"It wasn't made," Lady Hamilton said in tones of deepest mystery. "It was found. Esmeralda has been possessed of visions concerning it for weeks, and though she told me the import of each, none of it made sense until she saw what I recognized as a peculiar stone in the walk behind Hamilton House. I ordered it pulled up, and beneath, in a little casket near rotted with age, was this extraordinary necklace!"

Even as those light words elicited the proper admiring noises from Lady James, Thomas felt a chill cut through him. Lady Hamilton turned to show the necklace in the best light as she expounded upon the story in answer to Lady James' inquiries, and it glittered in the light. Necklaces did not come from nowhere—and they certainly were not found through otherworldly visions. It had to be a ruse, a beautiful millstone to tie about his mother's neck in order to drown his family. There could be no good hidden in such a carefully woven plot.

Thomas wanted the thing gone—and with it, Esmeralda. He stood, silent and immobile, until Lady James moved off so that he could confront his mother alone. He stepped forward, taking Lady Hamilton's elbow. She started when he touched her, and he tamped down a surge of anger against the statuelike form of Esmeralda.

"Madam," he said quietly, "you did not tell me that Esmeralda had given you that necklace."

His mother looked confused, the dark painted lines of her brows drawing together. "Given me it? No, I had the gardener dig it up—"

"Nevertheless." Thomas cut her off. "It is a gift. Her visions led you to it, you say. How easy would it have been for her to keep silent about them and keep the necklace for herself? No, she wanted you to have it, and I mistrust her reasons."

Her face grew stony. "You are simply speaking from your prejudices."

"I simply do not like the intentions of a stranger who has no reason to be kind and may have many other motivations you know nothing of," he returned, forgetting in his annoyance to pander to the illusion that the spiritualist possessed supernatural gifts. "Did it not occur to you that the piece might be stolen? Imagine the damage it would do to your husband in Parliament if our family were connected to a theft. Madam, I would ask you to remove the necklace and to conceal it until we reach home. Then put it away and pretend it was never found." He looked down at her, ruthlessly exploiting the uncertainty in him that Esmeralda had fanned into fear. "Do not wear it—or even refer to it—until that spiritualist is gone."

The color drained from her cheeks, and with it went the traces of her girlhood beauty. "You are punishing me," she whispered, "for not getting rid of her as you told me to."

Thomas stretched his lips in a smile he didn't feel. "No, madam. I am trying to save you." And with that, he let her go, praying that she would accede to his demands.

He turned to face the woman who sat so still across the parlor, who had been sending shadows for him to duel for the better part of a year and who had insinuated herself so fully into society that her presence had become well nigh inescapable.

He had never spoken to her. Never acknowledged her, knowing that she would, in time, be tossed away like last season's fashion in hats. That had been a mistake, for society had not tired of her quickly enough—a mistake he would commit no longer.

He closed the space between them, weaving between belling skirts and through the archipelago of chairs. The air was heavy with the sickly sweet scents of sherry and sweat, cologne water and drooping flowers, the stench of tobacco hanging upon the coats of the men who had indulged themselves over the supper table after the ladies had retired.

Esmeralda did not stir in her corner, though he would have sworn that her eyes were fixed upon him as he drew near. He stopped so close to her chair that his boot tips touched the stiff dupioni of her dark crimson skirts. He could tell almost no more about her from that vantage than he could from across the room, for she was still just as motionless, the fabric of her veil revealing nothing but a hint of the shape of her face beneath. Her high-necked dress ended far beneath the veil's edge, her tight sleeves coming down over her wrists to meet short black gloves. She was slender but tall for a woman; he had seen her rise from a chair and use that height and her eerie quietness to silence a room. She could be any age, any woman, really, beneath the armor of silk. If it were not for the small movement of her chest as she breathed, echoed by a flutter of her veil, he could almost believe that she was not even alive.

But she did breathe—and he could feel the tension radiating from her body as he stood over her, looking down.

She said nothing, so neither did he. Instead, he walked slowly, deliberately around her until he stood in the gap between the corner of her chair and the wall, directly behind her left shoulder and out of her peripheral vision.

"We need to talk, *Esmeralda*," he said. "I think I would like to have my palm read." He put a hand on her shoulder. He could feel the muscle over her collarbone, rigid through her silk dress.

"I do not read palms," she said. It was the first time he had ever heard her voice, and it sent a shock through him, for it was neither the exaggerated Gypsy accent nor the cronish cackle he had expected. Instead, it was low and melodious, with the merest trace of an accent he could not place. "I read souls."

Thomas tightened his hand upon her shoulder. "You lie."

"You sound so sure." The reply was swift, practiced; she had met doubters before.

"I am sure," he countered. "If you could read my soul, you would be trembling now."

She gave a swift intake of breath; whether it was a

gasp or a kind of laugh, he could not tell. "Reading souls is not as simple a matter as seeing a face."

Thomas refused to continue to be drawn along that track. "You have been giving audience all evening long. I ask for one now."

"In private." For the first time, he detected an unmistakable tremor of fear.

He leaned on her shoulder slightly, deliberately. "Most assuredly."

"And if I refuse?" she asked, unbending even though the fear still lay there, underneath her words.

He bent so that his mouth was level with her ear. "How mysterious do you think Esmeralda will be once she has been unveiled?" He wound the fabric of the veil around his hand.

"I will come." The words were unhurried, but he felt for the first time that he had found a weapon to use against the word knives she wielded.

"I am pleased," he said, and he shifted his grip so that he held her arm, half lifting her from her chair. "Do lead the way. I will follow."

The veil was smothering her, and the man's hand on her arm felt like a vise. Esmerelda forced her breathing back under her control, willing her racing heart to slow. She had seen the exchange between Lord Varcourt and his mother—had seen Lady Hamilton's hands flutter at the antique necklace at her neck, had seen the terror on her face as her son stalked toward Em. Stalked—not the vain, preening walk of a peacock but the deliberate movements of a predator.

She had now seen him exactly six times. The first time had been when he had thrown the door open in the midst of a séance at Hamilton House, causing half the women present to emit faint shrieks and reach for their smelling salts. Then, he had simply called from the doorway, "My lady, mother. Mary. Elizabeth." And the giggling twins had been instantly silenced, following their ashen-faced mother from the room.

That had ended that afternoon's session, but she had received a letter—and a payment—the following week to continue to meet more privately with Lady Hamilton alone. Em had been glad enough, for large shows were only good to impress an audience. It was only the small sessions in which her skills were best put to use—and her patron could be convinced most thoroughly of her powers. Still, whenever Em mentioned any sense that she had received from the events following Lord Varcourt's interruption, Lady Hamilton would grow pale and nervous and would bring the subject firmly around to her dead son Harry.

At first, Em had given her the usual palliative communications, feeding the poor woman a constant stream of reassurance about her son's happiness on the other side of the veil. After that scene, though, a sense of self-preservation and a bone-deep dread had caused her to let doubt about the countess's surviving son seep in to her communications, how much out of fear for herself and how much out of a genuine concern for her patroness, she didn't know.

Since then, Em had seen Lord Varcourt only across a parlor or a dinner table, as she had begun being included in social invitations during the past two months as a kind of joint entertainment and curiosity. When he had looked at her, she felt the animosity of his eyes boring through her, and she had grown cold inside at the thought that those eyes might have been the last things that his brother had ever seen. And now she was walking beside him, her arm in his hard grip as everyone in the parlor stilled to watch the two of them—the spiritualist and the skeptic—leave the room together.

No one asked whether she was going willingly. It did not occur to anyone that she was a being whose will meant anything at all.